"You forget, my lord. You bought me.

"You have only to send for me if you wish to speak to me."

"And I was vain enough to think you had come back to talk to me," said Lord Ambourne wryly. He took Perdita's chin in his fingers and pulled her head up.

"The first time I did this, you bit me, Perdita. Do you remember? Are you going to bite me again?"

He pulled her mouth to meet his and gently kissed her. At first she tried to push him away, but then as the kiss grew sweeter and deeper, he drew her into his arms. This time when they parted, the earl was shaken.

Perdita swiftly moved to the door. "May I go now?" she said.

"Yes, you may go," the earl said curtly. But he had a feeling that Perdita, the lost one, had found herself, and now it was he who was lost.

Regency England: 1811-1820

"It was the best of times,
it was the worst of times...."

As George III languished in madness, the pampered and profligate Prince of Wales led the land in revelry and the elegant Beau Brummel set the style. Across the Channel, Napolean continued to plot against the English until his final exile to St. Helena. Across the Atlantic, America renewed hostilities with an old adversary, declaring war on Britain in 1812. At home, Society glittered, love matches abounded and poets such as Lord Byron flourished. It was a time of heroes and villains, a time of unrelenting charm and gaiety, when entire fortunes were won or lost on a turn of the dice and reputation was all. A dazzling period that left its mark on two continents and whose very name became a byword for elegance and romance.

PERDITA

SYLVIA ANDREW

Harlequin Books

TORONTO • NEW YORK • LONDON
AMSTERDAM • PARIS • SYDNEY • HAMBURG
STOCKHOLM • ATHENS • TOKYO • MILAN
MADRID • WARSAW • BUDAPEST • AUCKLAND

Published April 1993

ISBN 0-373-31195-8

PERDITA

CHAPTER ONE

THE GIRL STOOD shackled to the post in the corner of the huge courtyard. Someone with a belated sense of decency had covered the shreds and tatters of her clothing with a cotton cloak, and a trick of the moonlight silvered the folds and gave grace to the emaciated body. Her head was slightly raised, and a sudden breath of wind lifted her matted hair away from her face. The moonlight flooded over her, revealing the pure profile, the proud lift of her chin and the slender lines of her throat. The man standing in the shadows caught his breath. His instinct had not played him false this afternoon. She was perfect—Artemis the huntress in person. Indeed, she resembled nothing more than one of the statues he had so recently seen on the Acropolis, an impression which was increased by her immobility, the apparent indifference with which she faced her fate, and the cool silver light in which she was bathed.

"Sir! Sir—there's the guard now."

The whispered warning drew his attention to the figure making its way along the battlements towards the courtyard.

"It'll be some minutes yet, Tom. Are you ready? You remember what you have to do?"

"Yes, your lordship. I can't answer for them two heathen, though."

The Earl smiled. Tom would never admit that the two Berbers standing behind him might prove necessary or useful. But on tonight's adventure they were essential. Danger was in the air. The Pasha had accepted his bribe, it was true, but that did not necessarily mean he would keep his word and see that the guards were blind. His mind turned to the scene in the Dey's palace that morning.

"I'm obliged to you for the provisions and water, Mehmet Pasha."

"It is nothing, Lord Ambourne. A trifling gesture of hospitality to a storm-tossed traveller; nothing more. If I can serve you in any other way, of greater significance, then I am honoured to do so."

The Earl hesitated, then spoke. "There is one other thing you could grant me . . ."

Mehmet Hussein Pasha, Dey of Algiers, grinned his shark's grin and said gently, "All I have is yours to command, my lord. My poor people have already experienced your princely generosity in return for the water . . . You have only to tell me, and it is yours."

"You have some prisoners in your courtyard—not, I think, of your race?"

There was a little silence. The Pasha's thoughts were racing, in spite of his appearance of judicial calm. What was this Englishman up to? Behind the Earl's air of indifference lay a purpose which the Pasha had not yet divined. He carefully considered the man before him. Hair that was almost black, a strong face with cool grey eyes, an arrogant high-bridged nose and a hard, disciplined mouth. There might be passion there, but if so it was well under control. The Pasha was in the habit of looking for men's weaknesses and exploiting them for his own ends. It would be difficult to find any in this man. What was his interest in the wretches below? Was it that they were French and therefore should be deported or tried in their own country? Or was he anxious to make sure that they would be punished adequately here? Europe, as the Pasha knew only too well, had strong views on piracy in the Mediterranean. Only two years ago their ships had bombarded Algiers, and since then the Pasha had walked an uneasy road between his former associates and the ever-watchful Mediterranean fleets.

"They are French, my lord," he said finally. "French pirates. We captured their ship, *Le Faucon*, two days ago after they had attacked one of our own merchantmen. Unfortunately the captain and senior members of the crew were blown to pieces attempting to escape from the sinking ship in a longboat. What we have here are the pathetic remnants of the crew, not worthy of your attention, I assure you. They will all die tomorrow."

The Earl got up and walked to the window overlooking the courtyard. "They are not all men, Excellence. One of them is a girl. I might pay well for her."

The Pasha was startled out of his customary urbanity. "Pay for a pirate? A girl? What girl? Ah—my lord, you jest. The woman in the courtyard? That is nothing for you. She is a pirate's drab, a piece of scum, not worthy of your slightest breath. Her own master left her to drown or be captured." Then, as the Earl remained silent, he added, "The other members of the band shun her. They say she has the evil eye, that she is what you call a witch. That is nothing for you." He sat back, his composure restored, and smiled knowingly. "No, no, my lord, there is little enough to comfort a man in that one. But if it would please you to look through this window..." He led the Earl over to the other side of the room. A fretted window overlooked a scene to delight the eye of any wanderer. Fountains played in a sheltered courtyard full of flowers and sweet-scented shrubs. Cushions were scattered on the lawns, and on some of them lay members of the Pasha's seraglio. "The choice of them is yours, my lord."

"Tempting as these sights are, Mehmet Pasha, I regret I must forgo the pleasures they promise. The girl prisoner would not be for such a purpose, I assure you."

The Pasha frowned. The Englishman's directness annoyed him. This was not the way business was conducted in Algiers—at least not with a Pasha in the Ottoman Empire and high in favour with the Sultan himself. Still, the girl was to die tomorrow, along with the rest of the trash in the courtyard. She was worth little enough to him. How much would she be worth to the Englishman? He looked at the face above him, but the lean, tanned features revealed nothing. He sighed. "Alas, my friend, the girl is the Sultan's prisoner, a condemned associate of pirates. It would be difficult and dangerous to release her."

The Earl restrained his impatience with difficulty. Until recently this old fox in front of him had been a close associate of the pirates that had ravaged the Mediterranean for centuries. However, to remind the Pasha of that now would hardly further his cause. He said carefully, "But, Excellence, does not the Koran say that women should be protected and treated gently, as befits their weaker constitution?"

"The girl is one of a band of infidels, my lord. The Koran says nothing of such a woman."

The Earl decided not to fence any longer. He had come prepared, after all. As he spoke he drew from his finger a pearl ring of singular beauty and contemplated it. "I understand your scruples, believe me. But is there not a way this matter could be arranged to our...mutual benefit?''

The Pasha's eyes gleamed. ''My lord, the Sultan's laws are absolute. On the other hand...the guards, it is true, are sometimes less vigilant than they should be. I have often spoken to their commander on this subject. A prisoner might well escape—especially when, for example, the muezzin calls the faithful to prayer...''

''One hour after sunset. I think I understand you. There remains but one detail.''

''What is that, my lord?'' asked the Pasha eagerly, his eyes on one of the largest and most lustrous pearls he had ever seen.

''I must see the girl at close quarters. I must be sure.''

In spite of his curiosity, the Pasha was too anxious to possess the pearl to make any objection. They descended to the courtyard, where the late-morning sun was blazing down mercilessly on the wretched band of prisoners. The Pasha had spoken the truth. The men had distanced themselves from the girl, who was crouched, head bowed, in the minute amount of shade afforded by the post to which she was chained. Squatting down beside her, the Earl took her chin in his fingers and pulled her head up. Startlingly dark blue eyes blazed into his, then sharp teeth bit hard into his thumb. The Algerians gasped when they saw the drops of blood on his hand, but the Earl did not release his hold.

''Take the drab away!'' screamed the Pasha. ''Take her away and beat her!''

''No!'' said the Earl. ''The injury is nothing. Leave her where she is, I pray you.'' Then, as the Pasha, resenting this usurpation of his authority, would have spoken, he added deliberately, ''Look at her. She is a pearl beyond price.'' He looked at the Pasha and smiled. The Pasha slowly smiled back, and the smile turned into a laugh and then a roar.

''Truly a pearl,'' he spluttered, pointing at the bundle of rags on the ground. The courtyard rang with the sound of his laughter.

''Then we are agreed?'' said the Earl, frowning at the fury in the girl's incredible eyes. He slowly released his hold.

''Agreed,'' said the Pasha, still chuckling. ''A pearl beyond price.''

NOW, EIGHT HOURS LATER, as the moonlight streamed over the girl, the Earl smiled grimly. The success of his plan was worth a dozen such pearls. This step was but the first of many. Away in the distance a ghostly wailing began, was taken up by others until the air was filled with the sound—the muezzin. It was time. He nodded to his three companions. One of the Berbers went swiftly to the stairs, where the guard might appear. It was wise to be cautious—the Pasha might have taken the pearl without actually earning it. The other Berber ran forward to the girl, wielding a murderous-looking axe. With one mighty swing he severed the chain which bound her to the post. Meanwhile the Earl, with Tom's help, had taken hold of their prize.

"Quickly, Tom, the gag in her mouth. Ouch! The devil! Yashid, take her feet! Hold up the rest of the chain, man!"

Struggling, kicking, uttering muffled little cries, the girl was carried out on to the causeway, which led to their dinghy. Halfway along it she stopped her struggles, as if she was suddenly drained of energy, and the Earl gave her over to Yashid to carry. She was no weight, except for the fragment of chain still attached to her ankle. They waded out to the dinghy and the Berber dropped the girl in the bow, where she lay motionless as they cast off, making for the ship, which lay at anchor in deeper water. No sound of pursuit came from behind them. The night was tranquil under the moon and there was just enough breeze to make sailing sure. But when the ship was almost within reach the Earl gave a sudden shout. "Tom! Catch her! Quickly!"

The girl had taken advantage of their preoccupation with the ship ahead to slip silently into the water. Tom just touched the chain, which was sliding after her, but it was dragged from his fingers. Within seconds she had nearly disappeared, pulled down by the weight of the chain. Calling to the Berbers to hold the boat steady, the Earl leapt in and dived after her. With some difficulty he managed to drag her back, and with the aid of the others they were soon in the dinghy again. The Earl was furious. "You stupid bitch! What Satan's mischief are you up to now? Tie her up, Tom, and don't let the she-devil out of your sight till we have her safely locked in the cabin! You two, make for the ship as quickly as you can!"

The rest of the journey was completed in silence. The girl was ignominiously hauled on board, and the Earl strode off to his cabin, giving the order to the captain to set sail as he went.

"But sir!" called Tom as he scurried after him. "My lord, what about the girl?"

"Get her carried into my day cabin and fetch one of the men to take the chain off her leg. Then you can start preparing a bath for her. But don't untie her yet! We don't want any more tricks. Keep a close watch on her!"

"But what are you going to do, sir?"

"I'm going to change into dry clothing—without your help, Tom! No, do as I say. Get that girl seen to!"

"I'm not a blessed ladies' maid, sir! I'm your manservant..."

The Earl's voice came from behind a closed door. "Get on with it, Tom!"

Tom went off to get on with it, and the girl was soon in the large forward cabin, the chain removed from her ankle. However, it was clear that he was seriously worried, for while he worked he carried on a muttered conversation, ignoring the girl standing at the porthole.

"I'd like to know what's in your mind now, my fine lordling. Dealing with dirt like this! Nothing good, I'll take my oath on that. I've known you since you were knee high, and I ain't never seen you like this before. Not when you was injured, and not even when Miss Linette was took so ill. Mark my words, no good will come of this. I feel it in me bones."

"You'll feel more than that in your bones if that bath isn't ready in five minutes, Tom!"

The Earl was standing at the door between the two cabins, looking coldly at his man. Tom took a deep breath, drew himself up to his maximum height and gave tongue. "His lordship may remember, if I may be so bold as to remind him, that I was brought along as his personal manservant. It is no part of a valet's duties to attend to...to...any kind of female." Then, with a sudden descent from his dignified air, "What's more, you wouldn't find that snotty-nosed valet you keep at home in London doing it neither!"

The Earl's tone was silkily dangerous. "Exactly so! Perhaps that's why he's in London now and not here on board with us. Is it your wish to join him, Tom? Is that it?"

"But it isn't right, your lordship! I don't...I don't know about females and such."

"I don't suppose our guest will complain, Tom. I doubt very much that she has ever enjoyed the privilege of a maid's services. Not even the pleasure of a bath. Look at her."

Indeed, in the clear lamplight the girl was a sorry sight. Even the dip in the sea had not washed away the dirt on her clothes and person. Nor had it removed the noisome smell acquired during her brief sojourn in the filthy courtyard.

"So which is it to be, Tom? The bath or London?" When the man still hesitated, the Earl said impatiently, "Believe me, Tom, if I have to bathe the slut myself you will return to England as soon as I can arrange it." Tom remained silent. "Dammit, I need your help, Tom. The matter needs discretion. Who should I trust but you? I've known you all my life. You know very well we have no abigail, so what am I to do if you refuse?"

Tom nodded reluctantly and set to. The bath was filled and waiting when he looked curiously at the girl by the porthole. She had taken no interest in the discussion but was staring out at the night. "Er—madam? Will you step this way, please? Miss?"

The girl ignored him. The Earl gave a snort of laughter and said, "I fear your courtesies are wasted on the jade, Tom. Tell her simply to take her clothes off and climb into the bath. Meanwhile I need some food. I'll find the steward."

"Oh, no, sir, don't leave me. I'll do it, but don't leave me alone with her! Come on, girl, do as he says and get in the bath! I don't think she understands English, sir. You tell her in French."

When the girl continued to ignore them both the Earl grew impatient with what he saw as an assumption of modesty on the part of a woman who had been living with a gang of pirates. He strode over, picked her up and dumped her in the tub, clothes and all. "Now get on with it, Tom!"

He disappeared. Nervously Tom approached the girl, only to find her shivering uncontrollably. "Now, don't take on so. I'll do your face first, shall I? That's the ticket. That's the way; you help, then we'll both be happy. Look, I daresn't turn me back because of what you might do, but I promise not to look, if you know what I mean. Let me take some of these rags off your back. That'll be a start. Lord love us!"

Tom's concern was not because of the girl's emaciation, bad though that was. What had caused him to exclaim was the state of her back and shoulders. They were covered with a network of bruises, weals and burns. Tom had been with his master at Waterloo, and had travelled widely with him since, but this evidence of deliberate cruelty shocked him. With gentle fingers, which no ladies' maid could have rivalled, he quickly removed the rest of the girl's rags and helped her out of the bath. He fetched salves and one of his master's fine linen nightshirts. When the Earl returned she was dry and lying in a makeshift bed on a couch in the day cabin.

"The steward is bringing some food for you and the girl, Tom. I've dined. Are you ready for it? Ah, good! You've dealt with our little friend, I see."

"I have in a manner of speaking, sir. But I'd like you to see this. I wouldn't treat an animal like this and that's a fact."

The girl was still shivering as Tom gently lifted her up, pulling the nightshirt from her back to reveal the dreadful scars. The Earl frowned.

"Do you think the Pasha's men did all that, sir?"

"No, some of those scars are old ones, though I very much fear she had that beating today after all. What a life she's led, poor devil! I see you've put something on them."

"What we've got, which ain't much. What do you think we should do, sir?"

"I think she needs some food—something easy; a little gruel, perhaps. Then she probably needs sleep more than anything else. After that we'll see." By now Tom had lost his inhibitions about looking after a female, and he dealt with the girl with an unexpected deftness before tucking into a hearty meal himself. Meanwhile the Earl sat in his chair, frowning at his thoughts.

"We must put back our plans for a month or two, Tom. The girl is little use to me the way she is. I'll leave her with Sheikh Ibrahim when we call there to deliver the two Berbers to their home. I think I can persuade him to treat her. We should be there in two days, not more."

Tom was still preoccupied with what he had seen. "I suppose she might not have felt it as much—being brought up to it, so to speak," he said to himself without much conviction. "But how's she borne it? Sir, do you realise that if we hadn't of found Miss Linette when we did she might . . . she might have . . . It doesn't bear thinking about!"

"But I have thought about it, Tom," said the Earl softly. "Ever since we brought Linette back from that doxy's house in

London I've thought about it. And about the animal that put her there."

"This plan you were mentioning, sir. Is it something to do with Miss Linette? I shouldn't have thought this one'd be fit company for Miss Linette. I mean, look at her! What are you thinking of doing with her?"

"I'm using her to teach someone a lesson, Tom," said the Earl grimly. "One he won't forget. I mean the girl no harm, but I bought her for a purpose. She's a tool; no more. Let's hope she survives, for she's the key to my whole scheme."

Later that night, when Tom had gone to his bed, the Earl sat considering the slight figure on the couch. She was in a restless sleep, muttering unintelligibly and occasionally moaning. Where had she come from? She was probably French, of course. It didn't really matter—French or English, she would do for his purposes. But she'd need a name, a new one, for her own would probably be highly unsuitable. He sat in thought for a moment or two. "Perdita. Yes, that's perfect. Classical but apt. Perdita, the lost one!" Her eyes flew open, and once again he was astounded by their depth of colour. In that pale face they burned like a dark blue flame, like sapphires. There was something in them… He got up calmly, and walked to the door of his cabin. On his way out he looked back, smiling sardonically. Perhaps the Pasha had been right after all. The slut was a witch! All the better for what he had in mind.

THE VOYAGE WENT smoothly, and in two days they were close to their destination. This was a small bay to the west of Tangier, where lived a man skilled in those arts of medicine for which his ancestors had been famed throughout Europe. The Earl had made his acquaintance some years before, and had good cause to be grateful to him. Sheikh Ibrahim was now an honoured friend, and though the two men met infrequently they were able to pick up the threads of their friendship with ease. It was the Sheikh who had persuaded the Earl to take the two Berbers with him on his journeys through the eastern Mediterranean.

The Earl and Tom were much relieved at the prospect of making an early landfall. Perdita, as she was now called, had been in high fever ever since the first night. Tom had done what he could, but the resources of the ship were small. If she was to have a chance of survival the sooner she was in a doctor's hands, the better. Throughout her illness the girl had muttered and even shouted, but never so clearly that they could deduce who she was. Even her nationality remained uncertain, though they assumed that, like the rest of the pirate band, she was French. The Earl felt some pity for the girl, but he was impatient at the threat to his plans. He could, he supposed, replace her, but it would be difficult to find another so ideally suited to what he had in mind. He was intrigued by her, too. How did someone who had lived in primitive squalor come to have an air of such dignity and grace? These were attributes which could serve him well, but he wished he knew where she had acquired them!

They were received with great joy by the Sheikh and his household. He declared Perdita's condition bad but by no means hopeless, and saw her safely bestowed in his private apartments under the care of his own daughters. Then he led his guests into the salon, where he regaled them with refreshments and demanded an account of their travels. The Earl knew what the Sheikh wanted to hear. He had little interest in the antiquities of Greece, Turkey or Egypt, but was eager to hear what was happening in Athens, Istanbul and Cairo. It was not difficult to satisfy him, for the Sheikh had friends all over the Ottoman Empire and the Earl had been charged with numerous messages for him. But though he talked freely of his adventures in these great cities the Earl was singularly reticent about the girl—a fact which did not go unnoticed by the Sheikh.

When they had exhausted their supply of news—at least for the present—the Sheikh sat back and looked quizzically at his friend. "And now, my lord? Do you make for home and England? Or are you to visit your estate in France? You will note that I am far too discreet to ask you outright what you intend to do with your. . . protégée through there."

"What I do now depends in some measure on what you suggest. The girl, as you have seen, needs care and treatment. I was hoping you would undertake that."

"Of course, of course. It isn't necessary even to ask. I think we can cure her—to some extent at least. You realise that some of those scars will fade, but they may never disappear entirely?"

The Earl nodded soberly.

"But what then, my friend? I hope I do not presume on our friendship too far when I point out that she is a most unlikely companion for the Earl of Ambourne—here or anywhere else." The Earl raised an eyebrow, and the Sheikh said apologetically, "I could not help noticing, even in my brief examination, that the scars on her body are not those one acquires in the salons of London or Paris, or even in the houses of joy in those cities. You are not indulging in some generous but unwise act of chivalry, I hope?"

"My days of chivalry are over, Ibrahim."

"I know, I know. You will tell me that they disappeared when you lost the use of your arm at Waterloo. But my treatment seems to have cured that. I notice you are using it quite freely. Why is it that I could not cure your soul? Or is it not the injury, but something else that eats away at your spirit? My friend, my dear friend, you are not seeking some form of vengeance, are you? Perhaps for what happened to Mademoiselle Linette?" The Earl's face darkened and he walked to the window. The Sheikh continued gently, "Now I have offended you. Forgive me. I must not judge when I know so little of the story. You will, I am sure, talk to me if you feel you can do so. Meanwhile I will use all my skills to heal the flesh of that poor wretch in there. Damage to the spirit is more difficult to repair, but we shall do what we can. Let me take you to your room."

The Earl turned again, and the Sheikh was distressed at the implacable look on his face. "You have never seen Linette, Sheikh Ibrahim," he said. "She was a lovely child. Open, generous and happy. Linette is a pet name, but indeed I think it is apt. We have a little English bird, the linnet, and Linette was just such a happy spirit—not clever, but infinitely lovable. She spent her early childhood in France, but when her father died she and my aunt came over to live with us in England. They lived with us at Ambourne for over twelve years, and they were happy years. My own father died when I was still quite young and I became the head of our house, with all the responsibilities that held. Linette was one of them."

"Did you fall in love with her?" asked the Sheikh.

"Not as a man loves a woman he wishes to marry. But Linette needed all the protection we could give her—she was so trusting. Even when she grew older she felt nothing in the world

could do her harm; evil simply did not exist. Yes, she trusted us,
and we failed her," he said bitterly.

"What happened?"

"My aunt had been in ill health during the autumn of 1814,
and it was decided she should take the waters at Bath. She went
in November, leaving Linette with my mother at Ambourne. I
was in Vienna all that winter and I suppose my mother felt dull
and lacking in company. She invited friends to stay, among
them my mother's goddaughter, a lady who had at one time
persuaded herself that she would like to become the Countess
of Ambourne. I had disabused her of the notion. She brought
with her a new acquaintance, a certain Piers Carston. Spurred
on by her ill will towards me, Georgiana Compton persuaded
Linette to believe herself in love with Carston. She encouraged
secret meetings, overcame Linette's scruples and later aided the
pair to elope. Carston must have had some hold over her, for
she would not otherwise have abused our trust so grossly."

The Earl had obviously reached a difficult point in his nar-
rative. His voice remained calm, but his hands were clenched
round his glass. "Carston himself was motivated by greed. You
see, he had been deceived by the apparent affluence in which
Linette lived into believing her an heiress. When he discovered
this was not the case..."

The Earl paused and the slender glass cracked. Drops of
blood appeared on his thumb, which he absently wiped away.

The Sheikh put out his hand. "Take your time, my friend.
This is very painful."

"I have nearly finished, Ibrahim," said the Earl sombrely.
"Piers Carston had taken Linette to London. When he found
that she was not the heiress he'd imagined, he refused to marry
her and abandoned her there in one of the worst quarters of the
town. It took us a week to find her, and when we did...we were
horrified by her condition. She very nearly died. Our innocent, who had never had a malicious thought in her life, who
knew nothing of evil or inhumanity, had been deserted by the
man she loved and left to God knows what sort of life in the
stews of London. She was sixteen years old. Would you say that
this man should not be punished? I am not so forgiving. But I
am not seeking vengeance, Sheikh Ibrahim. That is too melo-
dramatic a word. Say rather that I am about to exact justice. I
have sought this man for over three years. He is now in London and I have found the weapon with which to punish him."

"You draw a fine line between vengeance and justice," said the Sheikh gravely, "and if, as I suspect, the 'weapon' is now lying sick in my apartments, then you must take care it does not rebound on you. To use human beings thus is a dangerous exercise."

The Earl smiled. "When have I ever shunned danger, Sheikh Ibrahim? Tell me that!"

CHAPTER TWO

THE BIRDS IN THE OAK trees outside had been arguing for some time. The noise of their angry chatter coming in through the window had woken her. Her skin was hot and sore and her head was aching. Her limbs were stiff. She must be ill. Mama would come soon, she was sure, and then all would be well. Mama would send for Dr. Williams and then she would be better... She closed her eyes and slept again... Strange! She was asleep, and yet she could feel herself being lifted and turned. Gentle hands were bathing her forehead, then putting something soothing on her back. That hurt! She drank gratefully from the cup that was put to her lips. Had she fallen from her horse, perhaps? She couldn't remember. Mama would tell her... Later...

When she next woke up the pain in her head was less severe. The birds were quiet, but she could hear voices outside. She slowly turned to look at the window. What was wrong? This was not her room! The window was in the wrong place. Perhaps they had moved her bed... No, the room was completely strange to her. Where was she? Where was Mama? Then she heard a voice she recognised. It was a man's voice, crisp, decisive, talking in French. The last time she had heard it he had been speaking English... Suddenly memory came flooding back in a series of pictures—the two men on the Englishman's ship, the courtyard in Algiers, the capture of *Le Faucon* and her life with the pirates. Oh, God, no! She remembered it all now. She was back in the nightmare that was reality. In her weakness and despair she groaned, and slow tears forced themselves down her cheeks. There was an instant flurry of silk and a breath of perfume, then cool hands were wiping her face and forehead and giving her a drink. She slipped into sleep again.

It continued like this for some days. The girl hovered between sleeping and waking, while her poor battered body re-

gained strength. In her more lucid moments she forced herself
to face what had happened to her in the years up to the sinking
of *Le Faucon*, and as her body grew stronger so did her determination to return to the stoicism she had possessed before her
illness. She accepted the gentle care of the Sheikh and his
daughters passively, but met all overtures of friendship with
silence. This act of will took its toll, and the Sheikh became seriously worried about her state of mind. On the morning of the
Earl's departure the Sheikh voiced his concern. "I am satisfied that the battle for the girl's physical well-being is almost
won. All she needs now is rest and care. When you return I
hope she will be fully recovered. But I am more concerned
about her refusal to communicate with her fellow humans. It
is not only a question of language, I am sure. She has erected a
barrier, which will take time and skill to overcome. I wish I
knew more of her history. What is her name, for instance?"

"I know very little, Ibrahim," said the Earl. "Only that she
was arrested on the pirate ship *Le Faucon* one or two days before I found her in the Pasha's courtyard. I don't even know her
real name, but, as it is almost certainly unsuitable, I named her
Perdita."

The girl was shamelessly listening in the room overlooking
the garden court in which the two men were sitting. She smiled
ironically. Her real name was most certainly inappropriate.
Perdita would do very well.

"You English and your Shakespeare," murmured the
Sheikh. "Yet I suppose it is apt—the lost one. However, if I
remember correctly Shakespeare's Perdita was found to be a
princess."

The Earl laughed. "Oh, I very much doubt that my Perdita
is anything of that nature, Ibrahim! That's the crux of my
plan—the slut is so very unworthy, so absolutely low. She's part
of the scum of the Mediterranean, and she's perfect!"

The Sheikh looked serious. "I do not wish to bore you again
with my anxieties about your plan, my friend. But I beg you to
be very careful when you are playing with the lives of others.
That is Allah's prerogative—and Allah is jealous of his powers."

"You are too concerned, Ibrahim. The girl is a tool, no more
and no less. I promise you that when I have finished with her
she will be no worse off than she was—in fact, she will have a

much better life. Why, she will have an establishment of sorts, and fine clothes and jewels.''

"I cannot believe that your values have become so crassly material, Lord Ambourne!''

"No, they are not, I hope. But hers might well be. Now, how long must I wait before coming again?''

The Sheikh considered, pulling at his beard. "I would like to keep her here until she is fully restored—in mind as well as body. But I fear that would be too long for you. Shall we say three months?''

"Two at the most, Ibrahim. Concentrate on curing the girl's body. Leave her mind to me!''

They went into the house soon after, and silence fell in the garden. Upstairs in her room, Perdita was left with much food for thought. She was to be involved in a plan, that much was clear. It was also clear that the man who had brought her here did not think of her as a person at all, only as a—what had he called her?—a tool. He had called her other things, too. She wrinkled her brow in an effort to remember. It wasn't only 'slut' or 'scum'. There was something else ... She had it! He had called her a 'pearl'. When she'd lain in the filth of that court-yard he had called her a pearl, and then the courtyard had filled with cruel laughter—more cruel than anyone there realised. Well, over the last two years she had taught herself to expect nothing more. She would survive this, as she had survived the catastrophe that had put her on the pirate ship in the first place and the torment and isolation that had followed. But she had only done that by learning to be strong, by refusing to be affected by the world around her, by shutting it out. She must exert herself. It would be so disastrously easy to relax her guard with the Sheikh and his daughters, for it was a long time since she had experienced such loving care. She must not let it weaken her.

TWO MONTHS PASSED, and the Earl's ship had just been sighted. He was expected within the hour. The Sheikh was sitting in the garden with Perdita. Rest and food had transformed her. She was still slender, but her face and figure had acquired the bloom of health. Her long hair was a cloud of dark brown silk held back in a jewelled cap, and the combination of her sea-green kaftan and those deep blue eyes made of her a picture to delight

the most critical eye. The Sheikh regarded her with pleasure,
but then he sighed. In spite of all his efforts she was as distant
as ever. He had reasoned with her, tried persuasion on her, had
asked his daughters to amuse her—all in vain. She suffered their
ministrations patiently, was always courteous, but refused to
talk to them. He had tried to trick her by speaking at length in
Arabic and then suddenly switching to French or even English. He knew she understood at least one of those languages,
but she was never caught out. He was astonished at the strength
of purpose to be found in such a delicate frame. Over the weeks
he had become increasingly certain that there was a mystery
about the girl. He had the absurd impression that she could
easily be the princess the Earl had so laughingly dismissed, for
she had breeding in every line. He was anxious for the Earl to
see her, but not at all happy at the thought of Perdita's departure.

Perdita, too, regarded the Earl's imminent arrival with mixed
feelings. She, too, was apprehensive about her unknown future. But she was much more eager to go. She knew that if she
stayed much longer with the Sheikh and his family she would
be unable to keep the detachment she had so painfully regained. She was beginning to return their regard for her, and
she dared not let that happen. She looked at him now, his eyes
full of kindly concern. He took her hand and addressed her in
French, "And so, Perdita, the Earl will be here very soon now.
Are you ready to go? I doubt it. I wonder whether he would let
me keep you a little while longer. But would that serve any
purpose? You widen your eyes. You're afraid, but of what?
You do not wish to stay here, is that it? Are you afraid of us?
Or can it be that you are afraid of yourself? If that were so it
would be progress indeed. You shake your head. Perdita, I beg
of you, do not shut us out like this. I know a little of what you
have suffered, and I believe you have armed yourself against
any further pain by rejecting human contact—even life itself.
Oh, yes, you may shake your head again, but I know of your
attempt to end your life in the sea . . . I have surprised you?"

Perdita had never been more strongly tempted to confide in
this man, to explain to him why she had jumped into the sea at
Algiers. For twenty-four hours she had believed herself to be
close to death in the Pasha's prison. She had come to terms with
the thought of death, even welcomed it as a way of escape from
a life that had become insupportable. When the Earl had re-

moved that way of escape she had impulsively tried to take her
own life. She knew it was wrong, and knew she could never do
such a thing again. Life was to be borne, stoically if necessary,
but never thrown away. She looked at the Sheikh. He seemed
to see through to her very soul. He said softly, ''Well, Perdita,
I think we understand something of each other after all. Perhaps words are not always needed. Fight your battle, my child,
but if ever you should need a refuge I would be happy to offer
you one. Lord Ambourne is a man of honour and feeling, but
in this instance I fear his judgement is impaired by his hatred
of the man who betrayed his young cousin. Ah, you understand hatred? You have felt the same emotion? For the captain of *Le Faucon* perhaps? No? I wonder who? You will not
tell me? Well, then, I will say to you what I will say to Lord
Ambourne: hatred is destructive. You might or might not succeed in destroying the object of your hatred. You will certainly
succeed in destroying your own happiness.'' Then, when Perdita smiled bitterly, he added, ''Happiness is still possible for
you. Do not shut the door to it. And now that is enough. Remember what I have said. You have the courage and spirit to
help Lord Ambourne. Use them wisely.''

A bustle inside the house warned the Sheikh that his guest
would arrive within minutes. He bowed to Perdita and went in.
She got up and walked restlessly about the garden, her thoughts
in turmoil. The Sheikh's words had made a deep impression on
her. But she would not, she *could* not now surrender the fortress she had built to protect herself. So much courage she did
not possess. As for Lord Ambourne, she would wait to see what
was to come. Of one thing she was certain. His opinion of her
was so low that nothing she felt or thought would hold the
slightest interest for him. It was better it should be so, for then
she could remain indifferent to him in a way she could never
dismiss the Sheikh. All the same, she was curious to see this
man who held her immediate future in his hands. She remembered very little—grey eyes in a tanned face, an impression of
strength, an authoritative voice, an ability to speak French as
fluently as he spoke English. That was all.

She looked up to see the object of her thoughts standing in
the garden doorway. Her memory had not been at fault. He had
grey eyes, hair that was almost black, and a strong, rather hard
face. He was tall, and dressed well but plainly in fawn buck-
skins and a dark maroon coat. For an unguarded moment his

eyes widened with astonishment and something more. She did not know what it was, but it filled her with a peculiar excitement, almost a sense of recognition. But of what? He took a step towards her, but then stopped abruptly, and his face, which had been alive with feeling, became expressionless. When he finally spoke his tone was cool. "I would not have thought it possible that you could be so changed. I must congratulate the Sheikh on his work."

She looked at him silently, still dazed by what had happened.

"Ah, yes, Sheikh Ibrahim did say you were not yet talking to us. A pity. But he is sure you understand French, so in the absence of any other evidence I will assume you understand me. I am returning to Europe tomorrow, and you will accompany me. In your room you will find some European clothing." He looked her up and down. "Fetching though those garments are, as I'm sure you are aware, they are hardly suitable for the rigours of a northern European winter. You will consult with the seamstresses here. They have my orders and will see that you look respectably dressed. I expect to see you ready to sail with me at nine in the morning." As she continued to stare at him he said irritably, "Go, girl, go!"

Sadly she returned to her room. Now that the moment had come she was reluctant to leave this oasis in the desert that was her life. She refused to admit, even to herself, that the Sheikh and his daughters had taken a place in her heart. But she had been reminded of her status by the Earl's tone. To him she would always be something lower than a servant.

In this she did the Earl less than justice. He would never normally have spoken to a dependent in such tones. The truth was that he had been disorientated by the unexpected feeling that had overtaken him on seeing Perdita. For years he had prided himself on his self-control. Born into a family with large estates, he had inherited the title early and accepted its responsibilities as fully as he enjoyed its privileges. As a young man in Regency London he had, of course, enjoyed the favours of various ladies in that pleasure-seeking world. And his birth and wealth had made him a tempting prospect to ambitious mamas and their marriageable daughters. But he had easily avoided all the traps laid for him, had never experienced any emotion he could not control, other than hatred for Piers Carston. Not, that was, until he had looked into Perdita's eyes on

the night he had taken her from Algiers. Now, at the sight of
Perdita in the garden, his calm assurance had deserted him
again...! He reminded himself that he had been abroad for too
long. Such unaccountable lapses would soon be forgotten after his return to Europe.

The time for them to leave was soon upon them. Perdita had
been caught up in a whirl of fitting and stitching, with little time
left to come to terms with her departure. Before she knew it she
found herself on the shore in her new European clothes, waiting patiently while the Earl took his leave of his host. Then it
was her turn. While the Earl looked sardonically on, the Sheikh
kissed her cheeks and said with a mischievous look, "You
would make an ideal wife, Perdita, for you never answer
back!" Then more seriously, "Remember, my daughter, you
have a refuge here if you should ever need one. Now farewell!
Go with Allah's blessing and protection!"

The Earl was making for the ship and the girl followed him.
Suddenly she turned back, caught the Sheikh's hand and kissed
it. "*Merci*, Sheikh Ibrahim," she whispered so softly that no
one else could hear, "*merci*." Then, without looking at him
again, she followed the Earl to the ship for France.

PERDITA SAT IN HER CABIN, examining her new clothes. There
was nothing else to do, for a cold wind was blowing outside and
the seas were rough. Besides, Tom had brought a message that
she was to remain inside. He had obviously been coached, for
he made no comment on her appearance, nor even gave any
sign that he had seen her before. She wondered if the Earl was
suffering from seasickness, and rather hoped he was. It was
therefore a disappointment to hear his incisive voice on the deck
a few minutes later, giving some directions to Tom. No seasickness there. She turned back to her clothes with a sigh. They
were very pretty, of course. It was a long time since she had seen
such lovely materials—pink Italian silk and pale blue jaconet
muslin for two of the dresses, midnight-blue merino wool for
a third, grey kerseymere and dark blue velvet for the pelisses.
The undergarments were all of finest cambric or lawn. There
were even two matching hats and a luxurious cashmere shawl.
The gloves were Limerick, and the slippers of softest leather.
Perdita was still feminine enough to enjoy parading in her new
wardrobe, curtsying and bowing. She was pleased to discover

that she had not forgotten the art. It had been so long...dear
God...so long! She sat down, overcome with a sudden vision
of herself at her first party. It had only been a small affair, but
it had promised to be the door to a delightful new world. She
had worn pink silk then, and it had been a great success. Afterwards Mama and she had planned what she would wear for
her come-out the following year. The question of whether white
lace would be too 'old', and if it should be worn over white,
pink or blue satin had seemed overwhelmingly important. Of
course as the heiress to the Taverton estates she would be assured of an excitingly successful season...But by the following June, when she would have been dancing at her first
London balls, her mother was dead and she...and she...She
hid her face in her hands. Whatever happened to her in the future she would never go back to the happy world of her girl-
hood. That would remain closed to her forever, for she was now
unacceptable in any decent society. She sat there for a moment, then rallied herself angrily. What was she doing? This
was no way to survive! This was what happened when one relaxed one's guard! She had been closeted in her cabin without
air or exercise for far too long. To hell with the Earl and his
stupid commands! She flung open the door of her cabin and
marched out on to the deck.

A gust of wind caught her as she came out, forcing her to
clutch her bonnet. The kerseymere pelisse was not really thick
enough for the weather, but she was determined not to go back.
She walked briskly round the deck, enjoying the strong fresh
air. However, her enjoyment was curtailed when she turned a
corner and walked into the Earl. The ship gave a sudden lurch
and she found herself clutching his sleeve. When they were
disengaged he turned on her.

"What the devil are you doing out on deck? I gave strict orders you were to remain in your cabin!" In the face of his anger she adopted a stratagem she had learned to use with
Legrand, the Captain of *Le Faucon*. Looking as stupid as possible, she behaved as if she had not heard him. He continued in
tones of contempt, "I know you heard me, so don't try your
tricks on me! Or were you too anxious to show yourself in your
new finery? That's not meant for pleasing the sailors, my girl.
The bonnet's an expensive one from Paris—it's wasted on
them. Save it for London!"

Perdita's mind was racing behind her expression of stupidity. How could she punish him for his unpleasant insinuations? With a masterly look of hurt incomprehension she took her hand away from the bonnet. She regretted the necessity, for it was a fetching grey velvet lined with pink silk. The wind swept it into the air. It hovered for a moment, then went sailing down into the churning sea. Then she put her hand to her mouth.

The Earl was furious. He narrowed his eyes and said softly, "If I were sure you had done that deliberately, you little slut, you wouldn't sit down comfortably for a week." She could see him debating whether to pursue the matter, then he suddenly turned on his heel and left her. As he went he shouted to Tom to escort her back.

Perdita returned to her cabin well pleased with her short expedition. The Earl, it seemed, was not as in control as he would like to be. There was scope here for some fun. She did not deceive herself that she could win any serious battle between them, but it was pleasant to have got the better of him in that little skirmish. Detached she would remain, but she might derive some mild amusement from needling the great man! The fact that she refused to talk was already a source of annoyance to him. She must see what else she could think of. It might while away the weary hours.

Unfortunately the Earl proved very elusive for the rest of the voyage. When he saw her he treated her with apparent indifference, but since she had all her meals in her cabin they did not often meet. Until she learned what sort of establishment was to be her home it was difficult to make plans, so she spent most of her time in stultifying boredom. However, the Earl did arrange for Tom to escort her on a walk round the deck every morning. It did not disconcert Tom that she was silent. He talked enough for both of them, and Perdita learned a great deal about the Earl's home on these walks. She found it difficult to reconcile the man she knew with the picture Tom drew of him, and put it down to an old servant's partiality. Towards the end of their voyage he said in some embarrassment, "I wouldn't never have thought you could turn out so well, miss. You might not talk much, but you do have an air about you, no mistake. I take back what I said. I think you and Miss Linette would do well together. I hope you'll be very happy at Belleroi."

He scuttled away, leaving Perdita in a rueful frame of mind. After years of isolation from gentleness, concern, even good-will, she was now meeting them wherever she went! She jumped as a voice behind her said, "What a pity Tom isn't going to be at Belleroi to act as your champion! How do you do it, Perdita? First the Sheikh, and now Tom. Well, I have a use for those arts of yours. But do not employ them too indiscriminately. The cowherds at Belleroi are very susceptible!"

Thank you, my lord, thought Perdita. It is a relief to know that if I am ever in danger of forgetting my true position I can be sure you will remind me. Though I cannot like you, I am truly grateful to you. And she went into her cabin without looking round.

They landed at Cherbourg and were soon in a carriage, on the last stage of their journey. She had learned from Tom that, in addition to his estates in England, the Earl had inherited a small estate in a quiet corner of Normandy, and guessed that he was taking her there. It was dark as they came through a cluster of cottages and up the long straight drive that led to the house. She was so travel-weary that she noticed little of their arrival. She was taken up to her room by a stout woman in black, who gave her some soup, undressed her, and put her to bed. She was asleep before the door was shut.

CHAPTER THREE

PERDITA WOKE EARLY the next morning after a refreshing sleep. She lay there for a moment in the darkened room, and then got up to open the curtains. It was barely light. The long straight drive along which they had driven the night before stretched in front of her. It seemed to go on forever. At the far end were two massive cast-iron gates, flanked by wide stone pillars. To the left and right, about a hundred yards from the house, stood two identical little lodges, and flowerbeds and lawns were laid out in rigorous symmetry around them. She shivered. It all looked so cold, so formal. She shivered again and realised that it was, in fact, very cold! She had spent so long in the Mediterranean that she had forgotten how sharp autumn mornings here in the north could be. After all, it was already November. She splashed her face with water from the jug on her wash-stand and dressed, putting on the thickest of her three dresses—the dark blue merino. Hastily throwing the grey pelisse over her shoulders, she slipped out of her room and sought the stairs. In two minutes she was outside.

The air was intoxicating. It had a crisp freshness that no wind of the Mediterranean had ever possessed. She savoured it for a moment while she stood listening for signs of movement around the house. The servants were astir in the kitchen, which must be behind the house, and she could hear a child's voice among the other noises. But the main rooms along the front were curtained and silent. She had time to explore. When she reached the lodges she turned and looked back. The house was a small château. The symmetry of the gardens and lodges was echoed in its façade, but the grey stone was softened by creepers, which had been allowed to grow over the lower half. Two rows of windows stretched across the front. The lower ones obviously belonged to a series of large reception rooms on the first floor, and above them were the bedrooms. A line of small windows in the roof probably belonged to the servants' rooms. The whole building showed signs of recent repair—perhaps since the restoration of the monarchy in France.

A servant, dressed in black, was walking stiffly up the drive. He bowed when he reached her and said in a voice that was formal but managed at the same time to convey his disapproval, "*Mademoiselle*'s breakfast is served in her room." Meekly she allowed herself to be conducted back to the house. There was little point in ignoring him; she needed to find out more about the house and its occupants before deciding how to behave. Besides, she was ravenously hungry!

Her room was charming in the fresh morning light. Draped muslin softened the tall windows and furniture, and rose-printed chintz hung from the brass curtain-poles. The same rosy chintz covered a small couch and two chairs. A fire burned in the pretty marble fireplace opposite the bed, and in front of it stood a tripod table with a tray. She drank the hot chocolate and ate the crusty rolls, butter and quince jam with relish. She was just exploring a tiny dressing-room, which opened off her room, when a maid appeared to escort her to the library. After hastily washing her hands and face she followed the maid downstairs.

The library was a lovely room on the first floor. She was gazing in admiration at the long windows and the books lining three of the walls when a cool, well-known voice said, "Come here, Perdita."

The Earl was sitting in a wing chair by the fire, dressed plainly in a dark tobacco-brown coat and buff pantaloons. On the small table at his side was a pile of papers and books, one of which lay open on his knee. She contemplated disobeying him, then decided it would be better not to challenge him until she knew more.

"Sit down," he said, without looking up from his book. This was too much! She looked at him blankly, her stupid expression firmly in place.

"Do not, I beg of you, imagine I am deceived by that bovine look. You understand French perfectly, and I have no time for tricks. There's a great deal to say to you. Please sit down." Happy to have wrung a "please" out of him, she sat. He shut his book and looked at her thoughtfully for some minutes, while she stared into the fire, trying to shut out all consciousness of the long figure sitting in the chair on her left.

"You are about to embark on a strenuous course of study, Perdita. During the next six months you will be trained—I will not say educated—in what is necessary to give you the outer appearance of a lady. You will have a chaperon, who will also instruct you in deportment, and tutors in dancing and music. You will be given the elements of reading and writing—at least enough to write your name."

He paused, and Perdita looked at him in astonishment. Could this really be happening? Was this man telling her that he was about to make her into a lady? She did not know whether to laugh or cry at the bitter irony of the situation. She had spent two years trying to forget all she had learned of gentleness, concern for others and the courtesies of polite Society. Now she was to have six months' training to 'acquire' them. Life was surely full of strange twists!

"Perdita, I have told you I am not deceived by this idiot's stare you employ. I am convinced that you use it to hide what you do not wish the world to see—such as, God knows why, triumph at the loss of a very pretty bonnet." Caught off guard, she turned her head swiftly to look at him. "Yes, I thought as much—you did it deliberately! Was it a somewhat childish effort to annoy me? The loss of the bonnet was yours, not mine! But then, I have long given up divining the thoughts of women. To return to the tasks ahead. I will assume that before the time is out you will regain the use of your tongue, and when that happens you will be taught to speak correctly."

Perdita found herself wondering what use this high-born aristocrat had for a pseudo-lady. What was he up to? Well, she would wait and see—the situation would not be without its piquancies. She realised he was talking again. She must concentrate on what he was saying.

"When I have finished with you, which will be within a year, I will see that you have enough clothes and jewels to set yourself up in the profession I imagine will suit you best. There is no reason why you should not enjoy a very comfortable existence from then on. It will at the very least be an improvement on your mode of life with the pirates."

Perdita was torn between resentment and laughter, but finally forced her mind into its preferred mode—that of detachment. She would need a clear head if she was to succeed in the delicately balanced game in front of her. The man was no fool.

"However, I should warn you, Perdita," the cool voice went on, "that if you refuse to do as I have said you will be sent back to the Pasha in Algiers with my compliments. Do you understand me?"

She stood up quickly. There were some things to which she could not remain indifferent. It was as she had thought. She might win skirmishes, but she would never win the major battles. He had all the heavy weapons in his hands. But that wouldn't stop her from resisting his attempts to destroy her self-respect. Whatever had happened in the past she had always kept an inner core of integrity. She wasn't going to let Lord Ambourne succeed where so many others had failed.

He let her go then, merely saying that she was to present herself in the library at two o'clock that afternoon to meet the first of her tutors.

In her room she found the stout woman in black, who had helped her to bed the night before. She introduced herself as Madame Lebrun, the housekeeper. She was obviously curious about Perdita and disappointed not to be able to converse with her. Perdita ignored her as far as possible, and at length the woman finished what she was doing and went out with a sniff. Madame Lebrun was indiscreet enough to recount her experience to the other servants, and this, coupled with their uncertainty about Perdita's true position in the household, caused them to treat her with unfriendly suspicion. This well suited Perdita's passionate determination to remain totally self-contained, depending on no one for friendship or company.

"I SHALL DO what I can, milor'," said Monsieur Champollion doubtfully. They were in the library, and Perdita had just met the little music master for the first time. "The time is very short. And *mademoiselle* does not talk, you say?"

"Not yet, anyway," murmured the Earl, looking sardonically at Perdita. "However, we have every reason to believe that she will eventually."

"But how am I to teach her the theory, or test her knowledge, if she cannot answer me? She could perhaps write it down?"

"Well, not yet, Champollion. Mademoiselle Perdita has not yet mastered the art."

"Not write?" faltered Champollion. "She can't write?"

"Champollion, if you cannot manage to teach her some rudimentary little tunes—enough to tinkle out at some insipid evening party—then say so. I will find someone else," said the Earl, growing impatient.

Perdita surveyed them both in silent amusement. What fun she was going to have. Who would have thought that such an unpromising episode in her life would turn out to be so diverting! She straightened her face when she saw the Earl's eyes on her.

Monsieur Champollion was hastily protesting his complete confidence in Mademoiselle Perdita's ability. "She will soon have a repertoire of the most delightful little tunes, milord. You will see. Very soon." He left, looking doubtfully at Perdita and mopping his brow.

"What amused you just now, I wonder?" said the Earl. "Was it Champollion? The poor man is convinced he has an impossible task, but he would not dream of admitting it. Are you so unmusical? You must not underrate yourself, Perdita. You may well discover you have an unexpected talent for music. It will complement your other... talents." Perdita's eyes flashed and she jumped up. "What has angered you now?" said the Earl impatiently. "The ladies in the kind of establishment I imagine you would aspire to—in London, or Paris perhaps—are not simply stripped and bedded, Perdita. They must entertain their clients. A little ability in music will not come amiss."

Perdita walked to the window, struggling for calm. Whatever he said she must not let it affect her.

He continued scornfully, "Oh, come, now! You surely don't imagine that I am ignorant of what you have been, Perdita? I assure you, your assumed indignation is really quite unnecessary. By all means act the modest young lady when we are in the public eye, but abandon these histrionics when we are alone. I bought you, knowing you for a strumpet, and you are of value to me because of it. Sit down, and listen to what I have to say." Perdita turned round and gazed at him defiantly, staying where she was. He said softly, "I am not accustomed to being defied in my own house, Perdita. Come here and sit down!"

When she still refused to move he got up swiftly and caught her by the arm. "What is it, Perdita?" he said dangerously. "Are you trying to have me believe that no man has ever held you like this? Kissed you like this?"

He kissed her violently, even passionately, but though he was angry there was an innate tenderness in his kiss that turned Perdita's heart over. She had never experienced anything like it before, and for a moment it filled her with a surprised delight. Then she struggled to pull herself away. He released her with a laugh and stood looking at her contemptuously. "My God, I must congratulate you, Perdita. If I did not know you for what you are—a slut, a drab from the dregs of the Mediterranean— that air of artless innocence might well deceive me." Perdita walked swiftly to the door. He made as if to stop her, but then hesitated and said merely, "Consider carefully what I have said, Perdita. You will have time, for I do not wish to see you again today. Tomorrow you will meet your chaperon and other tutors. Be here at the same hour. Go now."

Perdita was glad to be alone in her room. She needed a respite. The strange and lovely emotion she had experienced was so new to her that it would take time to recover her self-possession. But recover it she must. Bitter unhappiness lay ahead if she allowed the Earl or anyone else any power over her real self. To him she was a tool, no more. It was essential she returned to her former detached dislike of him.

When they met the next morning it was as if the afternoon before had never been. The Earl's behaviour was intimidatingly formal. He presented her to Madame d'Espery, the elderly aristocrat who was to chaperon her, Signor Calvi, her dancing master, and Père Amboise, the local *curé*, who would teach her to read and write. If she had not been so antipathetic to the Earl she could have admired his competence in dealing with them all. Not only were the lessons admirably arranged throughout the week, he had also seen to it that she had free time in the afternoons for fresh air and exercise. He soon dispersed any gratitude she might have felt, however.

"Understand me, Perdita, you are not to stray far from the house on your outings, nor are you to indulge in any of your tricks with the fellows of the neighbourhood. They are simple souls and I am quite sure you could bewitch them out of their senses." He looked at the lovely face before him. "Quite sure. If you are wise, however, you will resist the temptation to do so."

PERDITA'S TIME was soon heavily engaged with her lessons, so-
called practice sessions and walks. She saw very little of the
Earl, for during the hours of daylight he was out on estate
business or closeted in the library with his agent, and in the
evenings he visited his neighbours or dined alone. But, even
when he was out, the château was dominated by his presence
and Perdita resented this. Her walks became precious to her, for
then she could escape. Madame d'Espery was content to let
Perdita walk alone, as she herself preferred to spend this time
"resting" in her room. As long as Perdita was back in good
time for their early-evening meal she was left to her own devices for the whole afternoon. She quickly discovered that the
gardens behind the house had none of the formality of the
front, but were designed in the English style, with large trees
scattered in the lawns, which sloped up to woods at the back.
In the distance to the right a large lake was a haven for flocks
of water birds. Though the weather was grey and cold, Perdita
loved her walks. The park was extensive enough to give her the
illusion of total freedom, and she was happier, discovering its
wild beauty, than she had been for some time. At this season
there was little by way of leaf or flower, but the undergrowth
was full of small animals that scuttled away as she approached, and when it grew colder left their tracks on the frost-
covered ground.

She was almost on the far side of the woods one day when
she heard a soft whimpering. Some animal in pain! Turning
swiftly in the direction of the sound, Perdita picked her way
through dead branches and brambles until she reached her goal.
A girl of about her own age lay there, holding her ankle and
crying. Her huge grey eyes were wide open in terror. "No! No!
Leave me! Don't touch me!"

"I'm not going to hurt you, I promise," Perdita quickly assured her, dropping on one knee beside her. "Tell me what's
wrong. Is it your ankle?"

The girl stared at Perdita for a moment and seemed to be reassured by what she saw. "Yes, I fell. I was looking for Toto."
Then, to Perdita's dismay, large tears gathered in her eyes and
rolled down her cheeks. She gave a helpless little sob. "I've lost
my dog. And my foot hurts. What am I to do?"

"Well, I should imagine the first thing is to see about your
ankle. Let me feel it." Perdita was not without experience, and
she soon established that the girl had not suffered any serious

damage. "I think you could walk if I helped you," she said eventually.

The girl clutched her arm. "Oh, no! I couldn't. The pain!"

"Then I must leave you to get help," said Perdita, rising. "It will be dark soon. We can't stay here."

"Don't leave me. Please don't leave me!" In her agitation, the girl rose to her knees. Perdita took advantage of this to help her to her feet, and they had soon struggled to the edge of the wood. Here the girl collapsed. "I can't go any further. My foot hurts," she sobbed. "And where's Toto?"

Perdita looked at her in exasperation. There was only an hour or so of daylight left. The girl must be made to walk. "Toto might have found his own way home," she suggested. "He might be looking for you there. Can't you try again? I'll help you all I can."

"Toto's a she, not a he," said the girl, looking up at Perdita indignantly.

Perdita was amused. It was cold, it was growing dark, the girl seemed unable to help herself, but she could still get annoyed with her rescuer over her pet dog! She looked at the flushed face before her. The girl was ethereally lovely, with silver-grey eyes, delicately pink cheeks and pale gold hair. The tear-stains on her cheeks only added to her air of fragility. Perdita sighed. She had already become far more involved with this spoiled child than she'd wanted—even to the point of breaking her rule of silence. What was she to do? "Come on," she said lifting the girl to her feet. "Lean on me and hop."

They had gone a fair way along the path when they were hailed by a man's voice. A minute later a young giant came running up to them. "Eliane, what's happened? I've been looking for you everywhere."

"My foot hurts dreadfully, Philippe, and I've lost Toto! Help me!"

"Toto came back hours ago. That's what worried us so much. Here, I'll take you home." He swept the girl into his arms and started off down the path. Perdita hesitated for a moment, then shrugged her shoulders and turned back through the wood. The girl was safe, and her task was finished.

IN THE DAYS that followed Perdita found herself wondering where the girl, Eliane, lived—perhaps on the other side of the

hill. She was certainly lovely, though probably spoilt. Perdita
had an impression that the girl had been ill—she was very thin.
How old was she? That was more difficult to judge. Eliane's
face and person were those of a girl of about twenty, Perdita's
own age, but her manner and speech had the simplicity of a
much younger person. And who was the young man who had
come so peremptorily to the rescue? From what she had been
able to see in the fading light, he too was fair, though his hair
was a darker colour than Eliane's. He was certainly handsome
and certainly strong—striding off over rough ground like that
with the girl in his arms! He'd seemed to treat her like some
precious jewel to be jealously guarded and protected. But then,
there was something about her which aroused a protective instinct. Look at the way she, Perdita, had rushed into speech in
order to reassure her. Well, whoever they were, she hoped they
were not too closely acquainted with the Earl. Explaining her
sudden ability to speak might prove difficult! For a day or two
she waited apprehensively for a summons to the library, but
when none came she decided with relief that either the Earl was
not on visiting terms with Eliane's family or that the girl herself had not thought Perdita's part in the adventure worth
mentioning.

The days grew shorter as November passed into December.
According to Madame d'Espery, the Earl would soon return to
England to spend Christmas with his family, and she redoubled her efforts to teach Perdita the usages of polite society. She
was sure the Earl would invite them to dine with him before his
departure and was eager to show that Perdita had made some
progress. Perdita was equally eager to demonstrate that she had
not! At first she had derived no little amusement from deceiving her tutors, and what the Earl had called her 'bovine look'
was much in evidence. However, for one of Perdita's lively intelligence the pleasure in fooling such easy prey soon palled—
it was far more difficult to hide her familiarity with the ways of
a great house and her growing appreciation of living in a civilised society once more. But, whether it was easy or difficult,
she remained determined to disguise her real self from everyone in the château—especially its master. Her refusal to talk
and her failure to "improve" satisfied her desire to thwart the
Earl wherever she could. In a situation where he had almost
absolute power over her future she cherished these small secret
victories over his domination. Accordingly, when Madame

d'Espery announced that they were invited to join him the following evening, Perdita felt both apprehensive and excited. However boringly simple it was to deceive her tutors, the Earl himself would be a far greater challenge. He wished to see what progress she had made. Well, so he should, thought Perdita, though if his expectations were high he was due for a sad disappointment!

She spent some time and considerable thought on her preparations the following day. She must leave some hope of improvement, for it would not do to give the Earl such a disgust of her that he would find her unsuitable after all and send her back to Africa. That must be avoided at all costs. Her resources were slender, but she made ingenious use of them. The unexceptionably simple rose silk gown acquired quite a raffish air when draped lavishly with lace from the top of her dressing-table and finished off with a purple spangled scarf given to her by one of the Sheikh's daughters. A painfully tight use of curl-papers the night before had enabled her to twist her hair into a riot of elaborate curls. She was pleased to observe that the addition of a small paper flower found in one of the bedrooms did not improve her appearance.

When this vision appeared in the salon before dinner Madame d'Espery dropped her fan and sank into a chair. It amused Perdita enormously to see the stunned look on the Earl's face, but his expression quickly returned to its normal impassivity. Madame d'Espery found her voice and suggested that she should take Perdita upstairs . . .

"I will not hear of it," said the Earl blandly. "Perdita has clearly spent a great deal of effort on her appearance tonight and it would be cruel to spoil her enjoyment. May I escort you into the dining-room, Madame d'Espery?"

Perdita was left feeling baffled by the Earl's reaction. She had fully expected to be ordered to remove her trailing draperies, and was somewhat disconcerted at being forced to manage them at the dining table. The Earl was at his most charming during the splendid meal that followed. Perdita knew that her chaperon had lost most of her own wealth in the Revolution and was almost one of the Earl's pensioners, but there was nothing to suggest this in his manner to her that night. Madame d'Espery positively sparkled in his company, and Perdita watched and marvelled. So fascinated was she by the exchanges between her companions, so relaxed in the conviv-

ial, candlelit atmosphere, that she almost forgot her own role.
She was reminded of it by the Earl. Part of her lace trailed on
to her plate, and had become caught in the cutlery. She was
making a discreet effort to disentangle it when she caught the
Earl's eye. His lips were twitching with amusement. Furious at
herself and him, she pulled the lace free, picked up the leg of
wild duck from her plate and, staring at him, defiantly bit into
the flesh with gusto. The look of amusement vanished, to be
replaced with a frown. At this she meekly put her duck down
and then slowly licked her fingers one by one. Madame
d'Espery's shocked "Mademoiselle Perdita!" made her jump,
so absorbed had she been with the Earl. "*Mademoiselle*, have
you forgotten yourself?"

Perdita looked apologetically at Madame d'Espery and
wiped her fingers carefully on her lace. At Madame's gasp of
outrage, the Earl said, "Pray, do not upset yourself, Madame
d'Espery. Your charge has by no means forgotten what you
have been teaching her. She is merely playing her favourite
game—'Bonnets', I think she would call it. She forgets what a
dangerous game it can be."

Madame d'Espery was too agitated to question the Earl's
cryptic remark but said, "I really think it would be better,
Mademoiselle Perdita, if you removed those...additions to
your very pretty dress. I do assure you, it does not need them.
And you would probably feel better if you cleaned your fingers with a little soap and water. Wait, I will ring for Jeanne to
take you upstairs to attend to it."

As Perdita reached the door the Earl's voice stopped her.
"Perdita!" He paused until she turned. "Remove that flower
from your hair. You need no such embellishments."

As Perdita followed the maid upstairs she was in a confused
frame of mind. On the one hand, she had undeniably demonstrated her lack of company manners. But, on the other, the
Earl had not been convinced, and she had only succeeded in
upsetting Madame d'Espery. But when she returned to the
dining-room Madame d'Espery was restored to good humour,
and Perdita found she had lost the desire to play any more
tricks. After dinner Madame d'Espery suggested that Perdita
should play something for them. "I am sure dear Monsieur
Champollion has taught her a little tune."

Perdita's flagging spirits were revived at the thought of what
she might do at the piano, but after a quick glance at her the

Earl protested that he had had enough entertainment for one
evening and took them into the library. "I set out for England
tomorrow, but I think we have made all the necessary arrangements, have we not? Perdita will continue with her lessons and
I expect to see much improvement when I return." This was
said with a warning glance at Perdita. "Now I would like a
word alone with Perdita, *madame*. Will I see you tomorrow
morning? I must set out in good time."

"Then I will wish you goodnight and *bon voyage*, Edward.
Pray convey my best wishes for the season to your mama. We
hope to see her at Belleroi before too long." At the door she
paused. "It is early days yet, Edward. Pray do not be too harsh
with Mademoiselle Perdita. She has much to learn, I know, but
she does try so hard. I cannot conceive where she has been, but
I am sure she means well." Her voice faded as she left the room,
and Perdita was left alone with the Earl.

"Madame d'Espery has a more charitable view of your intentions than I, Perdita. On the other hand, I believe I have a
higher opinion of your intelligence. You begin to intrigue me.
I ask myself if you are playing some deeper game of your own.
That would be foolhardy beyond belief, I assure you."

Perdita shifted uneasily. This was getting too close to the
truth for comfort. She would have turned away but he pulled
her back. "Am I right? Was tonight's display part of a larger
scheme? You surely cannot aim at being sent back to the Pasha? Or is it the Sheikh you long to return to? Answer me,
Perdita!"

He was growing impatient, and Perdita felt a sudden surge
of triumph. For a brief moment she had the upper hand. The
Earl would wait for longer than he imagined before she would
tell him anything of herself. Her lips curled in scorn as she
thought how easy it was after all to frustrate this autocrat, for
all his money and his power! But the Earl had seen her reaction, and her insolence enraged him. Her ridiculous curls fell
to her shoulders as he shook her like a doll. "Damn you, Perdita! What lies behind your silence? Tell me, you jade!"

He was white with rage, and such was the force of his anger
that Perdita's elation gave way to fear. She took an involun-
tary step back, but then her pride came to her rescue and she
stopped where she was, forcing herself to look at him calmly.
He seemed to sense her fear all the same, and with an expression of self-disgust he turned away. He said bitterly, "The men

on the ship called you a witch. I begin to believe them. You make me behave like a savage, like one of them." He stood in silence for a moment and then turned back to her. "There is some mystery about you, Perdita, and I intend to fathom it. But not tonight. It is late, and I have much to do before I leave for England."

Perdita's hand trembled as he led her to the door. He said abruptly, "You have no real reason to fear me, Perdita. Not if you deal honestly with me. But are you capable of honesty, I wonder?" He took her chin in his hand and held it for an ageless moment. Perdita was hypnotised by his eyes. They seemed to be reaching towards her innermost thoughts, and she saw them darken with a different emotion. Again there was the fleeting sensation of a wordless recognition. Slowly he bent his head and kissed her lingeringly. She willed herself to be still, fighting for self-possession, but it was hopeless. He seemed to be drawing her soul from her body. The kiss deepened and grew more passionate, and Perdita was lost in its spell. Gently the Earl released her, but then, cupping her face in his hand again, he murmured in wonder, "Such a lovely face. Such magical eyes. Such enchantment in the lips." Perdita looked at him, words trembling on her lips, but they died, stillborn, as he said, "Though I know you to be everything I despise, you still weave such a spell that a man could almost forget it all and ask for nothing more than to be your slave. How the devil do you manage it, Perdita? How can such corruption appear so damnably innocent?"

Perdita almost cried out at the pain caused by his words. She had to call on her considerable strength of will to hide her distress. There was a short silence, while the Earl stared at her broodingly. Then he shook his head as if to clear it, gave an incredulous laugh and said, "I can't believe it! Is that your game? To be my mistress? Oh, no, Perdita! Lovely though you are, I am more fastidious than you think. No, no, you are everything I looked for, but not for my own enjoyment." As she made no move, he said, "You will not be disappointed in the role I have in mind for you, Perdita. Remember the rewards if you play it well! Now it is more than time for you to go to your room. I will see you in the morning before I leave."

That night Perdita took herself severely to task. Her life had become too comfortable. A man had only to kiss her for her to forget the bitter lessons of the past two years. Trust no one, depend on no one. Life is not a game, but a battle for survival. Perdita against the world. Had she not learned that over and over again? She pushed away the thought that this particular man affected her as no one had ever done before—not even in her weakest moments.

By morning she was calm again. It was as well, for over-night the Earl's attitude had hardened. His parting words to Perdita were harsh. "Do not imagine my absence will make things easier for you, Perdita. Madame d'Espery will super-vise your conduct, and my servants, too, are vigilant. You may be sure I will hear of any...escapades. Remember the Pasha in Algiers, for I have not forgotten him."

After he had gone, however much she resolutely denied it to herself, Perdita felt his absence. His face was no friendlier than those of the servants, but, though there was danger in their en-counters, at least there was some excitement. The house seemed dead without him.

CHAPTER FOUR

SOON AFTER THE EARL'S departure Perdita was furious to find that she was being spied upon. She could never quite catch sight of the "spy", for whoever it was was adept at disappearing from view whenever Perdita turned round. So when one day she saw that her follower had whisked into a cupboard to keep out of sight she locked the cupboard door, and pocketed the key. Then she went to her music lesson, leaving her captive to cool his or her heels in the cupboard for an hour. When she came out of the music-room the house was fizzing with agitation.

"Have you seen Colette, *mademoiselle*? No, of course you haven't. Silly of me to ask, really," said one of the maids as she scurried past.

Colette? Who was Colette? Perhaps Colette was her captive. She went to the cupboard and gingerly unlocked the door. Lying asleep on the sheets and pillows inside was a little girl. The light woke her, and with a roar of fright she rushed out of the cupboard and down the stairs, shouting for her grandmother. Perdita laughed ruefully. Her "spy" had been a curious small girl!

"I am sorry to see that *mademoiselle* regards the terrorising of a little girl as amusing," said a frosty voice. It was Madame Lebrun. She swept past Perdita and went downstairs. Perdita started after her but then stopped. What was it to her? The child would find her grandmother and would get a great deal of sympathy from all the servants, who would be sure to lay the blame on the stranger in their midst. They would avoid her even more, and everyone would be satisfied.

Colette however had not been at all put off by her experience in the cupboard. Two days later Perdita found the child following her outside in the grounds. When she stopped Colette stopped too, some distance away. "You're not a witch, are you, *mademoiselle*?" Perdita smiled and shook her head. "The others said you were but Grandmère said no, and I think she's right because you don't look like one at all because you've got such a nice smile." Somewhat breathlessly Colette came along the path, and after a moment's hesitation took Perdita's hand. "Let's go for a walk, shall we?"

That was the beginning of a strange, secret friendship. Colette was an adventurous ten-year-old and, for her, forays into the main body of the house were a source of interest and excitement. They went on many walks together, and Colette's quick intelligence and quaint remarks kept Perdita constantly amused. Colette seemed to sense that Perdita did not wish to speak inside the house, but when they were outside Perdita's silence did not last long. The child simply bombarded her with questions until they were answered. So once again Perdita found her defensive wall of silence breached. Where the Sheikh's subtleties had failed, the need for an immediate response to Eliane's terror and Colette's curiosity had succeeded. Or perhaps it was just that time and a peaceful existence in civilised society had worn Perdita's resistance down. Whether she wanted it or no, life was sending out slender tendrils to catch her and draw her back into its fold.

CHRISTMAS CAME with a deal of celebration in the servants' quarters, but not much joy in the rest of the house. Perdita was on her own most of the time, for Madame d'Espery was confined to her room with a bad cold. She was touched when her elderly chaperon tottered downstairs on Christmas morning to escort her to church—so touched that she behaved beautifully, and was rewarded with an invitation to *madame*'s room for a glass of hot wine.

Madame warned her about Colette. "*Mademoiselle*, I hope you do not encourage the cook's grandchild to come into the house. I have caught her twice recently lurking about the corridors. She is harmless enough, but she knows very well that the servants' quarters are the proper place for her. She has no mother and, fond though she is of her, her grandmother Rosanne is too busy in the kitchen to pay much attention to the child. Colette should really be sent away to her other relations, but then her grandmother would be unhappy. Monsieur le

Marquis would never agree. And it is true that Rosanne is a superb cook."

Perdita looked her puzzlement. Who was Monsieur le Marquis?

"Do you not know? The Marquis de Belleroi. The Earl." As Perdita continued to look puzzled she went on, her tongue stumbling over the English names, "Edward Robert Justin de Cazeville Rotherfield is the fifth Earl of Ambourne and fourth Marquis de Belleroi. He inherited the French title and this estate from his mother's family, the de Cazevilles. Surely I told you that, *mademoiselle*?"

They spent an amicable hour together, after which Perdita persuaded the old lady back into bed, for she could see that the outing to church had taken a great deal out of her. The rest of the day she spent alone, for even Colette had deserted her in favour of the fun and laughter in the servants' hall. As she sat in the library, pictures from the past went through her mind. The great hall at Taverton, full of holly, ivy and mounds of spiced apples. Her father tossing her up on to the pony that had miraculously appeared in the stable one Christmas morning; her mother's face when Perdita gave her a penwiper she had made. And then that last Christmas. Perdita shuddered. Mr. Carston, with his white face and heavy features. How could her mother have married him? She had been lonely after Papa had died, it was true, and at first Mr. Carston had seemed all tender concern. She had paid for it dearly, poor little Mama. That last Christmas her mother had been so ill after the stillbirth of a child she should never have had that Perdita had hardly left her bedside. And Mr. Carston... That was enough! She must stop herself there.

She got up and looked along the shelves for her next book. Having been starved for so long of literature of any kind, she was having a feast of it now. French classics predominated, of course, but she had come across some modern English novels tucked away in a corner. She settled down to *Persuasion* and soon forgot her troubles in the world of Anne Elliot. She had just finished a chapter when the housekeeper came to put out the candles. She slipped the book down the side of the chair before Madame Lebrun saw it, and followed her disapproving back upstairs to bed. Christmas was over. Perdita lay awake long into the night, wondering where she would be and what she would be doing the following Christmas.

THE WEATHER DETERIORATED after Christmas Day. High winds whistled round the château, blowing flurries of snow against its walls and building up drifts along the roads. Perdita spent most of her afternoons in the library, eagerly reading all she could, for when the Earl eventually returned it would be more difficult to find the opportunity. However, on New Year's Eve the wind dropped and the sky cleared. The view from the library windows was breathtaking. White lawns and silver trees were dazzling in the bright sunshine, and Perdita could not stay indoors. Clad in her heaviest clothes, with her cashmere shawl around her, she ventured forth.

At first she stayed close to the house. The snow was still deep in places, and she was not certain of her footing. Then the crisp, clear air and the brilliant light enticed her to be more adventurous and she found herself eventually on the shore of the lake. It was completely frozen over and the waterfowl were having difficulty in landing gracefully on the ice. She stood there, laughing at their antics, for a while, but then reluctantly turned to go back—it was very cold.

"Hello! I say, hello!" It was the young man who had collected Eliane from her. He came skating across the lake, red scarf flying and arms swinging. A lock of dark blond hair had fallen over his eyes, and his cheeks were red in the cold air. "Don't go!" he said, coming to a swirling halt at the edge of the lake. "Mademoiselle d'Harcourt would like to meet you again. She's just over on the other side."

"Mademoiselle d'Harcourt?"

"Yes. Eliane," said the young man. Perdita had to hide a smile at his reverent tone. He continued, "We all met when Eliane hurt her foot. I'm Philippe Fourget."

"Of course. Where is she? I can't see her."

"Oh, she's not skating. She can't. She really isn't strong enough."

"Then how am I to meet her?" asked Perdita. "There's a lake between us, and I haven't any skates."

"Well, I thought," said the young man hesitantly, "that is to say, if you would permit me, I would walk you across the ice. It's really not difficult. There's a layer of snow on it." As Perdita hesitated he added, his hazel eyes pleading with her, "Do come! Mademoiselle d'Harcourt wants to thank you—and she needs company. It's not far."

Though it was clear that Eliane's wishes were the young man's command, Perdita was not at all sure that she wanted to meet her again. Furthering the acquaintance would almost certainly lead to complications. On the other hand, the house seemed very dull, and it would be fun to try walking on the ice. She held out her hands and they started moving slowly off. She fell once or twice on the way over but was quickly picked up, and arrived breathless and laughing on the other side.

Eliane was there, wrapped in furs and looking like the Snow Queen herself, with her silver-grey eyes and wisps of pale blonde hair peeping out from under her fur hood. "I'm so glad Philippe persuaded you to come, *mademoiselle*. Come quickly into the house; it's so cold out here, and you need to recover after your walk. You're very brave to cross the ice like that. I could never do it."

Taking Philippe's arm, Eliane led the way to a sprawling half-timbered house, which lay some distance back from the lake. Their wet outer garments were taken by a curtsying maid, and they followed Eliane into a large, low-ceilinged room. The outstanding impression was one of old-fashioned comfort. The huge log fire easily warmed the room to its furthest corners, and bowls of dried flowers and herbs scented the air.

A grey-eyed woman got up as they entered and came towards them. "Eliane, you're not cold, child, are you? Come near the fire. Philippe, I'm glad you've come. And this is Eliane's rescuer. *Mademoiselle*, you're welcome. Come, sit down here." Then, as they settled themselves, she said, "You see, we do not stand on ceremony here at Beau Lac, *mademoiselle*. I am Marguerite d'Harcourt, Eliane's mother. Eliane has not even told me your name."

Perdita was in a quandary. What was she to say? She knew of old that nothing was secret for long in the country. But the contrast between this house and the château suggested that the d'Harcourts' acquaintance with the Earl would be slight. Perhaps an abbreviation of her real surname would suffice.

"My name is Perdita, ma'am. Perdita...Taver. Is your daughter's ankle quite recovered?" This was enough to turn the conversation, though Perdita had the impression that Eliane's mother knew more than she was admitting. Her eyes had widened when Perdita had given her name.

During the next hour Perdita had opportunity to observe the little group. Madame d'Harcourt had been a beautiful woman, but now, in middle age, her face was lined, and in repose it was sad. Eliane had obviously been very ill some time ago and was still not fully recovered. Her mother watched her constantly and, each time Perdita caused Eliane to laugh, Madame d'Harcourt gave a small nod of approval. Perdita got the impression that the family was not as rich as it had once been— they apparently lived comfortably but very quietly. This encouraged her in her hope that the family had little contact with Belleroi. Philippe sat tongue-tied most of the time, only responding to direct questions, except when Eliane spoke. He was obviously head over ears in love with the girl, and she in turn seemed to draw on him for confidence and support.

It had been a long time since Perdita had enjoyed the company of people of her own age and upbringing. Through chance she had become acquainted with Eliane in the guise of her former self, with none of the problems that dogged her present life, and she was happier than she had been for a long time. It was a glimpse of what her life might have been if her mother had never met and married Frederick Carston...

Eliane proved to have a more attractive personality than had appeared at their first meeting. She had a delightful laugh, clear and childlike, and had obviously decided that Perdita was a friend. Perdita was often reminded of Colette, except that Colette was more robust and, she thought, more intelligent. They talked in generalities at first, and then Toto came in and their conversation turned to pets. The room often rang with their laughter as each in turn, including Madame d'Harcourt, told a favourite story. Perdita could see difficulties ahead, but for the moment she enjoyed the hour.

Refreshments were brought in, and when the tea-tray was removed Perdita suddenly realised that it was getting late and got up to go. By the time her cloak had been fetched the light was fading fast. Madame d'Harcourt insisted that she should come again. "It's some time since I have heard Eliane laugh so much, Mademoiselle Taver. You have been better than any physic for my daughter. She goes out rarely in the winter, and I am dull company for her."

"Thank you, I would like to come if I may," Perdita was surprised to hear herself say. "But has she no other friends in the neighbourhood, Madame d'Harcourt?"

"Until very recently my daughter was unwilling to meet anyone other than Monsieur Fourget, *mademoiselle*. You can-

not imagine how pleased I am to see her enjoying the company
of someone new.''

Perdita promised to come again when she could. Philippe
insisted on escorting her home, and together they set off on the
road to the château—the lake was judged to be too dangerous
in the half-light. Perdita was amused to find that Philippe
talked of Eliane all the way.

At the gates of the château Perdita paused. It was now almost dark, and if Madame d'Espery had found she was not in
the library she would be looking for her. But time had to be
found for a request. ''Monsieur Fourget, I would like you to do
me a favour and not ask any questions about it. Will you do
it?''

''I think so,'' he replied cautiously.

''Then will you please leave me here? Let me go up to the
château by myself. And...and...should anyone ask you about
me would you say as little as you can? I...I...well, I don't talk
when I'm in the château. Don't tell anyone I talk to you and
Mademoiselle d'Harcourt. Please.''

''But why ever not?''

''You did say you wouldn't ask. I'll tell you sometime, perhaps, but not now. I must go; they'll be watching. Goodbye,
Monsieur Fourget. Remember, you've promised!''

She ran up the drive and into the house, reaching the safety
of her room without, she thought, being observed. She quickly
changed into dry clothes and was waiting for Madame d'Espery in the salon when that lady descended for dinner.

FOR THE NEXT MONTH or more Perdita lived a kind of double
life. At Belleroi she was the silent, rather stupid ward of Monsieur le Marquis. She was dismally slow to acquire the requi-
site social graces, and failed to show much progress with her
tutors. Meanwhile she secretly continued to work her way
through the Earl's library, enjoyed her outings with Colette,
and when she was with the d'Harcourt family at Beau Lac she
behaved as normally as any other well-brought-up young lady.
She had a genuine love of music, and was delighted to discover
that the d'Harcourts shared this pleasure. She and Madame
d'Harcourt often played together, and even Eliane was occasionally persuaded to join her in a duet. They had a common
love of literature too. Madame d'Harcourt even had some

novels by the same English authors as Perdita had discovered at Belleroi. They read aloud from them, and Perdita's lively rendering of the absurdities of some of Jane Austen's characters was very popular.

Only once did she try to tell Madame d'Harcourt something of her true status. This was an act of heroism, for she was growing to depend on their friendship. But before she could get very far Madame d'Harcourt interrupted her.

"Mademoiselle Perdita, I am aware that your scruples are asking you to tell us something about yourself, which you would prefer us not to know. Let me say that I am content not to know it. I have observed you carefully since you have been visiting us. I know you will understand this, for you have seen how protective I am of Eliane. However, I do not believe you would willingly do her any harm, and your company has done her a great amount of good. As long as you are pleased to visit us I am well content to receive you. Now let us talk of something else. What is your opinion of *Waverley* —or have you not yet finished it? I have just received another by the same author, but I find the historical setting somewhat remote for me."

Afterwards Perdita was to ask herself how she could have been so blind. All the evidence was there, had she been alert enough to read it. Perhaps she was simply too happy enjoying the present to question it.

The snow disappeared, leaving behind it muddy paths and wet fields. Then came blustery winds to dry up the meadows and blow some of the newly placed slates off the roof of the château.

"You should not go out, *mademoiselle*; it is dangerous in these winds," protested Madame d'Espery, who was swathed in an exotic collection of shawls and scarves. "I cannot understand the modern passion for fresh air. We managed very well without it when I was a girl, I assure you. Monsieur le Marquis will be back any day now—what will he say if he finds you have been injured, or even killed? Tell me that."

Perdita would have said that Monsieur le Marquis would regard it as a great bore, since he would have to start all over again with another "tool", but she contented herself with giving an apologetic smile. She was not going to give up her visits to Beau Lac because of a slight breeze!

The winds were still high a few days later when she was returning earlier than usual from Beau Lac. Eliane had been slightly feverish, and her anxious mother had called the doctor. Perdita had been willing to stay to keep the invalid company, but Madame d'Harcourt had urged her to go home. "If Eliane is developing a cold, Mademoiselle Perdita, I would not wish you to catch it. You should go back in any case. The winds are dangerously high. Take care!"

She took the short cut through the woods. There were signs of spring wherever she looked. A few late snowdrops were tucked in among the dead leaves, and primroses and celandines could be seen on the edges of the wood. She came out on to the lawn and stood there, looking about her. The air was full of swirling movements and clouds were scudding across a bright blue sky. On her left ruffled waves were racing over a dark blue lake, and in front of her lay the château. She suddenly felt a sense of exhilaration. It was as if a great weight had been lifted from her shoulders. She was alive! She was a whole person! Whatever the future held, she could face it—not with stoicism, but with courage, not to reject life, but to challenge it. She ran laughing down the slope towards the house. A figure came racing up to meet her. Strong arms snatched her up and threw her to one side as a huge branch came crashing down from one of the lime trees on the lawn. She fell to the ground with the Earl on top of her.

"You stupid fool!" he said, fighting for his breath. "Don't you know better than to walk under old trees in a wind like this?"

She sat on the ground, dazed and bruised. "I'm sorry," she said. "I didn't look. You saved my life, I think."

"Not for the first time, either," he said. "Come on. Get up. You can come into the house and explain how you've suddenly found your voice. Or are you going to tell me it was the shock?"

CHAPTER FIVE

THE EARL AND PERDITA faced one another in the library.

"It was the shock," said Perdita with a straight face.

"I see," said the Earl resignedly. "I suppose I have only myself to blame for handing you that excuse on a platter. We shall no doubt eventually establish whether it is true or not. Meanwhile you will want to change, Perdita. Your clothes, I mean. Our tumble in the mud has made them rather dirty."

Perdita escaped to her room in some confusion. Little though she liked to admit it, she had been considerably shaken by her narrow escape. It was ironic that she had just discovered how precious life was when it had so nearly been snatched away from her. And it was the Earl who had saved her. What had he said? "Not for the first time." That was true, he had saved her life in Algiers, but life then had had no value for her. This time it was different, and she was grateful to him. She took some time to change her clothes, for she was strangely reluctant to go down.

Meanwhile the Earl was equally glad to be left to himself. He had dismissed his valet, and was sitting in front of his bedroom fire. The vision of Perdita laughing as she ran down towards the house was hard to dismiss from his mind. He had sent for her after his arrival, only to be told she was out walking, and was in the garden looking for her when she had suddenly emerged from the wood. She had looked magnificent. Her hair was streaming back in the wind, and her clothes were blown against her body, revealing its lovely lines. No marble Artemis this, but a vital elemental force. The sight of the broken branch which was threatening her had horrified him, and he had raced to save her without stopping to think. It had not surprised him that she had spoken, and he suspected she could have done so much earlier had she wished. But the quality of her voice was pleasing—low-pitched and musical. And, though

there was an elusive accent, her French was not as uneducated
as he would have expected. He wanted to hear more of it. He
began to be very interested in meeting her again. At last he
might have some answers to his questions.

Of the three at dinner that night only Madame d'Espery was
completely at ease. She was amazed that Perdita had so suddenly regained her speech, and said so often. She went into a
flood of reminiscence of other miraculous cures, which she or
her friends had witnessed.

Perdita was grateful to her. She was in an unusual state of
indecision, which reduced her appetite and made her reluctant
to engage in any conversation. What was she to do? Was she to
carry on the rest of her deception of the Earl and his household? After his prompt action that afternoon it seemed unnecessarily churlish, yet to confess that she had been wasting her
tutors' time, largely for her own mischievous amusement,
needed a degree of courage she was not sure she possessed.
Watching the handsome head bent towards Madame d'Espery, she was once again impressed by the Earl's charm tonight. She would not have credited him with the patience with
which he listened to the old lady's ramblings. She sighed,
crumbling the roll by the side of her plate into even smaller
pieces. She started guiltily when she saw the Earl's eyes on her.

The Earl too was quiet. While responding courteously to
Madame d'Espery he had been watching his pirate girl. This
afternoon she had been a vision of spring itself—Persephone
come to glowing life. This evening, with her rose silk gown,
bare of any ornament, her dark brown hair simply dressed on
top of her head, her sapphire eyes hidden under lowered eye-
lids, she could have been mistaken for a modest young lady of
fashion. Though she was nervous, her manners were unexcep-
tionable. Madame d'Espery had wrought a miracle, and the girl
herself was a revelation. He was amazed at the chameleon
qualities she showed. But which was the real Perdita?

After dinner he suggested they should adjourn to the library, since the salon was too large a room for such a small
company. He saw that they were comfortably settled, watched
as Perdita arranged Madame d'Espery's shawls, and then sat
down himself. One of the servants brought him a glass of
cognac, and he sipped it slowly, savouring its aroma.

"I compliment you on your pupil, Madame d'Espery," he began, lazily inspecting Perdita's face and figure. "She makes a charming impression."

Perdita looked up swiftly. Had there been a slight emphasis on the word "impression"? He stared blandly back at her and said, "And you, Perdita. Do you feel you have benefited from Madame d'Espery's time and patience?"

Madame d'Espery was not yet accustomed to the idea that Perdita could speak for herself. "She is a charming girl, Edward, and is slowly acquiring a modicum of decorum. Her behaviour at dinner tonight was, in my opinion, exemplary—a vast improvement from our last dinner together. Do you not agree?"

"Certainly, certainly. A little quiet, perhaps?"

"That is no real fault in a young lady. And you forget, until this afternoon Perdita did not have the power of speech." Perdita's colour rose as the Earl looked quizzically at her. But Madame d'Espery was pursuing her own train of thought. "I must confess, I have been somewhat puzzled by your ward, Edward. She appears to have no notion of sewing or drawing, and indeed her ignorance of all the uses of polite society is astonishing. Forgive me *mademoiselle*. I do not mean to hurt you, but you know it to be true. How can this be?"

Devilment lurked in the Earl's eyes. "Ah, yes, Madame d'Espery," he said. "Perhaps Perdita could explain that herself."

Perdita rallied. She would not let the Earl put her out of countenance. "Why, ma'am, I believe it is because I spent so much of my life removed from civilisation. I have only recently come to France."

The Earl listened in amusement to this evidence of Perdita's quick wit. She could not have chosen an excuse more likely to satisfy her tutor. For Madame d'Espery civilisation began and ended within the borders of royalist France.

"Of course," that lady said, gravely nodding her head. Then she continued, "However, I do not perfectly comprehend, *mademoiselle*, why you should find it so difficult to learn. Am I so poor a teacher?"

Once more Perdita was forced to rely on her wits. Somewhat desperately she said, "You are an excellent teacher, ma'am. Madame d'Espery has told me much of the great world she lived in before the Revolution, Lord Ambourne. Does his

lordship know the story of the Duchesse de Nevers and the
Duke of Hastings, ma'am?''

Madame d'Espery was not sure, but was happy to repeat it.
Perdita was safe for the moment from further questioning. Her
evasion had not been lost on the Earl, however, and he made a
note to pursue this matter on another occasion. Meanwhile he
sat back to enjoy Madame d'Espery's slightly scandalous reminiscence and to observe Perdita in the flickering firelight. He
was fascinated by her. He had seen her grace and dignity even
in the filth of Algiers. In the Sheikh's garden he had been surprised by her loveliness. But only now did he realise what a
barrier she had been putting between herself and the world.
Now that barrier seemed to have vanished. It wasn't just that
she now talked; as she sat quietly listening to Madame d'Espery her face was no longer closed and wary; it was alive, mo-
bile, even vulnerable. When Madame d'Espery's story reached
its ridiculous climax Perdita's eyes were alight with amusement, and a delicious gurgle of laughter escaped her.

Madame d'Espery sat back with a satisfied sigh. "And now,
Edward, I think I should like to retire to my bed. We live so
quietly here in the normal way that this evening's excitement
has quite done me up. Ah, you may smile, Edward, but when
one is my age one no longer has the resilience you younger
people take for granted. Come along, *mademoiselle*. Goodnight, Edward." Then she added with a roguish smile, "I hope
my story did not shock you!"

"I assure you, Madame d'Espery, till tonight I had always
regarded the Duke as a pompous bore, but your tale puts him
in a different light altogether! Wait—I'll have some candles
fetched."

He escorted them to the foot of the stairs, watched as they
slowly went up, then returned to the library. He was standing
looking into the dying fire when he heard a slight sound behind him. Turning, he saw Perdita coming into the room and
was filled with sudden pleasure. She, too, had felt the evening
incomplete. He walked forward and took her hands. They
trembled slightly as she said, "Madame d'Espery sent me for
her shawls, Lord Ambourne. They're on the chair."

"And I was vain enough to think you had come back to talk
to me."

"You forget, my lord. You bought me. You have only to send
for me if you wish to speak to me." Her head was bent and her

eyes veiled. He took her chin in his fingers and pulled her head up.

"The first time I did this you bit me, Perdita. Do you remember? Are you going to bite me again?" Once again dark blue eyes looked into his, but this time they were troubled. "What are you afraid of, Perdita?" he whispered. "That I shall kiss you again?"

He pulled her mouth to meet his and gently kissed her. At first she tried to push him away, but then as the kiss grew sweeter and deeper he drew her into his arms. She slowly put her arms round his neck and pressed more closely to him. After a while they drew back, and the Earl, holding her against his arm, looked at her searchingly. At first he was smiling slightly, but then with a muffled exclamation he snatched her back and kissed her again, more passionately than before. He kissed her as if he could not hold her closely enough, could not have enough of her. This time when they parted the Earl walked over to the fire. He was shaken. He had kissed many women, but never before had he felt so moved.

Perdita swiftly picked up the shawls and moved to the door. "May I go now?" she said, hugging the shawls to her as if for comfort.

"What is it between us, Perdita? And what am I to do about it? There's something about you ... Yes, you may go. Come, I'll escort you to the stairs."

At the foot of the stairs they paused. "Goodnight, Lord Ambourne," Perdita said in a subdued voice.

He had the ridiculous impulse to take her in his arms again and comfort her, but restrained himself. "Goodnight, Perdita." Then he added, smiling ruefully, "I have a notion that Perdita, the lost one, has found herself, and it is I who am lost. I wonder what will come of it?"

Perdita went up to her room, her head spinning. Found herself? Found herself? What a laughable notion! She was lost in a maze of rioting emotion. All her life, all her experience had not prepared her for this. She got herself to bed without noticing what she did. The treasured silk gown lay in a heap on the floor, the rest of her clothes on top of it. She lay there, her thoughts churning, for half the night. Finally she reached a measure of calm. The Earl still did not know her full story. Perhaps when he did he would treat her kindly, let her go to live a modest life somewhere in England. Tonight they had both

been in the grip of a strong emotion. If nothing was done to
change the situation the Earl might even overcome his repug-
nance for her past and suggest she should become his mistress.
That she could never do. Deep within her she knew that, for all
her self-discipline, the Earl of Ambourne could cause her more
pain than anything she had known before. She must prevent
that by telling him her true history. And then leave him.

Perhaps she could go to the Sheikh? Having decided that she
would tell the Earl everything tomorrow, she fell into a troubled sleep.

Unfortunately the decision was taken out of her hands. She
overslept, and by the time she saw him again it was too late to
attempt any harmonious solution to her problem.

The Earl, too, lay awake for part of the night, thinking of
Perdita. Where had she acquired her air of quality? How had
she retained it in the rough company in which he had found
her? Was she a victim of circumstance—or was she a consum-
mate actress? He debated what he should do. He had lived so
long with the thought of exacting justice for what had happened to Linette that he was reluctant to abandon it now. But
Perdita had somehow or other ceased to be a tool, had become
instead a real person, someone perhaps worthy of respect. He
felt he could not use her as he had planned, though what he was
to do with her he could not think. He fell asleep, still pondering the question.

The next morning was a busy one, and the Earl rose early.
Belleroi was once again a large and thriving estate and demanded a great deal of attention. The Revolution had passed
over this quiet spot in the heart of the Norman countryside almost without trace. But the land and more especially the house
itself had suffered from neglect during the period when its half-
English owner had been unable to visit it.

He spent the first part of the morning seeing his agent, the
master mason and various other members of his little community. Monsieur Champollion grew increasingly anxious as he
waited his turn. Finally he was admitted.

The Earl was sitting with his back to the window, at a huge
desk covered in papers. He was writing. The little music master clutched his hat nervously and waited to be noticed.

"Champollion, forgive me. I did not see you there. Now,
how have the music lessons progressed?"

This was the very question Monsieur Champollion had been dreading. "Monsieur le Marquis...milor', I...I..."

"Speak up, Champollion; it's surely not as bad as that?" said the Earl, smiling.

"But it is, Monsieur le Marquis. I have succeeded in teaching your ward nothing! She seems incapable of retaining anything at all, even the simplest tunes. She stumbles over the most rudimentary exercises, and appears to have no kind of ear for music. I think she is tone deaf! I apologise for my failure, milor'. I assure you that I have done my best."

The Earl got rid of the music master after a while, and then sat deep in thought. It was must unlikely that anyone with as musical a voice as Perdita's would be tone deaf. And he was absolutely certain that she was very far from stupid. Was Champollion being unfair, even malicious? He could imagine Perdita growing impatient with the fussy little man. But then Madame d'Espery had said something similar last night. That Perdita was very slow. And the relationship between the girl and her chaperon was clearly cordial—even affectionate. What had the girl been up to? He was just on the point of going to look for her when the housekeeper came in.

"There is a note for you, Monsieur le Marquis, from Beau Lac. Shall I ask the groom to wait?"

"No, there's no need," said the Earl, quickly reading the note with a frown. "Madame d'Harcourt has already departed for Paris. She will be away for some days. No, I will see her when she returns; there's no reply. Tell the messenger to go, but then come back here, *madame*. I wish to speak to you."

Madame Lebrun went out, and he returned to his thoughts. Last night Perdita had seemed a different person—open and honest. She might not have answered Madame d'Espery's questions completely, but what she had said was true. Later he had been deeply moved by her innocent response to his kisses. Innocent? Yes, he had to admit it, he had thought her response innocent. Innocent? said the devil inside him. A pirate's lover and innocent? Come, now! It was true, it did seem ridiculous to think so...

Madame Lebrun returned in a few minutes, and he invited her to sit down. "How is my ward, *madame*?" he began abruptly. "Is she happy in the house?"

"I'm sure there is nothing that Mademoiselle Perdita could complain about," said the housekeeper, pressing her lips to-

gether. "The staff all do their duty as far as she is concerned."
So the servants didn't like Perdita, thought the Earl. He wondered why. Madame Lebrun hesitated, then continued, "As for
being happy... well, she looks for her amusement outside the
house, not in it."

"I'm not sure I understand you," said the Earl. "What do
you mean by that, Madame Lebrun?"

"If I don't tell you someone else will, Monsieur le Marquis," said the housekeeper, and continued not without a certain relish. "She slips out most afternoons. As soon as Madame
d'Espery goes for her rest that girl is running out of these doors
and over the hills. I don't know what she gets up to out there,
but I can imagine."

"Be careful what you say," said the Earl coldly. "I will not
tolerate malicious gossip."

"Oh, I'm not the only one to have seen her, *monsieur*. The
others could tell you—"

The Earl interrupted her. "I do not propose to question the
other servants, Madame Lebrun. I will speak to Mademoiselle
Perdita myself. Thank you, that is all." As she reached the door
he asked, "Why do you dislike my ward so, *madame*?"

"She's a wicked, cold-hearted girl, sir. She terrified poor little Colette. Locked her in a cupboard just because she found
her in the house. I know Colette shouldn't have been there—
I'm not defending the child—but that was a heartless thing to
do."

"From what I've seen of Colette it would take more than that
to terrify her. But, if what you say is true, then yes, I agree. It
was heartless. Thank you, Madame Lebrun."

The Earl rose from his desk and paced the room. What was
he to believe? His old prejudices about Perdita were roused.
The devil inside him was mocking him—innocent? You fool,
you gullible fool! The strumpet looks at you with sapphire eyes
and you'll believe anything! He rejected the voice. He would
not condemn Perdita on servants' gossip. Neither would he
question the servants about her. He would see her himself.

However, Perdita was not to be found in the house. One of
the maids said she had seen her going into the woods some time
before. The Earl returned to the library, suspicion wrestling
with a determination to be fair to Perdita. Père Amboise was
waiting for him there, and the Earl remembered he had ar-

ranged to see him. Annoyed with himself for having forgotten
the *curé*, he apologised.

"Your excuses are not at all necessary, Monsieur le Marquis," the *curé* said sunnily. "I am glad to have an opportunity to examine your library. You have a fine collection of
books here."

After some discussion of the needs of the village the Earl reluctantly asked about Perdita's work.

"She's a good child," Père Amboise said. "She listens so
attentively. I fear I talk too long and test too little, *monsieur*,
but she seems to understand. The writing is coming along
slowly. She seems a little subdued in the house, but whenever I
see her outside she looks happy enough."

The Earl asked slowly, "Alone, Père Amboise? When she is
outside, is she alone?"

"Quite often. Her young friend is not always with her. But
whenever it grows dark he always escorts her to the château. Or
at least to its gates. I cannot say I have recognised him, but he
is a handsome lad and I am sure he looks after her well. Monsieur le Marquis needs have no fear on that score."

That the Earl finished the interview with the *curé* courteously and in no haste was a tribute to his iron self-control, for
he was in a towering rage. He escorted Père Amboise to the
door of the library, then returned to the desk, and with a vio-
lent gesture swept all his papers on to the floor. He stood in
thought for a moment, then strode out of the house to the stables. The servants scattered as they saw him coming, and the
grooms ran to do his bidding. His horse was saddled in the
shortest possible time and he was off, urging the horse to a
gallop as soon as he was clear of the buildings.

"Break his neck, he will, if he ain't careful," said one of the
grooms.

"He don't look as if he'd mind, neither," said the other,
shaking his head.

But when the Earl got to the trees he let the horse pick its way
slowly along the bridle paths, while he listened and looked for
Perdita. When he came out on the other side he turned to the
left, towards the village. Only Beau Lac lay to the right, and
since he knew the occupants of the house had left for Paris that
morning there was no point in calling there. Anyway, the last
place to look for Perdita was with his aunt and Linette. She
would be seeking her excitement elsewhere.

He got back late in the afternoon after riding through the
village and beyond without finding any trace of Perdita. The
white heat of his rage had been replaced by a cold and deadly
anger. During his ride the same thoughts had been churning
over in his mind. He had begun to trust her, had even begun to
wonder whether he should continue with his plan, since it involved her, and all the time she had been laughing at him,
playing him for the fool he was. She would pay for it. He would
catch her red-handed, and then she would pay!

PERDITA HAD TRIED TO SEE the Earl as soon as she had come
downstairs but had been told he was occupied with his man of
business. Too nervous to wait, she had gone to Beau Lac to take
Madame d'Harcourt into her confidence and consult her on the
best course to follow. But when she arrived at Beau Lac she
found its occupants gone. One of the maids had a note for her.

"I am sorry not to have seen you before we left. The
decision to go to Paris was taken very suddenly after our
local doctor had examined Eliane. As you know, *mademoiselle*, Eliane is not robust, and I think it better that the
specialist who treated her some years ago should see her
now. We do not plan to stay longer than necessary in Paris.
Eliane does not enjoy being in large cities, and I am sure
she will miss your company—as I will."

Madame d'Harcourt finished the letter with her most cordial greetings.

Tucked inside was a shakily written note from Eliane.
"Mademoiselle Perdita—I would be most obliged to you if you
could find time to see Philippe. I did not have the chance to
speak to him. Tell him I shall see him very soon. And I hope to
see you soon, too, dear *mademoiselle*."

Perdita was seriously worried about her friend, but reminded herself of Madame d'Harcourt's over-protective attitude. She would have to wait, and hope that they would be back
soon. Somewhat despondently she retraced her steps to the
château and went up to her room, where she sat in troubled
thought.

Shortly before dinner she was informed that the Earl wished
to see her in the library. The moment of decision was upon her.

Half hoping, half dreading the coming interview, she followed the maid downstairs. When she went in the Earl was standing at the window, looking out. Without turning round, he said, "Where have you been, Perdita?"

She did not wish to start her confession to this uncompromising back, so she hesitated, then said, "To the...to the woods, Lord Ambourne. They're very pretty at this time of year."

"Just to the woods?"

His voice was cold and harsh. Was he angry because he had found out about her visits to Beau Lac? She swallowed and said, "You told me I was not to go out of the grounds, Lord Ambourne—"

She was about to say more, but he turned round and demanded abruptly, "So you met no one on your walk?"

Well, that question could be answered with a clear conscience. "No, my lord," she said confidently. He stood there, a brooding look on his face. Finally he dismissed her, and she went with a last puzzled look at his silent figure.

The Earl was left with his thoughts. Obviously the girl was lying. He had searched the woods and found no trace of her. Where could she have gone? One thing was certain: he was going to find out, even if it meant following her himself!

That evening there was no pleasant dinner party. The Earl was not present when Madame d'Espery and Perdita had their meal. He took his late and retired to his room early. The two ladies chatted desultorily for a while in the salon, Madame d'Espery still amazed that Perdita had regained her speech, and then they also went to their rooms early.

CHAPTER SIX

WITH THE EXCEPTION of Madame d'Espery the whole household soon knew that Perdita was in disgrace. Madame Lebrun had wasted no time in spreading her account of the interview with Monsieur le Marquis, and most of the servants had witnessed his angry departure soon after. In the manner of a small community they gossiped about it and were eager to see what would happen. One thing they could all see for themselves—Monsieur le Marquis was polite to his ward but his manner was by no means friendly.

They were too well trained to make any comment in Perdita's hearing, but their sidelong glances as they passed her on the stairs or in the corridors of the great house made her uneasy. She was not quite sure why the Earl was so unapproachable—was it because of Beau Lac, or could it be that someone had told him of her walks with Colette? Surely not? He was autocratic, but not unreasonable. Such small offences could not have caused this change in him. Then she remembered his behaviour when he had first met her. Perhaps he was angry at her disobedience. She was worried, but could not bring herself to ask, and telling him her story was now out of the question.

When the Earl dined with them he addressed most of his remarks to Madame d'Espery, who was too delighted to have an audience for her stories to notice that Perdita was seldom included. Perdita was puzzled and unhappy, and at the same time angry with herself for being affected so strongly. Surely she ought to have learned by now that the only safe resource was herself? Just a few days ago she had felt ready to challenge life, to enjoy it again, and she admonished herself for being so feeble now.

Her preoccupation with her own misery made her clumsy and forgetful, provoking Madame d'Espery's strictures. Perdita was glad to escape from the dining-room as quickly as she could.

She had no comfort during the day, either, for her tutors too were conscious of the Earl's disapproval and redoubled their efforts to improve her playing and dancing. Some perverse demon made Perdita all the more determined to refuse to learn. Père Amboise alone remained blissfully unaware of the trouble he had helped to create. His pupil seemed a little listless, without the eager attention she had previously paid to his lessons, but he only thought he was being more boring than usual and resolved to make the lessons more interesting for her.

Meanwhile Perdita had not forgotten that Eliane had asked her to get in touch with Philippe. She knew he would be unhappy at Eliane's absence, and sharing what news they had might cheer him up a little. But how was she to accomplish this? She knew where Philippe lived. His family had a small *manoir* beyond Beau Lac. If only there was someone who could take a note arranging a meeting—perhaps Colette knew of someone.

Since the Earl's return it had been more difficult for Colette to reach Perdita's room unobserved, for servants were constantly on the move around the house. However, she appeared one day at Perdita's door.

"Psst...*mademoiselle*! I'm here! How are you? Oh, *mademoiselle*, you look so sad. Have you missed me? Do smile, please dear Mademoiselle Perdita!"

Perdita was pleased to see the merry little face—it was a change to see approval and affection directed at her! Colette spent a few happy minutes recounting what she had been doing, and then asked, "*Mademoiselle*, they say you talk now. Here in the house, I mean. Is that right?" Perdita assured her it was. "Oh, good, then you can talk to me as well! Why do you think Monsieur le Marquis is cross with you?"

Perdita had to confess she didn't know why they thought that. Perhaps Monsieur le Marquis *was* cross with her! "Well, never mind. I love you, *mademoiselle*!"

Perdita was touched by the little girl's loyalty, and wondered whether she was right to involve Colette in her problems. But Colette had no difficulty at all in thinking of someone. "My cousin Henri will do it, *mademoiselle*. He likes going to the Fourgets' house. He's got a friend there. Where's the note?"

Still doubtful that she was doing the right thing, Perdita wrote a short note, asking Philippe to meet her by the lake the next day. After checking that the Earl was at work in his li-

brary and Madame d'Espery had gone to her room, Perdita
slipped out the following afternoon. She hurried to the edge of
the wood, where she paused for breath and looked back. Except for the workmen still on the roof, the back of the château
was deserted. The servants were probably at their own meal.
She skirted the wood and ran down to the lakeside. Philippe
was waiting for her.

"Mademoiselle Perdita, do you know how Eliane does?"
was his characteristic greeting.

Perdita tried to reassure him about Eliane's state of health,
reminding him of Madame d'Harcourt's obsessive concern for
her daughter. He was not convinced, however, and indeed it
was not easy for her to be convincing, since she knew so little
herself. But she did manage to persuade him that Eliane's
thoughts before she had left had been of him.

"She is an angel, *mademoiselle*, I assure you, but, alas, I fear
she is not for me."

"Why ever not, *monsieur*? You are made for each other!
Eliane is dear to you, I know, and she needs someone like you
to cherish and protect her. It would be a perfect match."

"You do not understand, *mademoiselle*. The difficulty does
not lie with Eliane and me, but with our families. You have not
heard about my father?" Perdita shook her head. "My father,
mademoiselle, is an enthusiastic Republican. Do not mistake
me, he was not one of the rabble who caused the deaths of all
those people at the guillotine in '93 and '94. But he believed in
the Revolution and fought for it. When Napoleon became our
leader my father thought a new age of equality had come into
being. You can imagine how bitter he was when Napoleon in
turn took the crown and made himself Emperor. He gave up a
promising career in Paris to return to our estate here in Normandy."

"But it's very peaceful here. Could your father not have
concentrated on his estate and forgotten his disappointment?
And anyway, how does this affect you and Eliane?"

"The local landowners here regard my father—and his family—as traitors. Since the King was restored to power the old
families have returned, and we are treated as outcasts."

"But, Philippe, Madame d'Harcourt doesn't treat you as an
outcast! And, from what I have observed, she is no great land-
owner, either. She would not hold your father's defection
against you, I'm sure!"

"Madame d'Harcourt has been very kind to me, *mademoiselle*. But she is not the only one who has a say in what happens to Eliane. Surely you know that Madame d'Harcourt belongs to the de Cazeville family? Eliane is the cousin of Monsieur le Marquis."

"The ... the Marquis?"

"Yes, mademoiselle. The Englishman—the Marquis de Belleroi."

Perdita was stunned. She managed to ask, "But, Philippe, why should Eliane and her mother live so modestly if what you say is true? So withdrawn from the great world?"

"I think there is some tragedy in Eliane's past, *mademoiselle*. I am not sure what it is—they have never talked about it. When they came back from England it was assumed they returned at the Restoration of the Monarchy. But I think there was more to it than that. For more than a year Eliane refused to see anyone. Even now, three years later, she will only receive one or two—you, me, and Dr. Grondet."

"I see," said Perdita thoughtfully. Though she would not say anything to Philippe, she now knew something else about Eliane. Her English family called her Linette.

"So you see, Mademoiselle Perdita, I have not much hope of persuading Eliane's family that I am a suitable husband for her," said Philippe gloomily.

"Philippe, you must not give up hope," said Perdita, urgently clutching Philippe's arm. "I am convinced that you are the very husband Eliane needs. She needs you, Philippe. You must fight for her."

But Philippe was staring at a tall figure some distance away. It was completely still, but there was a menacing air about it. *"Le Marquis!"* he gasped.

Perdita turned to look, and her heart sank when she saw him. If he caught them now he would not be content until he had Philippe's story. He was sure to receive it unfavourably in his present mood. "Philippe, has the Marquis ever met you?" she said quickly.

"No, never."

"Then he won't know who you are. You must go quickly—now, before he comes!" Perdita pushed him towards Beau Lac.

"But, *mademoiselle*—"

"Go, Philippe! I am not in any danger. And if you meet the Marquis now your chances of winning Eliane will be worth nothing. Go!"

Philippe was not happy at leaving Perdita to face the Marquis alone. But this last plea of hers persuaded him. He ran to his horse, tethered behind Beau Lac, and was off. Perdita turned to face the Earl. She jumped when she found he was upon her. His face was white and his jaw was set. "Lord Ambourne—"

"Who was he?" he bit out.

She could think of nothing to say. Her ready wit failed her. "W. . . wh . . . who?" she faltered.

He grabbed her arm, holding it so tightly that she almost cried out. "Don't push me any further, you slut! Tell me the name of your lover."

"The . . . the name of my lover?" she asked in disbelief. "I have no lover, Lord Ambourne. And you're hurting my arm."

"Don't put on your airs with me, you little wanton," he said, giving her a shake. "You've been meeting him for weeks, whenever you've managed to get away from the château."

"It's not what you think—" she started to say, but once again he didn't let her finish.

"Don't try your lies on me, Perdita. I'm in no mood to listen to fairy-stories told by a lying, deceitful, heartless jade!" he said, giving her a shake with each of these last words.

She realised that he was deaf to any explanation she could give other than the one he expected from her. At the same time her own anger blazed up at this unjust treatment. She wrenched her arm out of his grasp and took a step back. "Then I won't tell you any," she shouted. "I won't tell you anything at all. Find out for yourself!"

"I won't need to; he'll soon come after you, like a dog after a bitch, when he realises you are not allowed to roam the fields any more! Or will he desert you when trouble threatens—like your previous keeper?" She looked at him wildly and made as if to strike him, but he caught her wrist and pulled it back, forcing her gradually to her knees. "You're coming back to the château with me, Perdita. There you will be kept like the chattel you are, until I am ready to make use of you. We have all been too lax. Leopards don't change their spots, nor do drabs become honest just because they're dressed up in fine clothes.

You'll buy your freedom, Perdita, but not till you've worked for it."

With that he pulled her to her feet and set off for the château, dragging her mercilessly behind him.

Though she was sure her undignified approach had already been observed by the people in the château, she attempted to release herself as they came to the building. He let her wrist go, but held her again by the arm. They passed Madame d'Espery on the stairs. "Why, Mademoiselle Perdita!" that good lady cried. "We were looking for you . . ." But she stared at them in amazement as the Earl strode on with Perdita close by his side.

Perdita was by this time fully as angry as the Earl. Six months before, when she was still with the pirates, she would have borne this rough treatment with stoicism. But now she had once again become used to life in a gentler society, a life in which respect for others played a major role. The Earl's treatment of her outraged her newly recovered self-esteem. As he opened her door she stood in stony silence, then she walked through into the room, turned and said, trembling with rage, "I will never forgive you for what you have said and done to me this afternoon, Lord Ambourne. You have made your low opinion of me quite clear. It does not begin to rival the depth of my opinion of you."

For a moment he looked surprised at the vehemence and confidence with which she spoke. Then he laughed sardonically. "My congratulations," he jeered. "But then we already know what an actress you are! Well, you're going to have plenty of time to rehearse your role. There won't be many distractions for you from now on, my little wanton. You won't have freedom to find them. I expect you down to dinner at the normal time. Take care to put your company manners on along with your fine dress!" With that he went out, pulling the door shut behind him.

Perdita threw herself on the bed and burst into a storm of angry tears. How dared he treat her in this manner? How dared he call her a liar? She'd show him! She'd throw his fine clothes and his stupid lessons back in his face. He could do what he wanted; she would not help him carry out whatever he had planned!

After a while she had cried herself out, and lay there in exhausted misery. As the afternoon wore on and the light began to fade other thoughts began to plague her. If she refused to

obey him he might send her back to Algiers—he was angry
enough at the moment. Her chances of escaping from her unhappy circumstances were much greater in France or England
than in Africa. There was no guarantee that she could reach the
Sheikh. When she was with the pirates she had tried several
times to escape, but it had all been in vain, for the seaports were
inhospitable places for anyone with no money and no friends.
They had all been afraid of the captain of *Le Faucon*, and she
had been unceremoniously returned to him. No, open defi-
ance was not the best way to solve her problems. She must
outwit the Earl—no easy task, for she knew that not much escaped those hard grey eyes. Of one thing she was certain: any
attempt on her part to gain his sympathy by telling him her
history would be greeted with jeering disbelief. She would not
expose herself to that, and that in turn meant she must try to
continue her deception.

A knock at the door startled her, but it was only a maid, who
had been sent to help her dress. Her toilet was completed in silence; then she was escorted downstairs to the salon. She had
always disliked this room—of all the rooms in the château it
was the most imposing. Spindly chairs and sofas upholstered
in dark green were arranged stiffly round its walls, the furnishings were of heavy damask silk and the walls covered in tapes-
tries from an earlier age. Crystal chandeliers held hundreds of
candles overhead, and tonight they were all lit. The windows
overlooked the rigid formality of the drive.

She stood in the middle of the huge room, still uncertain of
her course of action. Then, when the Earl greeted her, she put
up her chin and went forward to the fire. "Good evening, Lord
Ambourne."

"Playing the lady, I see," he said scornfully.

She looked at him coolly. "I do not perfectly understand why
you should be surprised, Lord Ambourne. I thought that was
what you wanted me to be."

"You could never be a lady, Perdita. I will be content if you
can act like one—for longer than five minutes before dinner."

The gloves were off, then. "I agree it will not be easy. It is
difficult to sustain courtesy where none is met. I will do my
best, however," she said, adding to herself, but not to please
you, my lord!

He seemed to read her mind. "You dislike me for knowing
what you are—that is natural," he replied. "But your games

are finished, Perdita. This afternoon, while you were in your room, I thought long and hard about your future. I must tell you that I am sorely tempted to send you back to Algiers.''

However hard she tried she could not prevent a shadow of alarm passing over her face. It was swiftly suppressed. The Earl continued abruptly, ''But I have decided against it. Time is growing short, and in many other ways you are what I need. It will only be necessary to keep a closer watch on you when you are not actually in your lessons.'' He paused for a moment. ''I have asked Madame Lebrun to assign one of the maids to your personal use. She will not be told that she is your keeper, but she will be expected to know where you are when you are indoors.''

Perdita frowned resentfully. The Earl might not intend the maid to know, but Madame Lebrun would see that she did. The girl would know herself to be Perdita's warder. But the Earl was saying more. ''It would, of course, be easier if we could confine you to the house until you are ready to go to London. However, I do not wish to deprive you of fresh air and exercise. You will be accompanied on your walks either by a groom or by me. Do not look rebelliously at me, Perdita. I assure you it is quite normal for a young 'lady' to be accompanied by a maid or groom when she goes out in London. Of course, we have learned from experience that in your case it is essential wherever you are.''

''And Madame d'Espery?'' Perdita asked stiffly.

''Madame d'Espery has been deeply distressed by your behaviour. She has decided to return tomorrow to her own house in the grounds of the château. She believes herself to have failed in her commission to teach you how to behave.''

Perdita made a small movement of protest. ''Madame d'Espery has nothing to reproach herself for, Lord Ambourne. She has been an excellent tutor—and a kind one.''

''Too kind,'' the Earl said harshly. ''She allowed you to cozen her into approval and even liking. She knows differently now.''

''I do not wish Madame d'Espery to be punished because of me,'' Perdita persisted.

''You should have taken that into your reckoning before you embarked on your tricks. It is too late now.''

That Madame d'Espery was to be sent away for her pupil's shortcomings was too much for Perdita's composure. She turned away in distress and walked to the window, stumbling over a stool on the way.

The Earl looked at the figure gazing blindly out on to the drive, then added in a slightly softer tone, "Madame d'Espery is not in good health. She herself requested me to release her. I did not ask her to leave."

"May I see her before she goes?" asked Perdita.

"Of course. She will be down in a few minutes."

At that moment Madame d'Espery came into the room. She was pale but very dignified. Her strict code of behaviour did not permit her to show how deeply she was hurt by Perdita's defection. She greeted her courteously and then talked about the weather, the state of the roads and the difficulties Père Amboise was having in the church. Her fund of anecdotes seemed to have dried up. Throughout dinner her manner was impeccably correct but bereft of any spontaneity.

Only now did Perdita realise how much the old lady had come to mean to her, but she found it impossible to approach her. After dinner she tried to say how sorry she was that Madame d'Espery was leaving and to thank her for her patience and concern. Her chaperon listened carefully, then said, "I thank you for the sentiments you have expressed, *mademoiselle*. They are not at all necessary, I assure you. I regret that I was not able to help you more."

In the light of Madame d'Espery's wall of politeness Perdita could not ask her if she might visit her. She felt she knew what the reply would be, and wanted to spare herself and Madame d'Espery any further embarrassment. The Earl rang for candles early and they were escorted upstairs by a silent maid.

The next morning, while Perdita was with Père Amboise, the Earl took Madame d'Espery to her house on the other side of the park, and a new phase in Perdita's life began.

The first surprise came in an interview with the Earl. This happened a day or two after Madame d'Espery's departure. He had been busy and her walks had been supervised by an elderly groom, who was uncommunicative and disapproving. He clearly felt his proper work was being neglected and was only anxious to get back to it. He walked Perdita round the path the Earl had recommended as if she were one of the horses—and not a very valuable one at that. They were both glad to return. Indoors, her time was divided between her lessons, meals and her room. Rather than give the maid the satisfaction of re porting her movements to Madame Lebrun, Perdita smuggled one or two books out of the library and spent most of her time reading in her room.

When the Earl finally sent for her he said, "There are several matters to be made clear between us, Perdita. Please sit down."

"I thought everything was perfectly clear," said Perdita. "We are working towards a goal known only to you, directed by decisions which are yours alone, enlivened by mutual antipathy."

He looked at her with a grim smile in his eyes. "That's exactly what I mean, Perdita," he said. "Where has a girl like you, apparently able neither to read nor to write, acquired a vocabulary more suited to a university dining table?"

Perdita thought hard and quickly. "Père Amboise?" she asked. "Of course, I don't always understand what the words mean—"

"I've warned you—don't try to play games with me."

The dangerous look in his eyes persuaded her to be prudent. She thought of her father and decided to tell the truth—at least partly. "I've always had a good ear, Lord Ambourne. I...I pick things up very quickly. And I once knew someone who loved books..."

"Another one of your lovers, no doubt. Who was he? And if he loved books so much why did he not teach you to read?"

"Teach me to read? Why?" she asked opening her eyes wide.

His lips curled in disgust. "I agree, it wasn't really necessary for what he needed from you. All the same, I think you do know how to read, Perdita. If not, why are there books from this library in your room?"

She jumped up. "You've had me spied on! How dare you? You've had my room searched!"

"Your room? You own nothing, Perdita. Not your room, not your dresses, not even yourself! Why should I not have any part of my house searched, if I so wish?"

"Would you search your servants' rooms?" cried Perdita angrily.

"No, but then I trust my servants."

With an exclamation Perdita swung round and made for the door.

"I have not yet finished what I wanted to say," said the cool voice behind her. She stopped with her back still towards him.

There was a small silence. "There is little likelihood of either of us achieving our goals if we continue in this fashion," the Earl said eventually. "Sit down again, Perdita. If you will refrain from provoking me at every turn I will attempt to have more patience with your foibles. I do not refer here to your behaviour outside the house, but to your determined efforts to mislead all who come into contact with you. Sit down. Please."

She came back slowly and sat in the chair opposite him. She was puzzled, intrigued and slightly afraid.

"First I will suggest that from now on, when we are not in company, we speak English to each other." She looked at him in amazement. Was there nothing this man did not perceive? Seeing her surprise, he went on, "Your French is excellent, except for a few words of argot which are inappropriate to a young lady's vocabulary and which I suspect you learned with your pirate friends. Fortunately Madame d'Espery did not recognise them for what they are. However, though you speak French fluently and well, I have no doubt in my mind that your native tongue is English. Do you deny it?" Perdita shook her head. "What? No words at all? Not even French ones? I am curious to hear you speak English, Perdita. You have a voice which is pleasant on the ear, but the accent is also important."

He paused, but when she still did not speak he continued in English, "And that leads me to my second point—your failure to learn anything from Monsieur Champollion. Ah, a reaction—one of scorn. Why? Do you despise him so much?" He leant forward. "Is it because he was simply too easy to gull, Perdita? I refuse to believe that a girl with as musical a voice as yours has no gift at all for music. Did he offend you with his ready belief that you were stupid? Or was your game a deeper one?"

"You all assumed I was stupid," said Perdita, feeling a sense of relief at talking in her own language again. "I merely fulfilled your expectations."

The Earl sat back. "There, I fear, you're wrong. I never for one moment believed you lacked intelligence—merely any moral sense. But at the moment we are not talking of your behaviour. We are discussing your lessons. Have you, in fact, learned nothing from Monsieur Champollion?"

Perdita answered with a sense of satisfaction, "Not a thing!"

"That has the ring of truth. So why do I have the impression that you are prevaricating?"

Perdita shrugged her shoulders and the Earl got up with an exclamation of impatience. He came over to her chair and leaned on the arms, trapping her in it. "You block every attempt I make to establish some ground on which to work. I told you once before, Perdita, I know you for what you are. I bought you from the Pasha in Algiers because of what you are. It isn't necessary for you to attempt to hide the truth about yourself—not from me, at least. But why can't you tell me more? Who was this man from whom you learned to read? Was he the one who taught you such purity of diction? You have a lovely speaking voice, Perdita. I think he must have valued you." When she remained silent he continued, "What happened? Did you play him false? Did you drive him to selling you to the pirates? What parted you from him?"

Perdita closed her eyes in pain. "He . . . died," she whispered. "And then . . . and then . . ."

"Yes, what then?" the Earl asked, bending closer.

Perdita stared at him in an agony of doubt. Should she tell him the real truth about herself? Would he believe her? And, if he did, what would he do then? Send her away, probably. She did not believe he would insist on keeping her once he knew the truth—that she was gently born and bred. He was sure to send her away—and, it came to her in a flash of self-revelation, she could not bear that. She did not want to be sent away!

"Perdita?" The Earl's voice seemed to come from a long way away. But she must escape from him for the moment—she must have time to consider this new dilemma. With a quick sideways movement she slid out of the chair and walked quickly to the door.

"Lord Ambourne, you said recently that drabs cannot become honest, any more than the leopard can change his spots. Why are you asking me to tell you the truth? In your eyes it is not to be found in me. And now I hope you will excuse me; I have the headache. I will waste no more of your time." She slipped out of the door before he could stop her and ran to her room. She needed solitude to sort out the tangle of her emotions. She was glad to note that, though the Earl's face had darkened, he had not followed her.

In her room, she sat down by the window and gazed out. What in heaven's name was she to do? The obvious course, the sensible course, was to confess everything to the Earl. He was autocratic, but not unjust—except to her. And had she not de-

served his lack of trust in her? She thought over their relation
ship. His first sight of her formed the background to everything
he had learned of her since. Was it so surprising that he should
assume the worst? She had done nothing, said nothing to dis
abuse him. Indeed, she had wilfully encouraged him in his
original belief that she was an unlettered, ignorant wanton. She
had enjoyed deceiving her tutors. It was a game in which she
had pitted her wits against theirs—or so it had seemed at first.
What she had really been doing, of course, was defying the
Earl.

Then she remembered his arrogance when he'd informed her
he was going to make her into a lady; when he had warned her
that she was to behave and threatened her with the Pasha; the
names he had called her—slut, jade, scum; his description of
her as a tool... She grew indignant. He deserved everything she
had done! But then...he had saved her life and brought her
back into an environment she had thought closed to her for
ever. Whatever his motives, he had restored her will to live.
Surely this was worth something? And, if her actions had been
right and just, why was she now so unhappy? She shivered as
she remembered the dreadful scene by the lake a few days ago
and its consequences. What could she have done? Tell the Earl
about Philippe and perhaps ruin Eliane's chances of happi
ness? He probably wouldn't have believed her anyway.

There was yet another problem. What was she to do about
the d'Harcourts? The Earl was bound to visit them as soon as
they returned, and they were sure to talk about her. If the Earl
remained in his present mood the fat really would be in the fire
when he discovered how far she had been deceiving him about
her abilities. He must then start questioning where she had ac
quired the attributes of a lady. And if he learned the truth he
would send her away...

Her thoughts had gone full circle and she was no nearer a
decision. One thing was undeniable: for whatever reason, she
did not want to leave Belleroi and the Earl. She stayed in her
room all evening. A tray was brought to her room, and, though
she left the food, she drank the glass of wine that had been
served with it. It enabled her to sleep. Her last conscious
thought was of the Sheikh's words. "You have the courage and
spirit to help Lord Ambourne. Use them wisely."

CHAPTER SEVEN

FOR HIS PART, the Earl was almost as confused as Perdita. He sometimes felt he could see right into Perdita's mind, and then a scene like their last one would leave him frustrated and angry, sensing there was something more he should know, yet unable to get it out of her. Why was she so reluctant to confide in him? Throughout the next day, whenever the business of seeing his tenants and discussing their needs with his agent left him time to think, his mind was exercised with this mystery. There were times when he cursed the day he had found Perdita. It should all have been so simple! Buy the girl, train her, and then use her to trap Piers Carston. The only difficulty he had envisaged was finding a suitable girl to act as his tool. And now, when his mind should be on the many problems the estate still faced, he was pondering about Perdita—not as a tool but as a human being with a personality all her own: her wit, her courage, her pride and grace, her concern for Madame d'Espery, the passion he sensed in her... and, on the other hand, her skill at deception, her lack of morals, her treatment of Colette... What was he to do with her? Use her? Or send her away? No, he didn't want that! With determination he banished her from his mind and concentrated on the business in hand.

When Perdita went back to her room after her lesson that morning she found Colette there, hiding behind the curtains. 'Oh, it's you, *mademoiselle*! I was afraid it was Jeanne. She's our maid now, isn't she? Do you like her?''

"She looks after me well, Colette. Aren't you frightened of being found here?"

"Oh, they're all busy on the other side of the house. That's why I came. Can we go out? I want to go to the old castle. Henri says it's haunted.''

"That ruin is dangerous, Colette. And anyway, I'm not able
to come out at the moment..."

"I know. Georges has to be with you, hasn't he? Monsieur
le Marquis told him to go with you whenever you went out."

Perdita's cheeks flamed. Did the whole household know?
The answer was probably yes, for Madame Lebrun was no
friend of hers. Why did the woman dislike her so much? She
began to regret that she had never taken the trouble to find out.
But when she had arrived at the château she had been indifferent to what anyone thought of her, and now it was probably too
late.

"*Mademoiselle, mademoiselle!*" Colette was tugging at her
skirt. "You don't have to have Georges with you if you don't
want to."

"What? Of course I do. He doesn't let me out of his sight."

"I know, but he doesn't like taking you. He'd much rather
be with the horses. If you didn't turn up at the right time he'd
go back to the stables and he wouldn't bother telling anyone.
Then you could come with me!"

Perdita was sorely tempted. Her walks had become pen-
ances—it would be wonderful to go into the woods once again
with Colette. She badly wanted to see Philippe again, too, for
he might have some news of Eliane. "I'll think it over, Colette," she said. "Meanwhile, you ought to go. Jeanne might
come any moment."

"Please come, *mademoiselle*. I want to show you the castle."

"I'll think about the walk. It isn't easy, Colette."

"Course it is!" Colette replied scornfully. "All you have to
do is be late for Georges. Bye."

She was gone. Perdita smiled—it was so easy for children.
They didn't think of the consequences.

However, the fates seemed for once to be on her side. Two
days later the Earl was called urgently to Paris. The household
was in a bustle until he left, but he did not forget to check that
Perdita would be properly supervised. In the rush to leave,
however, he did not find the time to see Georges.

Soon after the Earl's departure Perdita seized her opportunity to see Philippe. Colette objected strongly to her decision
to see him first, but Perdita refused to change her mind. She
would not spend long with him, but she had to find out if he

had any news of Eliane. She pacified Colette by promising to
go out with her later in the week.

The day dawned bright and sunny, and Perdita was so full of
anticipation that she had to laugh at herself. It was such a mi-
nor pleasure—her excitement was out of all proportion. It was
not the prospect of seeing Philippe. She was, if anything, not
looking forward to that at all. No, it was simply the freedom
offered by a walk without Georges's gloomy supervision. All
went as planned. Georges duly took himself off after waiting
in vain for five minutes, and Perdita slipped out and made for
the lake. She was pleased to see that Philippe was waiting for
her, but when she drew near enough to see his face she was appalled.

"Philippe, what's happened?" she cried. "Have you had
some bad news of Eliane? Is she very ill? She's not...she's
not..."

"No," he replied heavily. "No, Mademoiselle Perdita,
Mademoiselle d'Harcourt is not dead. Though it would be
better perhaps for her if she were."

"What are you saying? Is she injured? Philippe, don't stand
there making cryptic remarks—tell me what is wrong!"

Philippe looked at her. His cheeks, normally so pink and full
of health, were white, and his eyes were dull. "I cannot tell you,
mademoiselle. It is not fit for you to hear."

Perdita felt like boxing his ears, but she clutched his arm instead. She was desperate to know what crisis had caused this
change in Philippe's appearance. "Philippe, I am not a child.
Please tell me what has happened."

"*Mademoiselle*, you cannot imagine how distressed I
was...how deeply distressed." He gave a shuddering sigh, then
said, "The d'Harcourts have deceived me. Mademoiselle
d'Harcourt is not the innocent I thought her. She has had an
association with another man."

"A love-affair!" exclaimed Perdita. "When? Where?"

"In England. Before she came back here."

"That's impossible! Eliane is innocent, I'd swear it."

"*Mademoiselle*, there is no possibility of mistake. Before the
d'Harcourts came back to France Mademoiselle d'Harcourt
had an affair."

"Who told you this? Why are you so sure it is true?"

"Mademoiselle d'Harcourt told me herself."

"But when?" cried Perdita.

"When you told me that Eliane was ill in Paris I decided that I must find out for myself how she was. I set off that same day. It wasn't easy to see her but finally her mother came and took me into her room. She was so pale, *mademoiselle*, and...and we were so happy to see each other again. Her mother saw how it was with us and promised to see that the Marquis gave his consent. Then...then...Eliane told me—what I have told you."

"And now? You no longer wish to marry her? Is that it?" asked Perdita quietly.

"Marry her? Marry a woman who has been with another man? I don't think you understand, *mademoiselle*. She wasn't married to him! She ran off... Oh, God, I can't bear it! Eliane, Eliane!" Philippe turned away and a sob escaped him. At first Perdita's heart ached for him. He was so young and so full of ideals. He had put Eliane on a pedestal—an angel, he had called her—and now his world had crashed about him. But how had Eliane fared?

She waited until Philippe could speak again, then asked, "What of Eliane, Philippe? What did you say to her after her confession?"

"I...I don't remember. I ran out of the building and came straight back here. I never want to see her again!"

So this was the reason for the Earl's hasty departure for Paris, thought Perdita. She could imagine that Eliane might well have collapsed after Philippe's disastrous visit and that Madame d'Harcourt had sent for support. Poor, poor Eliane!

"Philippe, I can see why you should have felt like this in the first shock of discovery. But think of Eliane. What do you think she feels now, after you left her like that?" Philippe shrugged his shoulders, but said nothing. Perdita said suddenly, "When did you say it happened? In England? But how old was Eliane then?"

"Sixteen," said Philippe sullenly.

"Sixteen! Only sixteen? She was only a child! Don't you know any more?"

"Nothing. Isn't it enough? That she's had a lover?"

Perdita lost her temper with him. She cried passionately, "No, it's not nearly enough! You can't judge Eliane on this. I've known Eliane for no time at all but I'll swear she is an innocent party. If she did have an affair, then she was duped into it. How long have you known her? Hasn't she always looked to you for protection? Hasn't she always been afraid of strangers, reluctant to meet new faces? You cannot desert her. Think about Eliane instead of yourself. She isn't a fallen angel, she's a girl who needed you, and you failed her.'' She gave an angry sob and shook her head. "I'm sorry, I can't talk to you any more; I have to get back. Besides, there's nothing more to say. Goodbye, Philippe. You can reach me through Colette if you wish, but until you have reconsidered your attitude to Eliane I don't want to see you again!''

She spoke so forcefully that Philippe stared at her. However, he didn't say anything, and she turned abruptly and walked back in the direction of the house, brushing angry tears from her cheeks. Poor Eliane. Philippe's reaction was cruel but not unexpected. He was so young and inexperienced.

Her sad thoughts occupied her mind throughout the rest of the afternoon and evening. It was an ironic twist of fate that she and Eliane, two girls of the same age, should both have been so unfortunate. And who was to say which of them was the worse off? It was true that Eliane had a loving family round her now, whereas she had no one. But Perdita felt that Eliane was less well equipped to take the buffets life dealt out to her, that she could much more easily go under. She might well do so now. If only she could see her—perhaps telling Eliane her own story might help. She debated for a while how she might get to Paris, but finally decided this was impossible. She must hope that Eliane was brought back to Beau Lac. Would Madame d'Harcourt bring her here, where there were so many memories of Philippe? She went to bed with a heavy heart, thinking of her friend and wondering how she was.

Later that night she lay awake, remembering the conversation she had overheard in the cabin on the way to Tangier. Tom had said something about Miss Linette, about finding Miss Linette... That's right! And the Earl had replied that he'd been thinking about finding her in a 'doxy's house in London'. He was going to 'teach someone a lesson' for doing it. It was Eliane they had been talking about, she knew that. Then, from what the Earl had said after that, he intended to use her, Perdita, to accomplish this. Was this why the Earl wanted a pseudo-lady?

Well, if it was reasonably near legal, she would help him! She would willingly act as Eliane's champion, since Philippe seemed to have failed her.

Life continued in the château. The Earl must have conveyed
some of his scepticism to Monsieur Champollion and Signor
Calvi, for they were definitely suspicious of her. So for the first
time she worked properly, much to their surprise and eventual
delight. Here was a pupil any tutor could take pride in! Père
Amboise accepted the miraculous improvement in her writing
without question, but then he was used to living with miracles.
The fact was, Perdita no longer wanted to delay the Earl's
plans. She was burning to help Eliane in any way she could, and
was desperate to know how she was faring. When would the
Earl return?

The weather had turned cold and wet after Perdita's unhappy scene with Philippe, and it was impossible for her to go
out with Colette for nearly a week. They were both eager for
their walk. Perdita would be glad to exchange her depressed
thoughts of Eliane for Colette's lively company, and Colette
was anxious to show *mademoiselle* the old castle. When she did
eventually manage to get out Georges was less obliging than he
had been on her previous outing. He waited for fully quarter of
an hour before he hunched his shoulders and went back to his
horses. When Perdita got to the edge of the woods there was no
sign of Colette. Had she grown tired of waiting? Fifteen minutes might seem an eternity to a child. But she couldn't believe
Colette would so easily abandon their plans. Where was she?

A faint cry was borne to her on the wind. Colette! She looked
round, but saw nothing. Where had it come from? Again she
heard it. It was coming from further round the hill, where the
high road ran along the boundary. The castle ruins were in that
direction! Full of foreboding, she scrambled hastily round to
the pile of stones, which had once formed the original fortress
of Belleroi. The cries were louder here—Colette must be in the
ruins.

"*Mademoiselle, mademoiselle*, I'm here! Please come
quickly. I'm going to fall."

"I'm coming," Perdita called. "But where are you?"

"In a hole in the ground. It fell in and I fell too."

Perdita found the place. It had been an old well or store,
which had been filled in long ago. Now the top had collapsed
and Colette was standing on a narrow ledge, clutching the
fragile root of a small tree. Even as Perdita got down on her
knees to see, Colette slipped a little further.

"Hold on; I'll get your wrists. You'll be safe then." Perdita lay flat, her arms over the hole, and caught hold of Colette's wrists. It was just as well that she did, for the root suddenly snapped. Trying to speak calmly, she said, "How on earth did you get into this predicament, Colette?"

"I didn't go in the ruins, *mademoiselle*. I was just on the edge. You were such a long time and I got a bit cold. I thought it would be warmer in the shelter of the big stones. But I hadn't got very far when I . . . when I . . ." Colette's voice had developed a wobble. Perdita finished the sentence for her.

"When you went tumbling into a hole that wasn't there. That's clever! How are your toes?"

"They're all right, I think. But it's not very comfortable, *mademoiselle*. Can't you lift me out?"

"I'll try. Come on!"

After several attempts, however, she had to give up. Colette's weight, together with the uncertain stability of the ground, made it impossible for her to get enough purchase. Perdita began to grow worried. She dared not let go of Colette's wrists, for the child was standing on a very narrow ledge, beneath which was a long drop. But, if she couldn't go for help, how would they ever escape? It was getting very cold and a mist was coming up from the lake—Colette would soon be chilled through. For the next half-hour she tried desperately either to lift Colette up, or to anchor her so that she could go for help, but all her efforts were in vain. Her feet slipped on the wet grass, and, once, the ground started to give way on the edge.

Towards the end of the period Colette was getting tired, cold and frightened. Perdita took more of her weight, and went through her repertoire of funny stories to cheer them up. By the end of the period she was exhausted. It was with heartfelt relief, therefore, that she heard voices in the wood, which proved to be a search party for Colette. By this time she was too weak to shout, and lay there laughing with relief.

"Hey you! What are you doing with that child? You wicked woman!" Colette was snatched up, and rough hands pushed Perdita aside.

"Take her back to her grandmother; she's frantic with worry. There, there, little one, don't cry! You're safe now."

They started off, Colette held in a burly stable-lad's arms, leaving Perdita on the ground by the well. She called after them, but they ignored her, except for one who turned as he went and shouted, "You should be in prison, you should! Or a mad-house! Treating a poor little motherless child like that. What sort of woman are you, thinking it's funny to lock her up in a cupboard and hang her over a hole? Unless you're a witch." He gave her a fearful look, crossed himself and scuttled off.

Perdita was left alone. She was so exhausted that she couldn't move for the moment, and lay there, weakly laughing. She didn't believe it! They'd left her here because they thought she had been tormenting Colette. Madame Lebrun had surely spread her poison wide. Not one of them had doubted that it was so, and Colette had been too far gone herself to say any-thing. Poor child, she had really been very brave up to the last few minutes.

Now she must pull herself up and make her own way to the château. But the mist had grown very thick and it was difficult to get her bearings. She walked doggedly forward in what she guessed was the right direction, but suddenly found herself on the crumbling ground by the well again. She halted and lis-tened for any sound, but the silence was eerily complete. She shivered and felt a moment's panic, then made herself think calmly. The road must be on her left, so she set off again in that direction. It was now quite dark and the ground was rough... She tripped over a trailing bramble stem and fell heavily. For a moment she lay there, feeling dizzy, and when she tried to move again she found she was hopelessly caught up in a tangle of undergrowth. At least it was warm and dry here in the shelter of the trees and surrounded by leaves. She would have a rest and then try again...

PERDITA WOKE at first light, feeling curiously lethargic. The cold had penetrated to her very bones, though she was wearing her thick cape. She wondered why no one had come looking for her, for surely Colette had told the others the truth by now? Perhaps the little girl had fallen asleep as soon as she had got in and was not yet awake. But why hadn't Madame Lebrun or-ganised a search? Not for love of Perdita, but from fear of the Earl! For whatever reason, she was on her own. She forced herself to her feet and considered what she should do. The way through the wood was shorter, but the road made for easier walking. Besides, though it was early still, she might just meet someone who would help her. She got to the road and set off along it. Her head ached, her arms ached—in fact, there wasn't much that didn't hurt! She must get to the château.

CHAPTER EIGHT

THE EARL HAD EXPECTED to return to Belleroi the previous evening, but a cast shoe had delayed him and he had been forced to spend the night at a villainously uncomfortable inn on the road from Bayeux. He had left before first light, thankful to escape from the place. With luck he would be at the château for breakfast. The pathetic figure limping along the road touched him—it looked so tired and so determined. She must be making for Belleroi, looking for work or charity. The kitchen staff would give her something. As he passed he slowed his horses to tell her to be sure to call. But the words died on his lips as he looked down into Perdita's weary face. "What the devil...?"

He had no time for more. Perdita smiled radiantly at him, said, "Oh, you're back!" then slid to the ground. He leapt down and, kneeling on the road beside her, lifted her into his arms. She was very pale, with dark circles under her eyes. After a moment she opened them and looked up at him. She made a vague fluttering movement with her hand and said, "I'm sorry... I couldn't help it. Don't be angry. Please."

"What is it, Perdita? What's happened to you?" he said urgently.

A small smile came to her lips. "You'd never believe me, Lord Ambourne. I hardly believe it myself." Then she gave a small groan as he lifted her more closely to him.

"Where does it hurt, Perdita? Tell me!"

"Everywhere, I think. But it's not serious. I'll get up in a moment."

It was clear she was in considerable pain. Her gallant spirit touched him as no tears could have done. He carefully lifted her into the chaise, settled her as best he could in a vehicle that was built for speed rather than comfort, and set off for the château. The way was short, but the Earl had some time to re-

flect. Curiously enough, in spite of what he knew of her, he did
not doubt the truth of what she had said. Another instance of
the gap between his head and his . . . his what? His heart? No,
he dismissed that notion out of hand. The sooner he got Perdita back to the château the better. She needed care, and
he . . . he wanted some answers! He urged his horses into a
slightly quicker gait and they were soon bowling up the long
drive.

They arrived to find the château in an uproar. Colette had
woken up demanding to see *mademoiselle*. The servants soon
discovered they had made a serious mistake in their judgement
of their master's ward, and the men were frantically searching
in the village and further afield. When the Earl arrived at his
château there wasn't a groom to help him with his horses, and
the rest of the servants were all in a highly nervous state. Their
relief at seeing Perdita arrive with the Earl, however, was tem-
pered by the knowledge of the trouble that lay ahead for some
of them.

The Earl paid no heed to their greetings, nor did he listen to
any of their stammered excuses. Brushing these impatiently
aside, he carried Perdita up to her room and put her gently
down on the bed. Then he told Jeanne to look after her. As he
went out Perdita gave him a grin and said softly, "Aren't you
going to throw me into the bath?"

The Earl avoided Jeanne's shocked look and said, "Get some
rest now. I'll throw you in the bath when you're stronger. Look
after her, Jeanne." He went downstairs to his distraught
household, ordered one of the maids to bring at least some of
the search party back to tend his horses, and requested Madame Lebrun to see him in the library in two hours. Then he
went to his room to change. By the time he came down order
had been restored to the household and breakfast was waiting
for him in the small parlour. When he had finished he sent for
Madame Lebrun.

"Now," said the Earl coldly. "Now I am ready to hear any
explanation you can give me for what happened last night."
The housekeeper shifted uneasily. What was she to say?

"I am waiting, Madame Lebrun," said the Earl.

"Monsieur le Marquis, we were all so anxious about Colette . . . Rosanne was out of her mind . . . and . . . and . . . We're
so sorry for what happened, Monsieur le Marquis!" The

housekeeper was so far removed from her usual imperturbable
self that the Earl unbent a little.

"Sit down, Madame Lebrun. Now tell me first of all how it
was that Mademoiselle Perdita was out alone. Where was
Georges?"

"When *mademoiselle* didn't appear at her usual time
Georges thought she wasn't coming. He had a lot to do with the
horses so he...so he—"

"Forgot my orders and went back to the warmth of his stables. Right, that's one matter cleared up," said the Earl, making a note to take it further with both Georges and Perdita.
"Where did Colette come in? I'm surprised she was with the
mademoiselle in view of what you told me last time we talked
on this head. I thought you told me Colette had been frightened?"

"Oh, *monsieur*, we were all mistaken there. Colette is a
naughty girl. She kept her friendship with Mademoiselle Perdita completely secret. We had no idea that they went on so
many walks together. That's why we..."

"Well?" asked the Earl.

"That's why we jumped to the conclusion we did. That
Mademoiselle Perdita was tormenting Colette again, holding
her over the well."

"Of all the ridiculous ideas! Didn't it ever occur to you that
Colette might have fallen in by herself? Heaven knows she's
been in enough trouble before. Well, didn't it? The stable hands
might be stupid enough, but surely you knew better, *madame*?"

"I wasn't with the men when they found Colette, *monsieur*.
I only saw them arrive, and by that time she was worn out with
fright and cold. I couldn't question her then."

"How long was it before you decided to look for Mademoiselle Perdita?"

This was the difficult part for the housekeeper. She was
aware that she had left it far too long before doing so. "We
were so worried about Colette...and Rosanne, *monsieur*."

"When did you send the men out, Madame Lebrun?"

She swallowed and said in a low voice, "Some time after
nine, *monsieur*—but we couldn't find her in the mist. We
thought she had run away." His silence alarmed her and she
said defensively, "We all knew you didn't trust her, and she
wasn't very happy being taken for a walk like a dog every day,

so we thought she'd gone. I didn't think you would mind very
much . . ."

The Earl stood up. "Thank you, Madame Lebrun. That is
all."

Madame Lebrun hesitated at the door. "I was wrong, *monsieur*, to do what I did. I will understand if you wish me to go."

"What you omitted to do was worse," said the Earl with
grim humour. "You'll have to wait for my decision on whether
you should go or not. I haven't yet heard the whole story.
Thank you."

The Earl threw himself into a chair by the fire. He'd have to
see Georges, of course, though he knew what the groom would
say. Why had Perdita been late, though? He fancied her part in
this had not been totally blameless. But, from what Madame
Lebrun had said, Perdita hadn't used her freedom to find her
lover again. She had gone for a walk with Colette! Had the
young man he had seen by the lake been frightened off for
good? He hoped so. He stretched himself and sighed. He was
weary, not because of the journey to Paris and back, but because of what he had found when he'd arrived there. Linette
was like a little ghost. In itself her fever was not serious—a severe bout of influenza, no more—but she showed no inclination to fight it. Of course, removing her to Paris at the onset of
the attack had not been wise, but his aunt had always been in-
clined to panic where Linette was concerned and had taken her
to an eminent physician there. She would have been better left
here in Beau Lac. Then, perhaps, the unpleasantness with the
young man might have been avoided. Who was this Philippe
who had followed them to Paris? The young puppy deserved to
be whipped for his treatment of Linette—or Eliane, as he supposed he must now call her. She had grown hysterical when he
had called her 'Linette'—Piers Carston had made much of that
name. The Earl frowned. Piers Carston had not only destroyed Eliane's future. A whole happy childhood lay in ruins,
too.

He got up impatiently. It was useless bemoaning the past; he
must do something about Carston. It was time he suppressed
his scruples about using Perdita, stopped her nonsense with her
tutors, and prepared her for London. The sight of Eliane's
misery had hardened his resolve. Besides, whatever else she was
or had been, Perdita was undoubtedly a pirate's strumpet, and
she was penniless—two qualities he had expressly searched for.

No, he must dismiss any scruples about her—he could not afford them.

As the Earl had thought, Georges was unrepentant. His job was to look after horses, not silly girls who played tricks and got themselves lost. He would have said more, but the Earl sent him away. Georges was a genius with horses and knew it. He had always made it perfectly clear to the Earl that he let him ride his horses as a personal favour, and was most unlikely to worry about dismissal. Fortunately the Earl was fair-minded enough—and fond enough of his horses—not to pursue the matter. He had asked Georges to perform a task for which the man was not suited.

When he went up to see Perdita he found the door open and Colette sprawled on her bed, laughing at something Perdita had said. They made a pleasant picture, and he admired it for a moment from outside. As soon as she saw him Colette scrambled off the bed, gave him a somewhat inelegant curtsy and scurried out.

The Earl sat down in one of the rose chintz armchairs. "Are you recovered?" he asked.

"I was never really ill. I ought to be up."

"It's a great compliment to the Sheikh's treatment that you have survived a night out of doors so well," said the Earl. "Am I right to assume it was out of doors?"

Her mouth tightened as she said, "You have made so many assumptions about me, Lord Ambourne, that I am sure you will assume anything you choose. I could show you the clump of brambles, I suppose. But then you would merely assume that I was lying, or you would assume that someone was with me in the brambles. I assume you have some doubt?"

He laughed and said, "Pax, pax, Perdita. I believe you. Indeed, I can see the scratches on your face. Where was Georges?"

She hesitated and he could see her debating. Would she tell him the truth? Finally she said defiantly, "I tricked him. It wasn't his fault—though he deserved it! Tell me, did you choose him for his stimulating conversation, or his courteous ways?"

"Neither. I chose him because he's good with horses." At her indignant gasp he said, "When I engaged him initially, that is. He was the only one I could spare from the estate to walk with you. So you slipped the leash and ran off? Where?"

She looked at him for a moment as if she was assessing his question. "If you are simply trying to find out what happened yesterday I will tell you. But I don't like the manner of your questions. There are too many animals involved. Do you wish to know what happened?"

A smile tugged at his lips. He was to consider himself rebuked! "Yes, please," he said meekly.

She thereupon told him clearly and concisely what had happened in the castle ruins. The account was factual, but he could sense the fears and pain she and Colette had experienced. "So I started walking to the château," she concluded.

He hesitated for a moment and then asked, "Have you escaped from Georges on any other occasion, Perdita?"

"To walk with Colette? No," she said, not looking at him.

"So you've seen him again?"

"If you mean the man I was with when you were so angry, yes, I have," she said, lifting her chin and staring him in the eye. The Earl was conscious of a surge of disappointed fury, but he controlled it. In the light of his resolve to press forward with his plans for Piers Carston it was of little consequence if she had a hundred lovers. "I think you're making assumptions again," said a quiet voice from the bed. "My conversation with him—and that was all it was, Lord Ambourne—was short and unhappy. I doubt I will see him again."

"I doubt you'll have the time, Perdita. I wish you to be ready for England in a month. As soon as you are able to get up you will present yourself in the library. Things will be different from now on."

He got up and strode swiftly out of the room. As he went down the stairs he was frowning so heavily that little Jeanne pressed herself against the banister rail and prayed he would not notice her.

IN SPITE OF PERDITA'S brave words it was some days before she could go downstairs. The Earl had insisted on a visit from the local doctor, who had recommended that she should wait to the end of the week before attempting to get up. The Earl was all the more surprised therefore when Perdita presented herself in the library just three days after her experience.

She found him engaged once again with his agent. His trip to Paris had interrupted a programme of improvements to some of the farmhouses on the estate, and he was deep in discussion. When he saw her, however, he rose instantly and said, "Right, Etienne, see that it is all put in hand straight away. I don't want any more delays—I'd like to see it finished before I go back to England."

"When will that be, *monsieur*?"

"I'm not sure. In about a month, I think. It depends on *mademoiselle*, here. It won't be much later than a month, though, so don't delay! And Etienne—has the old well been properly boarded up? Good! Come and sit down, Perdita."

The agent looked curiously at Perdita as he went. He had heard strange stories about her, some of them contradictory. He hoped Monsieur le Marquis knew what he was doing.

When he had gone the Earl sat down again and contemplated Perdita. "Are you sure you're well enough to be downstairs? Dr. Grondet said next week . . ."

"I'm well enough, Lord Ambourne. My arms are still a little stiff, that's all. I'm ready for my lessons."

"Yes." He paused for thought. "Perdita, a short while ago I tried, and failed, to establish a working relationship between us. At that time I already knew you could read perfectly well. I established that you are a native English speaker, I learned a little of your history—though not nearly enough—and I attempted to find the truth about your lessons. As I told you, I did not believe you to be as stupid as your tutors suggested. Since my return from Paris I have had reports of amazing progress; one might almost call it miraculous."

He waited for comment from her, but when none was forthcoming he continued, "You already know I rescued you in Algiers with a specific purpose in mind."

"You bought me, Lord Ambourne."

"I prefer to say rescued, Perdita, but I am not about to argue the point; I haven't the time." Perdita stirred rebelliously, but her interest was caught. "I want some answers from you, Perdita. I do not wish to waste our time—yours, mine and that of your tutors—in trying to give you knowledge you already possess. I wish you to tell me without prevarication or evasion what accomplishments you have, and to what degree. I am ready to hear that now."

She felt as if a pistol were being held to her head. The moment of truth—some of it—had arrived. She got up. "Shall I play to you, Lord Ambourne?"

He rose and she led the way to the large piano in the centre of the music-room. She was nervous, but comforted herself with the thought of the hours of practice with the d'Harcourts. She played him a lively dance by Mozart and then, when he asked her to continue, she played part of a brilliant sonata movement by Scarlatti. Lastly, with Eliane in mind, she played a sad little tune from Lully. As the last note sounded she turned her head from him so he could not see the tears in her eyes.

There was silence. "You wicked girl," was the Earl's astonishing reaction. She turned back to him. "To have talent such as that, and to waste it playing tricks." He leant forward. "Why are there tears in your eyes, Perdita?"

Perdita shook her head, for she could not speak. What could she have said anyway? The Earl did not know of her friendship with Eliane, and she was not yet ready to tell him of it. "What about the rest? Of your gifts?"

"Madame d'Espery was right in one thing. I cannot sew. I think I know most of the rules of polite behaviour, though even when I'm trying I find it difficult to conform."

She had a sudden vision of her mother, shaking her head in exasperated affection and saying, "You are too impetuous by far, my love. A young lady always thinks before she acts and always acts according to the rules of society. When you go to London..."

She got up from the piano. Her impetuous behaviour had been the last link in a chain of disaster, but she must not think of that at the moment. What was the Earl saying?

"Perdita, are you all right? Come, I'll send for Jeanne. She'll take you upstairs."

"No, no. Thank you, I'm perfectly able to carry on. What else do you wish to know? As you probably suspect, I can write as well as read; I know the steps of most dances, but not the waltz; I have a knowledge of, though no talent for painting, but I think I will have little need for that in London. I have a basic knowledge of geography—especially of the Mediterranean," she added with a wry smile.

"Enough, enough," said the Earl, holding up his hand. "You seem to be vastly better educated than any of the respectable young ladies of my acquaintance. Tell me, Perdita, where did a girl of your background acquire all these skills? Was it with your first...protector?"

A cloud passed over Perdita's face, but she only replied, "Why did an aristocrat of your background acquire a girl like me? Isn't it time you told me, so that I know what you want of me, Lord Ambourne?"

The Earl was strangely reluctant to do this. Although she had not answered his last question, he had learnt more of Perdita during the last half-hour than ever before. He had the feeling that once he revealed his plans to her they would become strangers again. He said, "I will, but not yet. There are matters that should be cleared up before we embark on our joint enterprise. I hope it will be a joint venture, Perdita. You have something to gain from this as well."

"Yes," she murmured. "A discreet establishment in one of the better quarters of London, perhaps."

He looked at her sharply. She didn't sound grateful, yet to a girl of her history this ought to be the peak of her ambition. He didn't have time to think about that now, but he put it aside for later—part of the enigma that was Perdita.

He continued, "But first I must decide what to do about Madame Lebrun. You could have been seriously ill through her negligence. Have you anything to say about her?"

"Only that I think she has been punished enough. She must have been worrying for days about what was to become of her. I was certainly partially to blame for her antipathy towards me, and you yourself did not appear to value me very highly. The rest sprang from those two facts. Yes, she was wrong not to send out a search party sooner. But I am not much the worse for wear. And she has spoken very kindly to me since."

"No doubt," said the Earl with a cynical smile.

"No, I think she is sincerely sorry. You must do as you think fit, of course, but she is a most efficient housekeeper and would be hard to replace."

"So you think she should stay?"

"It is not for me to say. I should be sorry to see her go because of me."

The Earl nodded his head but did not say anything for a moment. Then, "Will you keep me waiting if I invite you to a walk this afternoon, Perdita? I must go over to one of the farms in the valley, and it is a pleasant afternoon's stroll. Will you come? We can talk on the way."

Perdita's face lit up and was then controlled. "Thank you, Lord Ambourne, I should like that. At what time do you wish me to be at the door?"

"I think two o'clock. That will give us time to walk in comfort before it gets cold. Are you sure you can manage it? You are not too stiff?"

"It will be good for me. Thank you." She went to the door, then paused. "Lord Ambourne, am I to understand that your visit to Paris concerned your cousin?"

"Yes," he said uncommunicatively.

But Perdita persisted. "I hope it was not bad news? Is she not well?" She seemed to be waiting anxiously for his reply.

"My cousin had an influenza, which she found hard to shake off. We are hoping the warmer weather will help her to recover. She is not strong."

"Thank you, Lord Ambourne," said Perdita in subdued tones. "I will see you at two."

He followed her out and went back to the library, asking one of the maids to fetch Madame Lebrun as he passed. She came so quickly that he guessed she had been waiting for her summons. Perdita had said she must have been worrying for days about her future, and if she could be so generous to her late adversary then surely he could not lag behind? He would let the woman stay.

Madame Lebrun was embarrassingly grateful to be given a second chance. Without saying so outright, the Earl let it be understood that Perdita had influenced his decision for Madame Lebrun's reprieve. Madame Lebrun was as ready to tell the other servants about Perdita's magnanimity as she had been indiscreet about her unfriendliness on her arrival. Soon Perdita found herself generally approved of—in the servants' hall at least. This, together with the approval of her tutors, made for an atmosphere of sunny harmony, which was a novel and attractive experience.

The Earl proved to be a pleasant companion on the first walk and the others that followed. He used the opportunity to tell her about current London society. He had a well-informed mind, and his observations on the world he was teaching her to know were astringent and witty. Perdita grew to look forward to her outings, though she was never allowed to relax on them. He expected her to remember every name, every fact he gave her. He could be impatient, and they often came dangerously close to an argument when she thought he was being unreasonably demanding. The sense of exhilaration when her mind was stretched to the limit more than made up for these lapses, however.

On one occasion he took her to see Madame d'Espery, and after a difficult start to the visit Perdita was able to convey her genuine regret that she had upset her former chaperon. The company of the Earl no doubt helped to soften Madame d'Espery towards her, for he was at his most charming, listening to her stories and making her laugh. When Perdita came to go, Madame d'Espery said, "I have had great pleasure in your company today, Mademoiselle Perdita. I should like you to call again—even if that rogue there is not able to come with you." Perdita looked at the Earl in amusement, and thanked the old lady.

That evening the Earl announced that he was going to teach Perdita the waltz. If she was to be presented to London society as a young lady of wealth she would need this accomplishment.

"But why can't Signor Calvi teach me?' she asked, slightly startled by this suggestion.

"You disappoint me, Perdita. I thought you had a feeling for style. Surely you've realised by now that Signor Calvi, while no doubt excellent for country jigs and *boulangers*, hasn't enough elegance about him for the modern dances. You would be labelled in an instant as a country bumpkin. You wouldn't want that?"

"How do I know what I want?" muttered Perdita, who was decidedly nervous.

The next day Monsieur Champollion was asked to play for them, and the lesson began. For one reason or another Perdita had already had the Earl's arm around her several times, but this was different. Though she normally moved gracefully, she stumbled and tripped until the Earl, never the most patient of tutors, sat her down in a chair and demonstrated by himself.

"Now you do it!" he said, pulling her up and placing her in the middle of the floor. She performed the steps with her usual grace. "I don't believe it!" said the Earl. "Come, we'll try again." Once again she stumbled, and he stopped where they were, demanding, "Are you playing your tricks again?"

"No! I just don't seem to be able to concentrate when you're holding . . . when you're holding me by the waist."

The Earl gave a roar of laughter. "That's rich! Come, Perdita, stop play-acting and do it properly. Look up, girl! Look up!" He took hold of her chin and pulled it up. The gesture reminded them both of other occasions when he had held her like this. For one heart-stopping moment the Earl seemed on the point of repeating his kisses, and then he gave a kind of groan and led her back to her chair. He bowed and said lightly, "Perhaps it would be better if you learned the basic steps from Signor Calvi. We can always add a little town polish when we go to London. Thank you, Monsieur Champollion; the lesson is ended. And now, Perdita, if you will excuse me I have some work to do in the library."

But by the time his agent came to see him two hours later the Earl had achieved very little. He had been thinking long and hard about Perdita, about Eliane and about Piers Carston. Pleasant though his interlude of walks and lessons had been, it was time he told Perdita of his plan. The next morning he sent for her.

CHAPTER NINE

"No, I WILL NOT DO IT! You cannot force me to, and I will never agree of my own free will!" Perdita stood before the Earl, her eyes flashing blue fire and her face white with rage.

The Earl was astonished at the strength of her reaction. It seemed such a little thing to ask of a girl with her experiences. "Perdita, did I not promise that once you have married the man, and we have made sure that the marriage is binding, I will provide you with the wherewithal to set yourself up as we agreed? What is wrong with that?"

"I do not recall ever having been asked, so how can I have agreed to anything? I have not agreed, my lord. I do not agree and will not agree!" She was so angry that her voice was trembling.

He looked at her and said, "I confess I do not understand this hysterical reaction. He may be a villain, but I do not believe he would mistreat you as you have been mistreated in the past. You have only to live with him long enough to validate the marriage. Then you will be free."

"And how is a marriage validated, my lord? Tell me that!"

The Earl turned away and stared out of the window. "I agree there will be a short time when you will be required to live with the man as his wife," he said shortly. "I am surprised this is distasteful to you. You are surely not claiming that your scruples would not permit it? You forget where and in what company I found you. This is not the time to claim any maidenly modesty—not to me, Perdita!"

She looked at his unrelenting back with something approaching despair. She would not do this thing he was asking, she knew that. But there seemed no way to reach him. The charming companion of the last weeks had turned into a monster. Surely love of Eliane could not have done this? "How will this plan of yours help your cousin?"

"Nothing will help my cousin," he replied, turning back into the room. "Her life is ruined. I explained that to you. But at least the man who destroyed her will live to regret it."

"But I don't understand how marriage to me will give him cause for regret. Other than the fact that I have nothing to offer him."

"He's an adventurer, Perdita. He lives on women. He ran off with Eliane because he thought she was rich, and abandoned her because she was poor. When the season opens in May he will be in London, looking for a rich heiress. He has to marry one very soon, or he will be thrown into Fleet Prison for debt. For the last two years he has been living off money he inherited in some way or other. Now that money has been gambled away and he is desperate for more. I will provide him with an attractive, modestly brought-up young lady with a rumoured fortune of thirty thousand pounds a year. He won't fail to take the bait. He would marry you if you squinted and had one leg. Your beauty will be a bonus."

He looked at her sombrely for a moment, then said, "By the time he realises that you haven't a penny to your name it will be too late for him. He will be ruined."

"But if you took me to London he would surely recognise you—if not your person, then your name. You can't do it, my lord; it's a mad scheme. And I won't help you." Her voice rose and she walked agitatedly to and fro.

The Earl was finding this interview more difficult than he had ever imagined. Perdita's distress perplexed and moved him, but he was none the less determined to carry his scheme through. "You will not be presented under my aegis, Perdita. It would not do in any case, since I am a bachelor. I have a lady in mind to act as your sponsor in Society. She will do it for a fee, and she will act as your chaperon, too."

He seemed to have considered everything. But however angry he might become he could not actually force her to marry this man. She went back to her original statement. "I won't do it!"

The Earl turned on her angrily. "I have waited for nearly four years to trap Piers Carston, Perdita. I am not going to be stopped now."

She stood as if turned to stone. He thought she was going to faint and came to catch her arm, but she shook him off. "Piers

Carston? Is that his name?'' she said through lips that hardly moved.

"Yes. Perdita, I can see that this has been too much for you, and I think you should go to your room. But I warn you I will stop at very little to make Carston pay for what he has done to Eliane. Do you understand?"

"Yes," she said, making for the door. "Yes, I understand. Please excuse me." She went swiftly out of the door and ran up the stairs as if pursued by the Furies.

The Earl, left in the library, sat brooding in front of the fire for some time. He had the feeling that he had just destroyed something precious, but did not know what it was. Then he thought of Eliane as she had been just before he'd left Ambourne to go to Vienna—a laughing, carefree girl, teasing him about his 'stuffy' work. That was the last he had seen of her until he'd found her in that filthy hole in London months later. Yes, he was right to act as he had planned. But why did he feel so out of sorts? He needed a hard ride round the estate to liven him up. As he got up to go, Sheikh Ibrahim's words came back to him: ". . . if, as I suspect, the 'weapon' is now lying sick in my apartments, then you must take care it does not rebound on you. To use human beings thus is dangerous."

Perdita reached her room, panting and dizzy, but she could not rest. She walked the length of the room and back again, to and fro, in a state of extreme agitation. Piers Carston! Piers Carston was intended as the victim of the Earl's plot! Even the name of Carston caused her to shiver with loathing, for the two men to whom she owed every misfortune were Piers Carston and his father, Frederick.

Memories that she had succeeded in repressing for years came flooding back to her—her gentle little mother, giving the news of her forthcoming marriage to Frederick Carston to her daughter. "You will see, he will be a new papa for you, my love. He's strong, and full of tender concern for both of us."

"I don't want a new papa; I loved the one I had, and I thought you did, too, Mama!"

"And so I did," her mother had said sadly, "but I have found life very difficult this last year. Taverton is a large estate and it needs a man's direction. I do not love Mr. Carston in the way I loved your father, but he is a good man and will look after both of us. Please don't be difficult, my darling. Life will be much more secure with Mr. Carston in charge."

Of course, that had been the trouble. Mr. Carston was not in charge, not really. Her father had left Taverton and all its rich acres in trust to his daughter, with a life interest for his wife, who would only own the estate outright if her daughter predeceased her. Perdita shuddered as she remembered the scene when Frederick Carston had discovered this. He had wanted to raise money by selling some of the land and found he could do nothing at all to the estate without the agreement of the trustees. He had bullied her mother mercilessly to attempt to have the terms of the trust changed, but this was one thing his gentle wife could not and would not do for him.

After that her new stepfather had changed almost overnight. Perdita had never liked him—his heavy white face and coarse features, his loud good humour and overbearing manners contrasted so sharply with her father's reserved charm. But now his good humour vanished except in the company of the London bucks he brought to stay, and he treated her mother with brutal contempt. Taverton was in Perdita's blood, for it had belonged to her family for generations. It now became a prison in which she could do nothing to help her mother, who was growing daily more fragile. The only solace in those dark times was Frederick Carston's son Piers, who was a frequent visitor and was everything his father was not. He had guinea-gold hair, frank blue eyes and a laughing, open countenance. He charmed her mother into an occasional smile, often made Perdita laugh and, whenever he could, bore the brunt of his father's ill humour. Perdita had reason to be grateful to him, looked forward to his visits, and was relieved and pleased when he decided to live at Taverton. When the crisis broke she readily turned to him for help.

A tap at the door brought her back to her room at Belleroi. "Who is it?" she asked, unwilling to see the Earl again until she had come to terms with this new and startling situation.

"It's me, Colette, *mademoiselle*. Can I come in?"

Colette probably wanted to go for a walk. Perdita had been neglecting her recently because of her walks with the Earl. She went to the door and unlocked it.

"Why have you locked your door?" was Colette's inevitable question. But, without waiting for an answer, she went on, "It's a lovely afternoon, *mademoiselle*. Do come out. There are some bluebells in the wood I want to show you."

Colette's bright little face looking up so expectantly made
Perdita's mind up. It would be better to give herself a respite
from the emotional stress of the day, and a walk with Colette
was just the thing. She found her pelisse and bonnet, and the
two were soon outside and on their way to Colette's bluebells.
These were duly admired, then they continued in the direction
of Beau Lac.

In spite of Colette's chatter, Perdita was often lost in sad
thoughts. Beau Lac looked forlorn in the spring sunshine, although some servants were certainly still there. Would Eliane
ever return? Her mother might well decide that it held too many
unhappy associations for Eliane to recover her spirits here.
Where would they go? At the thought that she might never see
Madame d'Harcourt and Eliane again Perdita grew even more
melancholy. She caught Colette by the hand and said, "Come
on, let's walk more quickly."

They went past Beau Lac and along a path winding away
from the château through a small copse. Philippe was leaning
morosely against a tree on the other side. Perdita didn't know
what to do. She was still angry with him, but felt she could not
ignore him. Colette would take in everything that was said, so
serious conversation was out of the question anyway. Colette
had no such inhibitions.

"Hello, Monsieur Fourget; how is Yvette? My cousin Henri
says he's going to marry her. Have you heard the news from
Beau Lac? Mademoiselle Eliane is dying."

Perdita felt as if she had had a blow to the heart. She cried,
"Colette, where did you hear that? It's not true! It can't be!"

"Yes, it is! Grandmère said so," asserted Colette firmly.

Philippe was staring at Colette as a rabbit stared at a stoat.
"No!" he said hoarsely. "No! It can't be true. It mustn't be."

Then without another word he ran wildly off into the trees.
They could hear him crashing through the undergrowth.

"He's funny. Why did he go like that, *mademoiselle*?"

"When did your Grandmother say that, Colette—about
Mademoiselle Eliane?" asked Perdita urgently, ignoring Colette's question.

"Oh, I don't remember... Yes, I do—it was before I fell
down the hole. She said Monsieur le Marquis had gone to Paris
because Mademoiselle Eliane was dying. There! So, you see, it
is true, *mademoiselle*."

Perdita was breathless with relief. "That was a long time ago, Colette! And Mademoiselle Eliane is no longer in danger."

"Isn't she? That's good. Have you seen those ducks over there, *mademoiselle*? I think they're going to land on the lake. Can we go and see them?"

They spent some time looking at ducks, and then returned to the château. Perdita felt that the walk had not exactly fulfilled its purpose of calming her nerves, for Colette's bombshell had taken its toll. And poor Philippe now believed that Eliane was dying. He would soon find out his mistake, but meanwhile his reaction was most interesting. It hadn't been that of a man who genuinely believed she was better dead. She went up to her room, pondering on Philippe and Eliane. If only there was a chance, even the slightest, that they would find some happiness together. That would be a far better outcome than any schemes hatched by the Earl. That thought recalled her own situation. What was she to do?

The meal that evening was a fairly silent one. Perdita was occupied with her own thoughts, and the Earl was reluctant to break in on them. He had asked her before the meal whether she had reconsidered her opposition to her part in his scheme, and she had replied briefly that she preferred to wait until the next day before discussing it. This seemed to be so much of an advance from her original position that he was content to let it lie.

Perdita sat at her window that night, thinking of Piers Carston. When she had first heard Eliane's story it had seemed strange that a gently bred girl, who had led such a protected life, should have acted so boldly in running off with the man who'd betrayed her. Now that she knew the man's name she understood perfectly. Piers Carston was a charming, smiling, plausible, ruthless villain—far more dangerous than his father because he seemed so trustworthy. With what sincere anxiety he had lied to her mother as she'd lain seriously ill! How protective he had seemed while he had been plotting to remove Perdita from the scene! Once again scenes from the past haunted her during the long night.

"My darling child, you must go away from here," her mother had whispered to her, clutching her arm and trying to raise herself.

"Mama, don't agitate yourself so. You must rest. How else will you get better?" Perdita had tried to put her back against the pillows but her mother had refused.

"I mean what I say; you must escape before it is too late! I am not going to get better, my dear. But you must go away from here before I die!"

"I can't do that, Mama. You need me here!"

"Your stepfather—oh, God, I can't say it. Your stepfather will do anything to inherit the estate—even murder!"

"That's not possible! He's not a good man, mama, but he's not capable of murder. No, I don't believe it!"

"His own son tells me so. If I die before you the estate will pass out of Mr. Carston's reach. But if you are dead, then he will inherit all through me. Now do you believe me?"

"Piers told you . . . How can he say this of his father?"

Her mother had lain back, exhausted, her face pale and her lips colourless. "He was very distressed. I felt such pity for him, but I believe him. You must go, my child. Piers will help you."

Perdita's eyes filled with tears as she remembered how her mother had pleaded with her. At first she'd refused to think of it, but then a coping stone from the roof had narrowly missed her as she'd walked on the terrace, the girth of her saddle had come mysteriously unfastened as she rode, and Piers had slowly convinced her, telling her that her mother would die in peace if she could know that her daughter was safe. Even now, three years later, Perdita could not bring herself to think of the parting with her mother, but she sat for a moment, clasping her hands in anguish, staring out on the moonlit garden.

Piers had suggested that he take her to his friends in Bristol, where she could stay for a while. Though neither of them had said it, they'd both known it would be until her mother's death. At least, that was what she had thought. He had been so considerate, had seemed so profoundly moved at her distress. The truth had never entered her head, not for one second, until they had got near Bristol and he'd drawn the chaise to the side of the road. It was nearly dark.

"I have a better plan," he'd said. "If we were to marry, you would be safe with me. I wouldn't allow my father to harm you."

She hadn't known what to say. It was the last thing she wanted, but she didn't want to hurt him by saying so. "You are kind, Piers, and I'm grateful for all you've done. But I can't marry you. I like and respect you as a brother..."

"But you could learn to love me differently," he said, smiling at her with boyish charm.

Her parting with her mother, the strain of the last weeks, had stretched her nerves to the limit. Though she tried for calm, her voice was impatient as she said, "No, Piers, I could not. I cannot marry you. I will not marry. I do not love you enough. Let us say no more on this subject. Please take me to your friends."

She should have taken warning there. Any normal man of honour would have heard the waver in her voice and taken pity on her. But he persisted.

"I don't believe you mean what you say, my sweet. It's only your inexperience that makes you talk like this. Can you imagine what it is like between a man and a woman? When they kiss and lie with one another and make love? Once I've taught you, my lovely one, you'll change your mind about me."

He tried to take hold of her and she struggled violently. She had never before been held so closely by a man, and his sudden attack put her into a panic. She hit out wildly, causing him to lose his balance, and he hit the side of the open chaise. He missed his footing, tried and failed to grab the rail, and fell to the road. While he lay there, dazed, she seized her opportunity, whipped the horses into action and drove them away in a frenzy of fear. She was desperate to get to a place of safety.

On the outskirts of Bristol she came to an inn. Trembling with cold and fear, she entered the parlour... It was like no place she had ever seen before. Living, as she did, in a remote corner of Somerset, surrounded by people she had known all her life, she had never seen the seamier side of life. Only desperation would have driven her into a strange inn now. This was a most unhappy choice. Even in the parlour the floor was covered with filthy sawdust. The settle in the corner may once have been red damask cushions, but now it sagged drunkenly against the wall, covered in greasy, greyish tatters.

A woman came into the parlour from the taproom. "Oh, la-di-da," she said in an affected voice. "Wot 'ave we 'ere? A *laidy*, no less!"

"Please... please, I need your help!" Perdita said.

"Wot's the matter, dearie? 'Ad a bit of a tumble, 'ave yer?" The woman gave a raucous laugh and summoned the men in the taproom to inspect the new mort come to pay a visit.

The girl now realised that she had made a very big mistake in hurrying in to the first inn she had come to. If only she had inspected it from outside! A more experienced traveller could have told her that inns on the outskirts of large towns, especially seaports, were seldom patronised by honest people. What better place to meet in secret than an inn near enough to the port for the smuggler or sea robber, near enough to the countryside for the highwayman or footpad, and far enough out of the town to avoid the unwelcome attentions of the watch?

She started to retreat to the door, but found her way blocked by a tall negro dressed in the loose trousers and striped shirt of a sailor. She moved away in terror as he grinned and mouthed words she did not understand at her. The rest howled with laughter, but suddenly fell silent as another sailor came in from the taproom. He limped slowly across to her, then turned to the others and said in a husky voice with a strong French accent, "Where's Carston?"

Several voices assured him that they hadn't laid eyes on him.

"He's late," the Frenchman said, examining the girl with eyes that were almost black. "Who's this?" Anxiously the ungodly crew hastened to tell him they didn't know. He seemed to exercise some kind of power over them.

Perdita remembered how afraid she had been, and yet how proudly she had faced him.

"I am Miss Taverton of Taverton Hall," she said. "I am on my way to Bristol to visit friends, and met with a...with a...an accident on the way. I see that there is no suitable accommodation here and I would like to be allowed to leave. Now."

The crowd roared with laughter, conjuring each other to listen to her fancy speech. One of the women sidled over and caught her skirt.

"That's a nice dress, dearie," she said. "I'd like that dress, I would. Perhaps yer'd like to give it me, ay?" She started pulling at the dress, but the man with the limp put his hand on her shoulder. She gave a squeal of pain and scuttled away, rubbing the shoulder and looking resentfully at him.

"Leave her alone, Peg—until Carston comes. Then we'll know what to do with her. You can have the dress afterwards, if she doesn't need it any more." Once again the Frenchman boldly examined her. "Though, if Carston hasn't a use for her, I know a thing or two I'd like to try..." He turned and winked at the crowd, who responded with sly leers and obscene gestures. Suddenly he cocked his head. "Someone's coming!"

In a flash half the occupants of the room had disappeared. The negro waited behind the door and the Frenchman stood facing it, his hand resting on a knife stuck in his belt.

Piers Carston appeared in the doorway, his clothing dishevelled and a bruise on his forehead. Three scratches ran down the side of his face. "Have you got her here?" he said menacingly as he came into the room. "Have you got her here, Legrand?"

But Legrand didn't answer straight away. He bared yellow teeth in a smile as he said, "What's happened Carston? Something has spoiled your pretty face for you. Was it..." he dropped his voice in an affected drawl "...was it Miss Taverton of Taverton Hall? Was the pretty boy unable to defend himself, then?"

He laughed, and sidestepped as Carston lunged for him. The girl, seeing the two men engaged, made a frantic dash to escape, but she was caught by the large negro at the door. Piers Carston whirled round and saw her. A look of fury made his face ugly for a moment, then a slow, cruel smile appeared.

"So you found my friends after all, my love. Let her go, Renard."

Though she was released, the three men surrounded her. She was sick with fear, but would not let them see it. Piers brought his face close to hers.

"Are you afraid, Miss Taverton of Taverton Hall? You should be, for I don't allow this—" he touched his face "—to go unpunished."

"We've got business to discuss. Leave the girl," said Legrand brusquely. "You can deal with her later."

"No!" Piers shouted. "She's going to pay now. I wasn't good enough for Miss High and Mighty, and she's going to pay for that too!" He gave the girl an almighty shove. She staggered, but was regaining her balance when he hit her. This time she went sprawling on to the filthy floor, hit her head on the leg of a settle and knew no more.

The gardens of Belleroi slowly grew visible in the early-morning light. Perdita could hear sounds in the kitchen—a new day was beginning.

CHAPTER TEN

PERDITA GOT UP and stretched herself wearily. In little more than an hour Jeanne would be coming in with hot water for her morning toilet, and she had not even been to bed. Reliving the terror of that fateful night had left her feeling drained, and in order not to upset her maid's susceptibilities she undressed and got into bed.

She smiled slightly as she thought of Jeanne. The little maid had become devoted to her mistress, forever coaxing her to try new ways of dressing her hair, and bemoaning the fact that Perdita was so indifferent to the way she looked. During Perdita's enforced rest she had been a constant companion, fetching small delicacies from the kitchen and bathing Perdita's temples with lavender water. Still thinking of Jeanne, she fell most unexpectedly asleep.

She woke later, feeling more refreshed than she would have imagined. Jeanne must have been in, for hot water was steaming in the jug on her wash-stand. She would return shortly to help her mistress to dress. Perdita leapt out of bed and busied herself. By the time Jeanne came she was standing by the window again, looking at the garden.

"As *mademoiselle* sees, it is a lovely day, but not, I think, yet warm enough for anything light. Would *mademoiselle* like to wear the blue merino today? Or the green wool?"

Perdita almost laughed at the expression on Jeanne's face, for her maid made no secret of the fact that she considered Perdita's wardrobe woefully inadequate.

"I don't know, Jeanne. You choose."

Jeanne chose, as Perdita knew she would, the blue merino. She admired Perdita's eyes and was always looking for ways to enhance their dark blue beauty. After Jeanne had twisted Perdita's hair into a knot on top of her head, not without her usual plea for a more elegant style, Perdita breakfasted and went downstairs. The Earl was out with his agent, so she had a peaceful morning with Père Amboise, who had just reread the *Iliad* and had a new theory on the location of Troy.

The Earl had still not returned at midday, so Perdita ate a light meal alone in the small parlour. Then, after looking in vain for Colette, she went out for a walk. This time she decided to avoid Beau Lac with its shuttered windows, and went instead to the front of the château.

The advancing season was softening the lines of the flowerbeds and lawns, and the twin lodges had a hazy background of young green branches. After her sleepless night the fresh spring air was like champagne. She walked for some time, going out of the drive and through to the other side of the village. Finally she took a rest on a bench in front of a small country inn. The landlord's apple-cheeked wife came to ask her if she wanted anything and stayed to chat for a few minutes. She knew who Perdita was—her sister's husband's niece, Jeanne, was *mademoiselle*'s maid, and Colette was her husband's great niece. Perdita knew this kind of network of relationships from her own home in Somerset, and she and *madame* chatted amicably for a quarter of an hour.

It might have been that Perdita was more tired than she realised, or it might have been that the talk with *madame* had once again reminded her of the past, but for whatever reason the château seemed depressingly far away on the return journey. Perdita was lost in unhappy thought as she walked up the long drive. She was remembering the last time she had seen Piers Carston. It had been in the inn . . .

When she came to she was on the floor of the inn, and her hands and feet were tied so tightly that she was unable to move them. Piers and the Frenchman were sitting at a crude table, and she could hear the clink of money.

"That's the last, I think," said Legrand's voice.

"I like the pearl. I think I have a customer for that—how much do you want for it?"

"Not so fast, my dear friend. What about the shipping information? What have you got for me?"

"The *Isabel* is due in Bristol on the twelfth of May—she'll have a cargo of silks and spices from the Levant. She may even have some gold. But better than that is the *Fair Maid of Richmond*. She's carrying gold bullion out of Istanbul to London, calling at Marseilles on the twenty-seventh of next month. Can you do it?''

"Don't you concern yourself with that. You look after the information, and I'll catch the cargoes. What else do you have for me?''

"That's all I can do for the moment. We've been too successful, Legrand. So many cargoes have been pirated in the Mediterranean recently that the people at Lloyds are getting suspicious, and I'll have to tread very carefully for a while. What's wrong?''

"Your little termagant is awake, I think. I wonder how much she heard?''

The girl on the floor shut her eyes quickly, but it was too late. She heard him get up and come across; then cruel fingers were pinching her chin. When she opened her eyes the Frenchman was bending over her and the smell of his sweat was in her nose. "Very nice," he said. "Very nice!" She tried to roll away, but he easily stopped her with his hand on her body.

Piers came over to join him. "What are we going to do?''

"That's your affair, my friend. Tomorrow I'll be away from here and safe on the high seas again. But if you want to get rid of her I'll take her off your hands.''

"She's worth something," said Piers.

"She's worth a hanging to you, Carston, if she heard your talk back there and passes it on," said Legrand, smiling wolfishly.

This thought hadn't occurred to Piers. He said slowly, "What'll you give me for her? What's more, can you guarantee she won't come back—ever?''

Legrand pushed the girl with his foot while he considered. "I can guarantee that, sure enough. But what I'll give . . . let me see . . .''

The girl could not help herself. She looked at her stepbrother with terror in her dark blue eyes. "Please," she whispered hoarsely. "I beg you, Piers, don't send me with him!''

Piers stood by Legrand, looking down at her. His face was as handsome as ever, blue eyes in an open face, red-gold hair tumbling over his forehead. Only the three scratches and the dark bruise marred his looks. He smiled charmingly.

"Oh, Miss Taverton," he said softly. "You should have married me when you could. I was willing to win the Taverton fortune by fair means. Now I have a double—no, triple reason to change my mind. If Legrand here will lose you for me there's a good chance the estates will eventually come to me, anyway—if your damned mother stays alive long enough. If you're allowed to tell others what you heard tonight I could hang. And..." he fingered the bruise "...I really cannot let this go unpunished, can I? No, Miss Taverton, if Legrand pays me enough you will go with him. How much, Legrand? What about the pearl?"

"You're surely not serious? That pearl is worth at least fifty guineas."

"On the open market, perhaps. Not otherwise."

The girl struggled violently in her bonds. She screamed, "Piers, don't do it! Please don't! Oh, God, I beg you not to!"

"You should have counted my virtues before you said you wouldn't marry me, my dear. It's too late now. Gag her, Legrand; I can't think when she's caterwauling."

Legrand went to tie a dirty handkerchief round the girl's mouth. She renewed her struggles, kicking her tied feet, twisting her head and biting. When he had finished he wiped his fingers, looking down at her thoughtfully, and said, "I could enjoy taming this one... If you give me the girl and thirty guineas I'll let you have the pearl. But what are you going to tell her people?"

"Oh, I don't know. Some story of being knocked out by footpads—this bruise will help to make it convincing. Then when I came to she was gone. Give me her scarf—I'll put some blood on it. This was all I found of her—you wouldn't believe how distraught I'll sound. Her mother will feel almost as sorry for me as for herself. Where's the pearl? Goodbye, Legrand. Goodbye, Miss Taverton, and good riddance! Enjoy your voyage!"

With a mocking bow he was gone. That was the last she had seen of him. She was taken in a closed cart, still gagged and bound, held tight by the negro. They went on board a small fishing vessel, where she was released from her bonds and locked in the cabin. After three days she was transferred to a larger vessel, which was called *Le Faucon*.

The nightmare that had begun in a sleazy inn near Bristol went on for more than two long years. The second time she was brought back to him after trying to escape Legrand gave her two pieces of news. Her mother had died a month after her daughter had disappeared, and the Carstons were living at Taverton.

Perdita sat down suddenly on one of the ornamental seats on the side of the drive. She had no doubt at all that she was going to agree to the scheme the Earl had so carefully prepared. She could, and would, bring ruin to Piers Carston in her own time. It would not be quite as the Earl had planned, but he wouldn't know that until the last possible minute. If, after the closeness they had experienced on their walks together, he was willing to use her in such an ugly fashion, then she could use him to get her to London and give her a background until she struck. As she sat there weaving her plans, the Sheikh's words came to her:

"Hatred is destructive. You might or might not succeed in destroying the object of your hatred. You will certainly succeed in destroying your own happiness."

She jumped up and walked impatiently along the drive to the château. Her hatred for Piers Carston had kept her alive these past years. She would not relinquish it now. As for Lord Ambourne—he was uninterested in her courage and spirit. He merely demanded her obedience. Well, he would have it—up to a point.

She dressed carefully for dinner that night, allowing Jeanne to arrange her hair in a more becoming style. The blue jaconet muslin was a foil to her dark hair, and her precious cashmere shawl gave her warmth and colour. She found that the Earl had also dressed formally in dark blue tailcoat, black breeches and a diamond pin in his immaculately tied cravat. They could have been any couple in fashionable Society. The Earl talked of the work going forward on the estate, and Perdita mentioned her meeting with the landlady on the other side of the village.

"Ah, yes," said the Earl, "Masson's wife. Between them they're related to three-quarters of the village. I don't suppose you escaped under half an hour, did you?"

Perdita was relieved that he made no comment on her going out alone, and indeed, since the adventure with Colette, he had not insisted on her being accompanied when he was not with her. She amused him with her lively report of Madame Masson's conversation.

After dinner she and the Earl went into the library. He waited while she sat down, then he stood by the fire and asked, "Well, Perdita? Which is it to be? Do I have your co-operation? Or will I be forced to remind you of the alternatives? I am persuaded the Pasha would take you back with pleasure—especially if you are looking as charming as you do tonight. He might even keep you for himself."

She said calmly, "I do not believe you would send me back to the Pasha. However, I will admit I am loath to put you to the test!" One slender hand was clenched as she asked, "You have known me for some time now, Lord Ambourne. We have discovered in each other a similarity of taste and temperament, and I at least have found pleasure in our recent walks and discussions. Are you still resolved to marry me to a man you know to be a heartless villain, to force me to live with him as his wife, to ask me to withstand his fury when he first discovers we have tricked him?"

The Earl was pale and his face was set. "I have told you my reasons. I do not propose to abandon my plans because of…because of a certain sympathy that has grown between us."

He looked down at her bowed head and clenched fist, and said in a softened tone, "Perdita, believe me, I would not do this if there were any other way."

For a moment she hesitated, half wanting to reveal the truth, but then he turned to the fire and continued harshly, "But, since there is not, I must use you as I planned to use you from the beginning when I rescued you in Algiers."

"You *bought* me," she said bitterly. "But at least you thought I was worth a pearl."

"Don't speak like this, Perdita! I will protect you as much as I can from Carston's fury. Afterwards I will see that you have a home and a source of income. What more can I do?"

"Nothing," she said. "I will do as you wish, Lord Ambourne."

He was conscious of feeling a curious mixture of relief and disappointment. Now that he had achieved his goal he realised that half of him had hoped she would continue to refuse. This confusion of mind was totally alien to his keen and decisive intellect, and he was relieved when Perdita asked if she might retire early. He needed time to restore order to his thoughts. It was past midnight when he finally went to bed, but he had mastered his weakness and was once again calmly resolved. Perdita had agreed, and they would work together to achieve his goal.

THE NEXT TIME Perdita saw the Earl he was sitting behind his desk, writing a note. In front of him lay a letter, much crossed and recrossed, which had been brought that morning. He replied absently to Perdita's greeting, finished his note and addressed it, then stood up and said, "Forgive me; I was somewhat preoccupied with my letter. Have you slept well? No second thoughts in the night?" Perdita assured him of her determination to help him in his aim. He nodded, then said, "This is a devilish thing! My mother is in Paris with Eliane and my aunt."

Perdita looked surprised. "Is that not desirable? I should have thought your aunt would welcome any support the family can give her."

"It's not that," he said impatiently. "I'm glad, of course I'm glad that Tante Marguerite has my mother to look to. No, it's just that Paris is too near Belleroi, that's all. My mother is perfectly capable of taking it into her head to visit me here and, much as I love her, the last thing I want at the moment is the distraction of a visit. Hence the note."

Perdita thought she understood. It would be embarrassing if his mother found her at Belleroi. Perhaps she could stay with Madame d'Espery during the Countess's visit? She was about to suggest this when the Earl excused himself and left the room. She was left to her own devices.

He returned a short while later smiling with satisfaction. "She'll get that before she has time to think of coming here. Now it's time to tell you of the lady I have engaged to chaperon you in London. She's unusual, but socially very acceptable."

For the rest of the time they were together he carried on telling Perdita about the people she would meet, and the image he wished her to create. "Young, innocent, a little simple, even— but I'm sure your powers of dissimulation will be up to it, Perdita."

She realised he was being deliberately provoking, but did not rise to it. If Lord Ambourne wished her to be a tool, then a tool she would be. Her energies were now channelled into arriving in London with her own plans complete.

She spent the next morning with Madame d'Espery, and was pleased to accept an invitation to nuncheon.

"Just a small repast, *mademoiselle*. I dine early and do not take much at midday."

The "small repast" proved to be so filling that she felt in need of fresh air and exercise. She walked over the fields and through the wood before coming back to the château. After tidying herself she went to the music-room, where she played for half an hour or more, finishing with one of her favourite, rather mournful airs. Eliane had been much in her mind. How would she react if she knew what her friend and her cousin were planning? Perdita did not deceive herself. What she and the Earl were doing was meant to satisfy their own feelings towards Piers Carston. As the Earl had said, nothing they were doing could put Eliane's life back together again. She put her hands on the keys and sighed.

"Oh, dear," said a voice behind her. "Don't do that. You'll blow the piano away."

For an instant she thought it was Madame d'Harcourt, and whirled round to greet her in delighted surprise. But, though Perdita could see a resemblance, the lady sitting in the large armchair had an air of gaiety about her that Madame d'Harcourt had never possessed. And her dress of striped *Gros de Naples* silk, with its slightly lower waist and flounced skirt, her beautifully dressed pale gold hair, showed a consciousness of fashion very far removed from Madame d'Harcourt's sober attire.

"I'm Ambourne's mother," said the lady, smiling at Perdita's astonishment.

"Forgive me, ma'am. I . . . I . . ." In great confusion, Perdita got up and curtsyed.

As she rose, the Countess said, "I know, I know. I've put you all in a bustle by arriving so unexpectedly. It's good for you, don't you think? Life can be very dull if we always know in advance what is going to happen. I can't wait to see Edward's face! Do you know where he is?"

Perdita pulled herself together and thought. The Earl was visiting one of the outlying farms, but would be back shortly. She told his mother as much and added, "Forgive me, ma'am, but did you not receive Lord Ambourne's note? Oh, how stupid of me, of course you couldn't have. He only despatched it yesterday."

"I expect he told me not to come," said the Earl's mother complacently. "That's why I set out before I could possibly get a reply to my letter. Besides, I have things to do at Belleroi and Beau Lac now, and Edward shan't interfere. You must be

Mademoiselle Taver?'' Once again in confusion, Perdita acknowledged this to be true. "My sister has told me a great deal about you. You were good for Eliane, *mademoiselle*—"

"Oh, ma'am, how was Eliane when you left her?"

The Countess smiled at Perdita's impulsive question, then grew grave. "She is making a slow recovery. I have persuaded my sister to bring her back to Beau Lac soon. But don't stand there, child. Come and sit down beside me."

"Lady Ambourne, I really ought not to be here," began Perdita bravely. "Lord Ambourne will be distressed if he finds us together like this."

"Rubbish, child! You're not his mistress, are you?"

Perdita gasped and shook her head vehemently.

"That's good, because, if you were, then, I agree, it wouldn't be quite the thing, would it? Imagine Edward's face!" She went off into a peal of laughter. "As for Edward being distressed . . . I'm sorry to tell you, my dear, but that I cannot imagine. Irritated, perhaps. Annoyed that his wishes have been ignored. But distressed, no! Besides, Edward has already told me about you."

"Told you? He's told you? About me?" Perdita exclaimed in horror.

"Well, I suspect he hasn't told me quite everything. And anyway, he doesn't know all of it, does he? I don't somehow think my son knows of the existence of Miss Taver, for example."

The Countess watched in evident enjoyment as Perdita's face grew scarlet with embarrassment. Then she said, "You know, *mademoiselle*, I get very bored at home in Ambourne with nobody but the servants and a shockingly dowdy cousin of Ambourne's to keep me company. And I went to Paris out of a sense of duty to my sister. I really didn't expect such a delightfully intriguing set of circumstances as I have found here. I will not be satisfied until I have fathomed it all. How interesting it is going to be!"

Perdita said hollowly that she hoped the Countess would not be disappointed, but was saved from any further comment by the sound of the Earl's arrival. While the two ladies listened, one appreciatively, the other apprehensively, the Earl exclaimed, questioned the servant further and then came striding into the music-room.

"Mama, what a delightful surprise!" he said as he bent to kiss her cheek.

"Edward, you have the best manners of all the men in my acquaintance. I cannot imagine where you acquired them!"

"Come now, Mama, you do not do yourself justice. And, if your flattery is meant to distract me from asking you why you did not let me know sooner that you were coming, then I assure you it is not necessary. I am well aware of your reasons! How is my cousin?"

"She is well enough to be moved, and I have persuaded Marguerite to bring her back to Beau Lac. That's why I am here. But, Edward, you are very remiss. Have you not observed your ward? She looks delightful, does she not? Are you not going to introduce me?"

Perdita had moved to the window when the Earl had come in. He now turned and saw her there.

"If I know my mother, Perdita, she has already made a bosom friend of you. She does not normally wait for formal introductions. However, since it is her whim . . . Mama may I introduce Mademoiselle . . ." the Earl paused and his mother's eyes danced wickedly as he looked at a loss; but he regained his urbanity ". . . Mademoiselle Perdita, my ward. My mother, the Countess of Ambourne and Marquise de Belleroi, *mademoiselle.*"

As Perdita curtsyed for the second time she looked up at the Countess. Was she about to have her friendship with the d'Harcourts revealed? But no. The Countess said with a solemn face, belied only by the laughter in her eyes, "I am enchanted to make your acquaintance, *mademoiselle.* I have heard so much about you."

The Earl looked startled. He had surely not told his mother as much as that? Perdita's lips twitched. This was pure farce! Each of them knew something one or both of the others did not know. How long would the conjuring trick last?

CHAPTER ELEVEN

THE COUNTESS'S relationship with her son was a revelation to Perdita. She teased him, exasperated him, tested his patience to its limits with her impulsive promises to the tenants. But he always ended by indulging her, and was clearly devoted to her. Perdita herself was rapidly falling victim to her charm, and a warm friendship developed between the Countess and 'Miss Taver', as she was teasingly called whenever she and the Countess were alone. However, her tormentor soon tired of that, and in a surprisingly short time was calling her son's ward 'Perdita'.

The Countess was as musical as her sister, and she and Perdita frequently spent time together in the music-room. This was where the Earl found them one morning. The two ladies were seated side by side at the piano and were a sight to please the eye of the most impartial observer. Inside the high-standing collar of Perdita's blue merino was a saucy little ruff the Countess had insisted on giving her. The Countess herself was wearing lilac. Her son was unmoved by this picture, however.

"Mama," he said dangerously as he entered the room, "Mama, am I to infer from Masson's comments to me this morning that you have promised to have the roof of the inn repaired before next Tuesday?"

"Of course I have, dear. The rain is coming in."

"Perhaps you are unaware that Etienne has drawn up a careful schedule for re-roofing the houses in the village. Large numbers of them suffered in the February gale, and Masson should wait his turn."

"Oh, do you think I shouldn't have interfered? But Masson has always been so kind to us, Edward, and his daughter is coming back home to have her baby in a month. Masson's wife was most distressed. I really couldn't not promise, wouldn't you say?" she said cajolingly.

"No, I would not, Mama. Etienne is going to have the devil's own job explaining it to the others."

"I don't think you should use language like that in front of Perdita, dear. I, of course, am used to it. But I'm glad you've agreed about Masson's roof."

He left the room with an exasperated groan and Masson had his roof by Tuesday.

This was not the only episode of its kind. Perdita marvelled that a man who normally had little patience for the foibles of others, and who was so disciplined in his own emotions, should be so indulgent with his wayward mother. When she expressed her surprise the Countess said, "That's because he loves me, my love. He's just like his dear father. When I first met Charles he seemed the completely traditional Englishman—so cold, so . . . logical! But somehow, after really quite a short time, I found he was just the man for me. I defied my family to marry him, and I never regretted it. All his life people who did not know him as I did thought him cold. But with me he was the most loving, most indulgent husband a woman could ask for."

The Countess wiped her eyes with a tiny lace handkerchief. "I miss him a great deal. That's why I find Ambourne so depressing. And I think Edward will be exactly like his father; it's just that he hasn't yet found the right woman to be his wife. And since the trouble with Eliane he has been obsessed with punishing Piers Carston. He thinks he failed her when she was his responsibility. That's why he's so set on this wretched plan he talks of. I haven't asked for the details; I'm afraid to. He means to ruin Carston, so much I know. But Eliane has had enough to bear. She cannot stand any more notoriety. She needs peace!"

Perdita squeezed the small hand in hers. If the Earl hadn't told his mother what he proposed to do then she could not betray his confidence. She said what she could.

"If you are afraid of scandal, or even danger, ma'am, then let me reassure you. Piers Carston will not harm Eliane or any of your family again, I promise."

"So you *do* know something of it. I suspected as much. And Edward means to include you in his scheme?"

Perdita withdrew her hands. "You must ask your son that, Lady Ambourne. I cannot tell you. But, whatever he says, remember my promise. There will be no danger to you or your family. And now, may I remind you that you promised to show me the dresses you bought in Paris?"

They spent the rest of the morning looking at the Countess's wardrobe, which was extensive, and by tacit agreement their conversation in the music-room was not referred to again. But, while she admired the delicate muslins, the *Gros de Naples* and barège silk dresses and the velvet pelisses, Perdita was aware that the Countess occasionally looked at her with sympathetic speculation.

Since the advent of the Countess life had become at once more formal and more lively. She hated to be without company, and a dinner party that did not have at least half a dozen covers she regarded as a bore. She said as much one night at dinner. In tones of deepest gloom the Earl said, "Alas, Perdita, we have failed in our attempts to entertain my mother. We must face the fact that we are dull fellows and not allow ourselves to be too cast down by it. But it is hard, especially for an only son!"

The Countess laughed and replied, "What rubbish you talk! How can I not enjoy my son's company? And Perdita is a darling. I must tell you, Edward, if she were my companion, instead of that boringly frowsty female relative of yours, I would not have to leave Ambourne so often."

The Earl raised his brows and protested, "Cousin Enid is a woman of sense and respectability, and well known for her charitable works. You ought not to be so unflattering in your description of her, Mama."

"There you are! As I said, the woman is a bore! Perdita, you surely agree with me?"

"Since I do not know the lady in question, ma'am, I cannot comment," smiled Perdita, holding up her hand.

"Yes, but would you describe me as a woman of sense and respectability? Ugh!" said the Countess, pronouncing the words as if they were insults.

Perdita laughed and said, "I think your son would be angry with me if I were to say you were not respectable, ma'am. And I am sure you have more sense than most people of my acquaintance!"

The Earl sat back, enjoying the exchange between the two women. They made a pleasant picture. His mother's face was alight with enjoyment, and the candlelight reflected the sparkle of diamonds at her throat and the sheen of her ruched wine-red silk dress. Perdita had laughter in her eyes too. She was wearing her pink silk, and, though she looked as lovely as ever, the Earl frowned slightly as he considered the simple way in which her hair was gathered on top of her head, and her lack of adornment. Was her maid incompetent? He must consult his mother.

His mother was observing her son with just as much interest. It seemed to her that Edward's eyes strayed constantly to his lovely...ward? Edward had told her a little of his plan for Perdita. He had sworn that he would see that she came to no harm, but how could he be sure? However, the Countess felt that Carston would find Perdita a more difficult prey than Eliane. Edward had not said a great deal about Perdita, but the Countess could see that she was no vulnerable child. Though there was an innocence about her, it did not stem from ignorance, and the girl had courage and intelligence. But why had Perdita not told Edward about her visits to Beau Lac? Her sister had talked at length of Perdita's kindness and charm, but Edward was not even aware that they knew one another. That was curious. How fortunate it was that she had come to Belleroi! Meanwhile she would insist that they did some entertaining. Apart from anything else she wanted to see Perdita's company manners. And she must talk to her son about clothes for the girl...

As a result of this Perdita found herself in possession of two or three very pretty dresses for the evening and a maid who was jubilant at being requested by no less a personage than Madame la Marquise herself to find new styles for Perdita's hair. Each evening from then on was enlivened by visits from the members of local society.

"And very tedious people most of them are, too," said the Countess one night after what had seemed a particularly long dinner. "I thought I should die of boredom during Monsieur de Sardet's eulogy of his estate—and especially his tale of the heifer. What on earth is a heifer, Edward?"

"It's a kind of cow, Mama. And you should not complain so of your guests—you insisted on inviting them. Most of them are only too glad to be back. After all, it's only three years since the monarchy was restored."

"There's another thing," said his mother. "Why do we have to have such a clod for a king? You may say what you choose about Louis XVI—he at least had style!"

"Style enough to get his head cut off, Mama. It's a new world we live in now, and Louis XVIII is doing his best. If the old aristocrats aren't able to change, then there'll be a second revolution. Let's hope it's less bloody than the first."

"Edward, why are we talking of such things? Perdita, I thought you looked particularly charming tonight; do you not think so, Edward? That jonquil muslin is very becoming. And Jeanne is growing skilful with your hair; I must tell her so when I see her. The flowers are an excellent idea."

Jeanne had parted Perdita's hair in the centre and, leaving a few curls to fall on her temples, had swept the rest back, twisted it and arranged it *à l'antique*. One or two tiny yellow roses were tucked into the back at the top. The Earl lazily admired this vision until Perdita moved restlessly and asked if they would give her leave to retire. The Countess looked disappointed, but Perdita left them in the salon and went upstairs.

Then came the news that Madame d'Harcourt and Eliane were returning within the week. The Countess immediately went down to Beau Lac to see that the house was suitably prepared.

"It's an old house, Perdita, and needs a great deal of heating up. I know—my family lived there in the old days."

"But, ma'am, I thought you lived at Belleroi!"

"Oh, no! My father was a younger son. All we had was Beau Lac. It wasn't until my uncle died that we inherited Belleroi, and there was no money, you know. I brought Ambourne a very poor dowry, but then he said all he wanted was me! My sister was not so fortunate, for her husband left very little. That's why—" her face clouded over "—that's why Carston abandoned Eliane. He thought she was rich, and she was not. But let us put these sad thoughts behind us, Perdita. Let us make Beau Lac so beautiful that Eliane will be happy to return! What is wrong? Why the sad face?"

"Eliane may be unable to enjoy Beau Lac, ma'am. I think she will be reminded of Philippe."

"Philippe? Ah . . . I see. The young man from Paris?"

"Not Paris, ma'am. He lives quite close, at Vauvron. His name is Fourget."

"Fourget? Fourget . . . not old Sansculotte Fourget's son? The Republican? I'd heard he was back in Normandy. Living in retirement, no doubt, the traitor!"

It was obvious that the Countess shared the prejudice of the local aristocrats towards the Fourget family, but Perdita decided to confide in her all the same.

"It is my opinion that Philippe still loves Eliane, ma'am. He found it impossible to face her when he learned she was not as innocent as he thought her. But when he thought she was dying he took it very badly."

"Are you suggesting that Eliane might conceivably marry Fourget's son?"

Perdita replied bravely, "If they can be brought together again I think it would be an ideal match. Philippe is really neither weak nor a fool. And, if he has discovered he loves Eliane in spite of what he knows, then I think he would look after her and love her in the way she needs."

The Countess thought for a moment and then said briskly, "Well, Perdita, what must we do to find out if Philippe has thought better? That seems to me to be the first step—and not the most difficult one. When I think of Eliane's state and my sister's reaction, my opinion of Fourget, not to mention my son's... What are you leading me into?"

"Perhaps Eliane's happiness, ma'am. At least we could try!"

However, Philippe proved to be away, so matters had to be left in abeyance till his return.

Meanwhile the Countess continued her social round in spite of her strictures on local society. Invitations to dinner were returned, and so it came about that Perdita and the Earl found themselves alone one evening. The Countess had been called for by what the Earl insisted was an old flame, which both annoyed and flattered his mother.

"You're a wicked boy to tease me so, but I confess he was quite particular in his attentions at one time—before I met your father, of course. But I forbid you to give so much as the batting of an eye when the poor man is here. He has put on a little weight since I last saw him, I must admit."

"Put on a little weight! That's rich. He can hardly get into the carriage, Mama!"

"You're very unkind, Edward, not but what you might be right..." At her apprehensive look the two who were being left behind burst into laughter, and the Earl assured her he would fetch her himself after dinner if her swain had eaten too much. He even offered to accompany her. "Oh, no," she said quickly. "Er—it would seriously discommode the Bonvilles. You forget, such an august person as yourself needs special attention. They aren't prepared for you. It might be too much.''

He declared it a great piece of nonsense, but seemed content to stay. The Countess, in a swirl of pomana-green crêpe lisse, was eventually driven away by her gallant, and Perdita and the Earl were left.

It was some time since they had dined alone, and the Earl sensed that, though she was disguising the fact, Perdita was ill at ease. But she talked with cool self-possession on uncontroversial subjects throughout most of the meal. He was once more impressed with her manners. Wherever she had learned them, they were impeccable. As the meal progressed, however, she started behaving more naturally, and by the end she was talking animatedly of Père Amboise and his theory on the position of Troy. Her face was slightly flushed, her eyes sparkled in the candlelight, and the curls at the side of her temples bobbed as she spoke. She looked enchanting in her lavender silk dress, and the Earl found himself loath to let her go. Since Perdita had agreed to his plan she had been cool in her manner to him except in the presence of his mother. She was different this evening. So he took the opportunity of asking her to play for him.

They went to the music-room, where she played for half an hour before her hands fell from the keys.

"Don't stop," he said idly. "Play the tune you were playing the other day—the Lully thing."

The sad little melody filled the room, and once again Perdita thought of Eliane. The prospect of happiness seemed remote for her—as indeed it was for herself. Would she ever be happy, really happy again? She doubted it. She felt tears come to her eyes again, and bowed her head.

"Perdita! You're crying! What has upset you?" With a muttered apology she would have left the room, but he caught her. "No, don't go! Come her to the fire and tell me what it is. Has my mother upset you?"

She assured him between sniffs and gulps that this was not so. He passed her an immaculate handkerchief and recommended that she should wipe her eyes. After a minute or two she was herself again, except for a red-tipped nose. He found it utterly appealing and suddenly kissed it. She looked up, startled, and he found himself kissing her mouth, then gently pulled her to him and folding her in his arms, resting his cheek on her hair.

They stayed like this for some minutes, and then she removed herself and said firmly, "I am sorry, I was foolish. The music affected me. Please excuse me; it will not happen again." She was twisting his handkerchief round and round in her hands. He removed it, and led her unresisting to the chair by the fire.

"I will not let you go to your room while you are so unhappy, Perdita. Can you not tell me what is wrong."

She looked at the piano and said sadly, "I was thinking of Eliane..."

"Eliane?" he asked in astonishment. "You were so unhappy about Eliane?"

She looked at him helplessly. What could she say? He couldn't understand because he didn't know of her friendship with his cousin.

"I...I did not tell you before...Oh, it's complicated, but I found it impossible to tell you. I know Eliane already. And her mother."

"When did you meet them?" he asked with a frown.

"When I was out walking one day I met Eliane in the woods. She had hurt her ankle...and I helped her."

"So you know my cousin? Yes, well you probably saw how helpless she is. And how unhappy. But why didn't you tell me, Perdita? Am I such an ogre?"

Perdita saw that she was going to have to explain at least some of her deceit. "When I met her I was sorry for her. She was frightened, so I...so I forgot not to talk. It was before I started talking here at the château, so it was awkward..."

He sat back, an amused smile on his face, "You little devil," he said. "So it wasn't the shock of the falling branch..."

"I didn't think you really believed that anyway."

The Earl laughed as he remembered the scene in the library the day he had returned from England. "You're right. I didn't. Tell me, when did you meet Eliane?"

She said in a small voice, "Before Christmas."

"Before Christmas...! So you were pretending not to talk for—how long, Perdita? Did you at any time find it impossible to talk?"

In an even smaller voice she said, "No...but in Tangier and for some time after I simply didn't want to. It wasn't until I met Eliane and Colette that..."

"Colette too? You talked to Colette? Was that why you kept your friendship secret?" She nodded without looking at him. Then he asked, "And the tricks with the tutors? When did they begin?"

"From the beginning. It started with Monsieur Champollion—he was so sure I was stupid. And of course there was you..."

"Yes, now we're getting to the interesting bit. What about me, Perdita?" he asked softly and silkily. She had heard that silken tone before. It was a danger signal, but she faced him bravely.

"I felt that I annoyed you by not speaking and by being so stupid, and that pleased me. You were in such a hurry to have me educated—no, not educated; you said trained, like a monkey—and by refusing to appear to learn I was defeating your purpose." She looked at him defiantly and he was disarmed once again by the frankness of those blue eyes.

"It was the episode of the bonnet on the boat all over again, was it not? Why were you so anxious to have the better of me, Perdita?" Her hands were twisting in her lap and the Earl reached out and took hold of one of them.

"I had to, to keep some spirit alive in me. You were so... You made me feel degraded. You wanted someone who knew nothing, had no self-respect, was worth nothing..."

"You're wrong," he said, examining the slender hand in his. "You were worth a pearl to me..."

She cried out in pain and pulled her hand away. "Oh, yes, you paid a whole pearl for me! Well, you were cheated. The last one who bought me only paid half as much." She caught her breath. What had she said? He stiffened.

"Ah, yes, I was forgetting... How could I have? The Pasha wasn't the first to sell you. There was the gentleman who taught you to read. Or was it someone else? I won't ask you who it was, Perdita. I don't honestly wish to know." He stood up and walked over to the piano, absent-mindedly strumming the little tune. "I wish things were not as they are," he said sombrely. "And I am sorry if I have said or done anything to make you unhappier than you would otherwise have been. If the future career I have suggested is distasteful to you I am willing to arrange something else. Would you prefer to live in England, in the country? Or abroad, here in France, perhaps? No, not near

here. Somewhere else. We will find something, Perdita. Try not
to distress yourself.''

She looked at him with eyes that were filled with pain, then
she got up, curtsyed and left the room. After she had gone he
struck the piano so that a great discordant note resounded
through the room.

CHAPTER TWELVE

IT WAS TO BE EXPECTED that the Countess would notice an air of constraint between her son and Perdita the next morning, but she made no comment. Instead she startled them both with her latest idea.

"Belleroi is going to have a ball before we leave for England!"

"Are you mad, Mama?" said the Earl. "Whom would you invite? There are hardly enough couples in the whole of Normandy for a ball. May I remind you that the old days are gone? Half the estates have disappeared, or are owned by an absentee landlord making his fortune in trade in Paris! A ball indeed!"

"Well, a small evening party with dancing, Edward. No, I will not listen to any objections. My reasons are perfectly good."

"Dare one ask what they are?" said the Earl, somewhat disagreeably.

"I really think you should see Dr. Grondet about your dyspeptic condition, Edward."

"I do not believe I suffer from a dyspeptic condition, Mama."

"You must be suffering from some stomach disorder, Edward, otherwise you would not be so disagreeable. But if you are not, then you must cheer up and help me with my ba...my evening party. I think Perdita should have an opportunity, before she goes to London, to dance in public. If she were at home in England she would have been to several small dancing parties by now, wouldn't you, my dear?"

Perdita opened her mouth to say she had in fact done so, before she suddenly recalled herself and stammered some disclaimer.

The Countess smiled and continued, "Secondly, I think it is time the servants had something to look forward to..."

"Mama, you cannot pretend that it is not a great deal of work for the servants. How can they look forward to it?"

The Countess contemplated her son for a moment. "Edward, dear, if you have not learned by now that servants enjoy the excitement of a ba...a small evening party as much as, if not more than, the hosts, then I despair of you. How are you going to manage your own household when you know so little about managing the servants? Think of the cachet they will have when Belleroi is *en fête*, and the vails and delicacies that will come their way."

"Delicacies? I see no need for delicacies for the servants. And why will they have gratuities for a mere evening party?" said the Earl impatiently. The Countess was exasperated.

"Well, of course, we must have a sit-down dinner party before the evening starts, and the servants always have a share of what remains, and naturally some of our guests will be unable to return home that night and will therefore stay here in the château. The servants will have vails from them when they leave. You are really being very tiresome, Edward. I don't think I shall tell you my third reason—you will only pour cold water on it!"

The Earl saw that his mother was seriously put out, and did his best to restrain himself. "I'm sorry, Mama. Tell me your third reason and I promise to listen with an open mind."

The Countess looked at him doubtfully, then decided he was being sincere. "If we have a formal evening here at Belleroi..."

"Yes...?"

"...Eliane will have to come," she said in a rush. "No, don't laugh at me, it's a very good idea. I'm sure Perdita will see that Eliane is properly cared for, they're such good friends— Oh!"

"It's all right, I know about Eliane and Perdita, though I wouldn't have said one meeting was enough to make them good friends." Here Perdita thought it prudent to explain to the Earl that she had met Elaine on several other occasions, whereupon he became quite annoyed. "I don't know any longer who has done what, or when, or who knows about it! I learn last night that Perdita met Eliane once, I learn this morning that not only does she know her rather better than that, but that my mother, heaven knows how, also knows she does! My opinion

about inviting Eliane to an evening party, Mama, is that it is an
excellent idea—if you can persuade Eliane to come. Now I am
going to find Etienne. Unless you have been visiting Masson
again, I ought to know at least what is happening on the estate!" He strode out, leaving the door wide open behind him.

"Lud, " said the Countess, "I've seldom seen him in such a
rage about so trivial a matter. I wonder what has happened to
upset him. Do you know what it can be, my dear?"

Under the discerning eye of the Countess, Perdita had difficulty in making her plea of ignorance convincing. The Countess seemed to accept what she said and continued to discuss her
plans for the party. Despite the Earl's doubts, it was decided
that twenty-five couples could be found from the neighbouring estates, and that about half of them would dine at the
château beforehand.

From then until the day of the evening party the house was
in a bustle. Servants scurried about the rooms, cleaning, dust-
ing, polishing already immaculate surfaces. Madame Lebrun
seemed to be everywhere at once, one minute chivvying the
maids in the bedrooms, the next arguing with the steward in the
wine-cellar. Even Colette was roped in to help her grandmother in the kitchen. A dressmaker came from Bayeux to re-
furbish one of the Countess's gowns for Perdita, since there was
little time to find suitable materials so far from Paris. Since it
was quite the loveliest dress Perdita had ever seen, she was
content with this arrangement.

But through all these preparations, and however busy she
was, Perdita found herself unable to forget her heartache. She
upbraided herself for it, she tried to find occupation for her
mind as well as her hands, she forced herself to maintain a
cheerful appearance. All was in vain. When she woke in the
morning the black cloud settled on her spirit, when she relaxed her guard for one second the blue devils appeared. Her
love for the Earl seemed to have been growing without her noticing it for so long that she had no notion when it had begun.
Yes, she had felt passion when he had kissed her before, but she
could have overcome that with time. It was when he had held
her so gently, so comfortingly in the music-room that she had
realised that this feeling for him would not go away—perhaps
not ever. She did not deceive herself. The Earl had felt something in return that night, she was sure. But he would never so
far forget the duty he owed to his family as to marry her. And

his mistress she was resolved not to be. So she busied herself
more and more frantically until the Countess was forced to call
a halt.

"Perdita! You must rest this afternoon. You look worn to a
shadow, child. What will my sister and Eliane say when they
arrive if you are in a worse state than Eliane? Come, up to your
room." And she forced Perdita to lie on her bed with the shut-
ters closed. She did not go away immediately, but sat on the
edge of the bed. "Can you tell me what is making you so unhappy, Perdita? Or can I guess?"

Perdita tried desperately to find the detachment she had
summoned to her aid in the past, but found it impossible. A sob
escaped her and she found herself folded in a scented embrace
and gently rocked.

"Perdita, Perdita, what are we to do? I feel in my bones that
you and Edward might be made for each other, but he is too
blinded by this stupid scheme of his to see where his happiness
lies. What can we do? Must we wait till it is all over?"

Perdita released herself from the Countess's embrace and sat
up. "No, ma'am, you mistake the situation. The Earl would
never marry me—not even when the matter of Piers Carston is
finished. I . . . I am not respectable enough for marriage to enter his head."

"Why not respectable enough, my dear?" asked the Countess, smiling slightly. "Are you a thief or a murderer?"

"No, ma'am, but I have associated with such. The Earl believes me to be a . . . a . . ."

"Really?" said the Countess, opening her eyes wide. "And
yet he is in a fair way to falling in love with you? He must be
more deeply affected than I thought." When Perdita would
have protested she went on, "Though he tries to conceal it, he
watches you constantly and is responsive to everything you say
or do. This was my self-contained son! Your precise origins and
the exact reason for your being here are unknown to me,
though Edward assures me that you are his ward, and I have
accepted that. But I have made my own observations and I
know you are of gentle blood and have been carefully brought
up. And I believe you know more about Piers Carston than
Edward thinks." Ignoring Perdita's gasp, she went on, "But
have no fear, I will not tell Edward of my suspicions. You gave
me a promise about Piers Carston and I trust you. Remember,
if I can help you at any time you have only to ask. Now get

some rest and come down with a bright face and a resolution to
have faith—in yourself and Edward. Will you do that?''

Perdita assured the Countess that she would try to rest. Then
she added, ''Thank you, ma'am, for your own faith in me.
Until you know the whole, I think you cannot judge Lord
Ambourne.''

''We shall see,'' said the Countess from the door. ''Eliane
should be here tomorrow or the next day and that should provide a different problem for you. What has happened to Philippe, for example?''

She went, and Perdita was left alone. Though she could not
see any happier outcome, her talk with the Countess had given
her mind a more cheerful direction. She must try to see Philippe as soon as possible.

Accordingly she caught Colette that evening and commis-
sioned her help in delivering a note. Perdita felt the need for
secrecy was almost past, since the Countess approved her efforts to reunite Philippe and Eliane. Nevertheless, she wanted
to avoid awkward questions from the Earl until she had established what Philippe's attitude would be. So, when Colette
brought a reply early the next morning and gave it to her in an
exaggeratedly secretive way, she smiled but did nothing to dis-
pel the child's sense of drama. Unfortunately she was observed by the Earl. He guessed immediately that the note
concerned the young man he regarded as Perdita's lover, and,
though he despised himself for it, he watched Perdita when she
later slipped out and hurried down to the lake. He would give
them time to meet and then he would get rid of the young
puppy once and for all!

Perdita was reassured by Philippe's appearance. He was still
very pale, but looked calmer. He asked after Eliane.

''Good news! She is much improved. How are you, Philippe?''

''*Mademoiselle*, Eliane has never been out of my mind. You
made me look at myself after I had been to Paris and I was
ashamed of what I saw. I did fail Eliane. Do you think she
would ever forgive me?''

Perdita answered honestly and carefully, ''I don't know. She
must have been hurt by your actions in Paris but your former
friendship must have some value for her. If you really wish to
be friends with her again you must ask her, Philippe. Am I to
understand that you still would not want to marry her ever?''

"Mademoiselle Perdita, if Eliane could forgive me enough to marry me I would be the happiest of men. But how could she?"

Perdita smiled at his intensity, but said, "If Eliane loves you she will. Do you know she is coming back to Beau Lac soon? If you wish me to deliver a note to her, I will do so."

"*Mademoiselle*, when?" Philippe's face lit up and in his excitement he grasped Perdita's sleeve.

"You have spoken to my ward for long enough. Too long! Now take your leave and go, sir!" said a cold voice behind them, and the Earl appeared. Philippe jerked as if to go, but Perdita stopped him.

"No, stay! It's time to introduce you. Lord Ambourne, allow me to present Monsieur Fourget to you. He is—"

"Charmed as I am to have a name at last for yet another of my ward's secret acquaintances, I must request you to leave, Monsieur Fourget." Perdita would have interrupted, but he turned on her savagely. "I have had enough of your machinations, Perdita! You will be silent until this gentleman has departed." He turned to Philippe. "Be glad, Monsieur Fourget, that I blame my ward more than you for these encounters. However, I do not wish to see you on my land again."

Philippe began hotly, "If it is because of your prejudices—"

"You may call it that, Monsieur Fourget. Now goodbye."

Realising that there was little point in argument, Philippe shrugged his shoulders and walked stiffly away.

Perdita was walking tempestuously up the path to the house. The Earl easily caught her up, but she ignored him. He caught her by the arm and turned her round, saying bitterly, "I will say what I have to say out here in the grounds, Perdita. It is not fit for my mother's ears. I had begun to respect you, had wished there was not this barrier of your previous life between us. I even thought that you regretted your past as much as I did. But as soon as you have some freedom you are running off to your paramours. How can respect or trust survive this? Have no fear that I will behave as I did on the last occasion. If I am angry, it is with myself for the way in which I wilfully allowed you to deceive me. You have made a fool of me in my own eyes. I wish to heaven I had never laid eyes on you." He left her and started walking up the path again.

"Lord Ambourne!" When the Earl continued walking, Perdita ran in front of him and blocked his way. Her cheeks were scarlet and her eyes were blazing. "I have two things to say to you, Lord Ambourne. You will do me the courtesy of listening, or I will say them in front of your mother, and anyone else in earshot!" He stood there, expressionless. "Philippe Fourget is in love with Eliane, and hoped one day to marry her. You have probably just destroyed that hope forever. And the second is this—you cannot possibly wish more heartily than I that you had never seen me. I have reasons of my own for continuing on this scheme, otherwise, I assure you, I would go back to Africa tomorrow!"

She ran swiftly indoors and up to the safety of her room. She was trembling with fury, but at the bottom of the anger lay a deep despair. The Earl would never forgive or forget her situation in Algiers. He would find out his error on the question of Philippe as soon as he talked to his mother. But there would always be other doubts, other suspicions. Because of the circumstances in which he had found her he would never trust her completely. As she stood there fighting for control the Countess walked in.

"I came straight in because I knew that if I knocked you would deny me. Forgive me, but I am very concerned. I saw you and Edward out on the path, Perdita. What was happening?"

"You must ask your son, ma'am. He wrote the lines of the play."

"Well, as I saw it, Perdita, you seemed to have quite a lot to say, too! You looked like a little turkey cock! What has my son done now?"

Perdita turned desperately to the Countess. "Ma'am, forgive me, I cannot talk at the moment. I am too angry."

"I had noticed," murmured the Countess. "Well, I will go to see what Edward has to say."

"Why is he so unkind, ma'am?" burst out Perdita. "Why does he always leap to the very worst conclusions about me?"

"Yes," said the Countess. "You should ask yourself that, Perdita. My son has always been the most reasonable of men. Why should he be so unbalanced where you are concerned? It couldn't possibly be jealousy, could it? Surely not?"

She went, but a few minutes later Jeanne came with some cloths soaked in the Countess's own lavender water and a glass

of the château's best claret. Then Perdita was left in peace. The
comfort, the wine, and the exhaustion after losing her temper
so thoroughly, gave Perdita the best few hours' sleep she had
enjoyed for days.

She was woken by the sound of her name and sat up in confusion. Who was it?

"Elaine!" she cried and leapt up to hug her friend, who was
standing at the foot of her bed. "Eliane, you're looking wonderful!" And indeed it was so. Eliane was flushed with the excitement of homecoming, her delicate features and pale gold
hair were surrounded by a pretty bonnet, and her green velvet
pelisse was in the very latest mode.

"Mademoiselle Perdita, it is very pleasant to see you again.
I've missed you."

"When did you arrive?"

"Five minutes ago. We have not yet been to Beau Lac. I
wanted to see you and Edward first. My mother is talking to
him now. Aren't you pleased he is here, too?"

Perdita found this difficult to answer, but managed to evade
the question by saying, "Your mother is here? I cannot wait to
see her. Excuse me, Mademoiselle Eliane, I will be downstairs
before you can turn around." Eliane left and Perdita hastened
to tidy herself.

Any embarrassment she might have experienced at seeing the
Earl so soon after their altercation was lost in the pleasure of
meeting Madame d'Harcourt again. If he had desired any evidence of his family's affection for Perdita he might have seen
it in abundance that afternoon. Eliane constantly referred to
her and Madame d'Harcourt grew quite animated as she told
Perdita of the subscription concerts she had attended in Paris.
Apparently the Earl desired no such thing. He stood morosely
in the background until Eliane drew him forward with a laugh.

"Edward, you must join in! You are behaving very stuffily.
Aren't you glad to see us?"

Perdita avoided looking at the Earl by observing Eliane. In
repose Eliane's face was still sad, and one could see signs of
recent illness once the excited flush had died away. But she was
very much better than Perdita had feared, and in the company
of the people she most trusted and loved she displayed greater
confidence.

"Edward looks such a crosspatch. Whatever had happened?" whispered Eliane as she and Perdita went for Eliane's bonnet.

"I think he has made a mistake in his calculations," replied Perdita. The Countess, who had heard this exchange, wagged a finger at Perdita and laughed.

"Poor Edward," said Eliane. "He has so much bookwork to do." Perdita was ashamed of herself for misleading her friend, but explanations were impossible.

Perdita never knew what the Countess said in the interview with her son. He appeared when she was alone in the music-room and asked her, "Who is he, Perdita—the fellow in the park? My mother seems to think I have misjudged you."

Somewhat stiffly Perdita replied, "His father has an estate at Vauvron. His name is Fourget, Philippe Fourget."

"Then, if his interest is in Eliane, why the devil could he not approach me openly, instead of behaving in this havey-cavey fashion?"

"His father is not generally liked by the other land-owners in Normandy so he didn't believe you would receive him kindly—and you have now given him every reason to believe this is so!" she added bitterly.

"Why should he . . . ? Oh, of course—Fourget! The Republican. But why should he think I would blame him for the sins of his father? If being true to your convictions can be so described."

"You mean you would have listened to him? You wouldn't have shown him the door?"

"I am not so unreasonable, Perdita." Her face was eloquent of disbelief. He added with a trace of hauteur, "It was very natural I should have misunderstood the situation—"

"Forgive me, Lord Ambourne, but it was not!"

"Very well, very well, I was unreasonable! And I regret that I misjudged you." He looked at Perdita's unrelenting face, took her hand and kissed it, saying in a gentler tone, "I am truly sorry if I offended you, Perdita. Both today and on another occasion when I misinterpreted the evidence. My behaviour was totally ill-judged."

Perdita looked at him sharply but he was perfectly sincere. She responded in kind. "My behaviour was not without reproach on those occasions either, Lord Ambourne. I expressed sentiments which were excessive."

"You mean you would not prefer to go back to the Pasha?" he said with a slight grin.

"Algiers was not the part of Africa I was thinking of. Sometimes I feel I would like to see the Sheikh again, but I know that is impossible."

"I could arrange for you to go there after... afterwards for a visit, if you so wished," he answered swiftly. "But I do not believe that to be your proper milieu for a longer stay."

"I do not know what my proper milieu will be, Lord Ambourne," said Perdita, with a sad smile. "But let us not, I pray you, broach that subject again. Perhaps time will provide a solution."

"I hope so," muttered the Earl. "I hope to God it will be so!"

They stood there at a loss for a minute or two. Then they both started a sentence and abandoned it in deference to the other. The silence that followed became painful to Perdita and she went to the door.

"Perdita," the Earl said, and when she turned he continued, "Why did you not tell me earlier about Philippe Fourget? Was it to punish me, because I misjudged you?"

"Not exactly, though it would have been reason enough. No, the first time you saw us I was afraid that if I told you who he was while you were being so out of reason angry you would dismiss him without listening to him—or me."

"I am far more likely to condemn him for making Eliane so unhappy in Paris. But why did you become so involved? Why not leave it to the two of them?"

"Because I love them!" cried Perdita. "I wanted them to have a chance of happiness and I thought I could help!"

The Earl moved restlessly and said, "There is little chance of happiness for Eliane. I saw what Fourget's reception of her story did to her. No, don't go! There is something else I want to ask you. What did you mean when you said you had reasons of your own for continuing with our scheme?"

Perdita took a step back. She had forgotten she had said that in her rage. She thought rapidly and said, "I would like to see England again and I have only once been to London. I think its sights will be interesting."

"Not half as interesting as your real reasons for going there, I am sure. No doubt I shall learn them in time." He looked at her in silence, then said, "I wish I knew what it is about you,

Perdita. You enchant everyone who crosses your path—the
Sheikh, Tom, my aunt and Eliane and now my mother. What
is it?''

''You are wrong, my lord. I know of at least one person in
this house who has failed to be enchanted.''

She curtsyed and left the room, but as she went she thought
she heard him say, ''Then I wish you would tell me his name,
Perdita, for I do not know him.''

CHAPTER THIRTEEN

MADAME D'ESPERY had been invited to dine before the party at Belleroi, and was as pleased and excited as a young girl. Perdita brought her a copy of the guest list and, as she had half hoped, Madame d'Espery gave her views on the company.

"Of course, the Bonvilles will be at the dinner, though in the old days Gaston Bonville would have thought himself fortunate indeed even to be included in the list for dancing. But there you are, *mademoiselle*; times have changed. So many of our friends died under the guillotine, and many others have never returned to France. It is difficult to maintain the old distinctions... I am pleased to see that the de Sardets have not been invited to dinner. The man has the soul of a peasant, though I have no reason to believe his mother played her husband false."

When Perdita gave a gasp of laughter, *madame* looked up from the list and said, "Oh, forgive me, child. I should not say such things—in front of you, I mean. I sometimes forget your youth." She looked at Perdita over her glasses and shook her head before she continued, "Now there's a name you should note, *mademoiselle*! I am surprised to observe that the Marantins are spending the night at the château, but then I suppose it is impossible for them to return home so late. I will not say anything more about them, but—" she bent forward and grasped Perdita's arm "—take care to lock your door firmly when Monsieur de Marantin is in the château. I will protect you during the evening, but I cannot be there at night. The story I could tell you of his visit to the Château de Joignet... Of course, he said he mistook the door of his bedroom, but... I will say no more."

The old lady finished the list with enjoyment, destroying the reputations of at least half of the guests on the way. Lastly she said, "I shall enjoy meeting my old friends again, *mademoi-*

selle. It is always pleasant to exchange news. Tell me what you are going to wear.''

When Perdita explained that the Countess was giving her one of her dresses, Madame d'Espery said, ''Eugenie de Cazeville was a very pretty girl, *mademoiselle*, and a charming one. Her husband was a clever, strong-minded man, yet she could wind him round her little finger. She was one of the best dressed women in London or Paris—is still, I suppose, for he left her very well provided for, and her interest in fashion is unchanged. Dear me, I fear my tongue runs away with me. I am too much alone and it is agreeable to have someone to talk to. But I should not discuss your hostess with you. Forgive me.''

Perdita assured her that she was as charmed by the Countess as the rest of the world. After Madame d'Espery had told her what she was proposing to wear and had described in detail what had happened on the last occasion she had worn it they parted with expressions of mutual goodwill.

After a great deal of persuasion Eliane had agreed to come to the party. Curiously, it was the Earl who prevailed on her to be present. As she told Perdita, ''Edward represented to me how difficult it would be for Maman to be present if I were not. And Tante Eugenie would be disappointed if neither of us came.''

''I am delighted you are coming for whatever reason, and think your cousin is quite right,'' said Perdita. ''But could you not call me Perdita? If your aunt and mother do so, surely you could?''

Eliane smiled with pleasure. ''I think Maman has caught it from Tante Eugenie, and I would be delighted, Mad...I mean, Perdita. It is so nice to have a friend again.'' Then her face clouded over, and Perdita knew she was thinking of Philippe.

''Eliane,'' she began tentatively, ''have you...have you heard from Philippe?''

''He visited me in Paris, Perdita. I cannot talk about it yet. Perhaps later...'' But Perdita knew that her time in France was now very limited and if she was to help her friend she must persist.

''I met Philippe after he came back,'' she said. ''He told me something of what happened. No, don't go away, Eliane. It's important I tell you this. Please stay.'' She led her reluctant friend back to her chair and held both her hands. ''Philippe regrets what he did—''

"And so he should!" cried Eliane. "I thought he was my friend!"

"Philippe did not regard you as only a friend, Eliane. He put you on a pedestal, thought of you as an angel, untouched and untouchable. That's why what he learned in Paris was such a shock to him." Eliane tried to pull her hands away, but Perdita refused to let her. "Philippe loved you and still does love you. He is bitterly sorry for the way he behaved. And I think you should forgive him."

"But how could he say those things—that he never wanted to see me again, and the rest . . . ?" asked Eliane piteously.

"Because he is human and he was hurt. Listen to me, Eliane. Philippe still loves you. If he should write to you please read what he says. Will you?"

"Do you think I should?" Perdita nodded and Eliane said finally, "Well, if he writes I will read his letter. But I wish my cousin were not taking you to London. It will seem very quiet here without you. Could you not stay a little longer?"

Perdita was forced to disappoint her. Their departure date had been fixed for three days after the ball. The Earl had wanted to leave earlier, but the Countess had announced that she would travel neither on the day after the party, nor on a Sunday. This was not the only point of conflict, for the Countess wanted to stay for one or two nights at Ambourne before continuing to London, and the Earl refused to countenance it.

"I HAVE NEVER KNOWN Edward so short-tempered," said Marguerite d'Harcourt to her sister. "Is he not well?"

"I fear he is suffering from an incurable malady," replied the Countess solemnly. Her sister looked at her in concern, but when she saw the mischievous expression on her sister's face she, too, smiled.

"Oh, lies the wind in that quarter?" she asked. "What about the lady?"

"I should not have told you, Marguerite, for neither of them seems to know where they are. There's some mystery about Perdita, of course, and I'm afraid that behind it lies a serious obstruction."

"Edward would be a lucky man if Perdita found herself able to marry him," said Madame d'Harcourt. Fond as the Count-

ess was of Perdita, no devoted mother could let this pass, and
she pointed out to her sister that her Edward was one of the
most eligible *partis* in England. He could, she said, have married any number of charming young ladies.

"But he has never shown the slightest inclination for any of
them," said Madame d'Harcourt. "Indeed, till today I had
never seen him display any strong emotion, other than his
hatred for Piers Carston. And that," she said bitterly, "is an
emotion I am forced to admit I share."

The Countess turned a troubled face to her sister. "You know
he is about to do something connected with Piers Carston, and
Perdita is included in his plans?"

"Yes," replied Madame d'Harcourt. "He told me when he
first brought her here that she was part of a plan. What is it?"
she asked, adding anxiously, "I hope it won't revive the old
scandal. Eliane is wonderfully recovered, but any further stress
would pull her down very quickly."

"No, no, there is no danger of that," said the Countess,
quickly reassuring her nervous sister. "Edward would never
risk such a thing, and Perdita has assured me of it, too. But
pray do not repeat any of our conversation to him. He is difficult enough, without learning that we discuss him behind his
back!"

THE DAY OF THE PARTY dawned. Flowers from the garden and
succession houses had been put in huge bowls all over the
house, the servants' uniforms and liveries had been brushed and
pressed, the gardens raked and the lawns cut. Rosanne, in the
kitchen with Colette and an army of helpers from the village,
was putting the final touches to the food, and Madame Lebrun was inspecting the bedrooms to be used for the guests.
Perdita noticed that Monsieur de Marantin's room was at the
furthest corner of the château from hers. She wondered
whether Madame d'Espery had spoken to Madame Lebrun,
and pictured the scene with amusement.

Perdita herself was up early and out in the garden. She
looked wistfully over the lawns, up the hill to the woods and to
the right towards the lake. In three days she would leave for
England, where the last scene of the drama that had begun in
an inn near Bristol would be played. She wanted to be finished
with it, wanted to start the next stage in her life free of the ha-

tred and misery of the past. Perhaps when she no longer saw the
Earl daily she would be able to forget him, or at least learn to
be content without him. Perhaps. She sat for a while longer,
enjoying Belleroi while she still could, before going in to start
the day.

The Earl had seen her sitting on a bench under the lime tree,
but had decided not to join her. The less time he spent in her
company, the more resolute he could remain. For weeks now he
had been in this unpleasant and unfamiliar state of indecision.
He had pursued his goal of ruining Piers Carston for nearly
four years. Now, when he should have been rejoicing that he
was so near its fulfilment, he found himself weakening. But, he
reminded himself, Perdita had been bought as part of his plan
and must not mean anything more to him than that. The sooner
they got to London the better. As for this scheme of his mother's that they should break their journey at Ambourne—he
would oppose that absolutely. He would not have Ambourne
haunted by Perdita's presence as Belleroi was. Taking one last
look at the figure on the bench, he turned away from the window.

The day wore on and evening approached without any serious disasters. Colette dropped one of the jellies Rosanne had
prepared, but a little adjustment of the other dishes made up
for this. Madame Lebrun found a snail in the middle of the
entrance hall, which had presumably escaped from one of the
arrangements of flowers and plants, and made three of the
maids search every bowl lest there should be any more, but
none were found. Colette later rescued the snail from the rubbish pail into which it had been thrown and carried it out into
the garden. At four everyone started to dress, for the first guests
would be arriving at half-past five. Madame d'Harcourt and
Eliane were to stay overnight and had arrived in the early afternoon. Eliane had whispered to Perdita that she had heard
from Philippe, but when Perdita eagerly questioned her she
merely said that she had not yet read his note.

"I have left it until I am alone, Perdita. I want to consider it
carefully and slowly." Perdita was content to leave it so. The
most important thing was that Eliane was prepared to read it at
all.

When the four ladies assembled in the salon shortly before
the guests were due, a prettier sight could hardly have been

found in Normandy. At least that was what the Earl said, carefully avoiding looking at Perdita.

"In Normandy! You are too cautious, Edward. I dare swear you will not find a lovelier sight than these two young ladies in the whole of France!" The Countess had some justification for her extravagant claim. Perdita and Eliane each looked pretty in their spring-like dresses, but together they looked like something out of a painting by Botticelli. Eliane, in primrose-yellow muslin and fine lace, with her delicate beauty and pale gold hair, looked like a fairy princess. Perdita was in pale green silk embroidered with rosebuds, flowers in her dark brown curls. The formal clothes might have subdued her vitality, but her grace and beauty had never been displayed to greater advantage.

The Earl, himself very formally attired in dark red velvet coat and white breeches, bowed and said, still not looking at Perdita, "Nor a finer one than you and my aunt, Mama." His mother laughed and disclaimed, but smoothed the heavy gold silk of her own dress and glanced at her sister in silvery grey with a satisfied air.

"But, Edward, do you not think Perdita looks lovely? I do," cried Eliane.

The Earl was forced at last to look at Perdita, and his face was expressionless as he said, "I congratulate you, Perdita. I predict you will capture all hearts tonight." Then he smiled down affectionately at his cousin and added, "Those that Eliane leaves untouched, that is!"

"Then I shall have a sad time of it, for I shall have none," said Perdita, looking warmly at her friend. The two sisters looked at one another, hardly able to conceal a smile, but they pulled themselves together when the first arrivals were announced.

"Monsieur Bonville and Madame! How pleasant that you arrive so promptly. Do you know my sister and her daughter?"

The Countess was in her element. As the guests arrived she moved from one to the other, introducing, reminiscing, mixing, but at the same time managing to observe Perdita and her son. Perdita's conduct impressed her. The girl's manner was apparently confident, yet modest. She bore with equanimity both the barely concealed curiosity of the polite and the impertinent questions of the less well-bred, and was able to dis-arm them both. She stayed close to Eliane until she saw her friend was happily engaged in conversation. Then she would leave her, only to return when Eliane was once again alone. Altogether a very nicely brought-up girl, thought the Countess.

The Earl was less pleasing to his mother. His manner was, as always, impeccably polite, and no one could have accused him of neglecting his guests in any way. But, to those who knew him, he seemed even more remote than usual, as if he was concealing his real person from the world.

Dinner was announced, and the Countess and her partner led the way in.

Perdita found herself next to Monsieur de Marantin, and conducted a harmless enough conversation with him until his wine glass had been filled two or three times. Then the tone of his conversation became less proper and she sometimes didn't quite know how to deal with it. On the one hand, she was not shocked by what he said: on the other, she knew that the sort of girl he imagined her to be—young, unmarried, delicately brought up—would be painfully embarrassed by his insinuating remarks.

She saw the Earl's eye on her once as Monsieur de Marantin laughed loudly at his own wit. Finally she leaned forward and looked at Madame d'Espery, who was sitting on Monsieur de Marantin's other side. That lady responded instantly. She was a formidable sight in her black velvet dress, which was twenty years out of date but had some of the loveliest Mechlin lace carelessly pinned to it with a large diamond brooch. She rallied to Perdita's rescue by monopolising the unfortunate Monsieur de Marantin for the rest of the meal, telling him stories of his father and, when he would have turned back to Perdita, hinting in the most delicate manner possible that she knew something of the events at Château de Joignet. He was held in thrall by the old lady till the end of the meal. Meanwhile Perdita was able to talk to her other neighbour, a dull but harmless young man, who was dazzled by her.

In London terms this was a very small ball indeed, but to the provincial society of Normandy, still trying to settle down again after the upheavals of the past thirty years, it was the event of the year. Long after it was over they would talk of the ball at Belleroi, and of Monsieur le Marquis and Madame la Marquise and their family. Eliane and Perdita soon found they were much in demand for dancing, and, since neither of them had had much opportunity before to be present at such an evening, they found to their surprise that they were enjoying themselves.

Madame d'Espery, true to her word, had kept a severe eye on Monsieur de Marantin, but during the supper interval she had unfortunately been carried off by the Countess. Perdita knew that Eliane had gone to find some fresh air and went in search of her. She found her in the music-room, struggling with an amorous Monsieur de Marantin. When Perdita arrived she could see that Eliane was becoming hysterical. How could she rescue her without causing the sort of scandal that would damage her friend? She hurried over and surprised Monsieur de Marantin into letting Eliane go by saying in enthusiastic tones, "Ah, *monsieur*! You too are a devotee of music. How charming! Eliane, your mama is looking for you. I think she is in the little parlour."

Eliane, with a grateful look at Perdita, ran out. Left with a befuddled adversary, who had imbibed too freely of the wine at supper, Perdita gathered her wits as she realised with a sinking heart that he was only too willing to transfer his attentions.

"A golden goddess departs and Pershephon ... Perphesh ... spring takes her place..." he said, making his unsteady way towards her.

She easily avoided him and went to the door, saying as she went, "Pray excuse me, Monsieur de Marantin. I should not be here alone with you, even for some music, which I adore." She turned to go, and ran into the Earl, who came storming in. He looked so murderous that she caught his arm, not only anxious for Monsieur de Marantin's safety, but also afraid that there would be the very scandal she had tried to avoid. "Monsieur de Marantin has been so kind as to express an interest in hearing some music," she cried, holding tightly on to the Earl's arm. "And I was just about to fetch your mother and aunt to play for him. He fully understands how improper it would be for me to remain here alone with him, is that not so, *monsieur*?"

Monsieur de Marantin was no expert on propriety, but he was fully aware of the Earl's anger and the tensed muscles under his elegant coat. He hastily agreed.

The Earl relaxed and Perdita let him go. He said smoothly, "It is always pleasant to find a fellow lover of music, Monsieur de Marantin, but I fear the dancing is just about to recommence in the salon and my mother is fully occupied there. Perhaps you could indulge yourself on another occasion? Indulge your interest in music, I mean, of course." He held the door open for his discomfited guest and ushered him out.

Perdita turned to him, her eyes brimming with laughter. "Oh, famously done! The poor man won't be able to look you in the face for a year." Then as she saw the Earl's serious look she said quietly, "I did not encourage him. Whatever you may think, I did not encourage him."

"I know," he said surprisingly. "Eliane told me what was happening."

"But Monsieur de Marantin—will he be all right? He was more than a trifle disguised."

"To the devil with Monsieur de Marantin. I am more concerned for you. Did he hurt you, Perdita?" She did not have time to do more than shake her head before he folded her in his arms, holding her tight as if he wanted to protect her against the world. "It is as well for him!" he murmured into her hair. "Though you look delectable enough tonight to drive any man out of his senses."

Though she knew it was an illusion, Perdita stood in the circle of his arms, feeling loved and cherished. It was a new and heady sensation. But after a short moment she stirred, moved away and, shaking out her skirts, said lightly, "I was only trying to divert his attention from Eliane. I was not prepared for such a lightning change of heart—I think he was comparing me to spring and it went to his head!"

The Earl grinned. "He was in some difficulty with your name, from what I heard, Persephone—or is it Perpheshone?"

Perdita laughed and said, "You should not make sport of your guests, Lord Ambourne, however badly they behave."

With a brief return to his grim manner the Earl replied, "If he had behaved any worse I might have done more than make sport of him! Now, Perdita, may I escort you back to the salon? We shall be missed." He held his arm out to her and, taking it with a smile, she accompanied him back to the ball. When they came into the room a waltz was just striking up. The Earl turned to face her and asked, "May I?" Then, without wait-

ing for her flustered refusal, he put his arm at her waist and
guided her on to the floor.

"I congratulate you, Perdita," said the Earl eventually.
"Your waltz has much improved since I last danced with you.
Now you should be able to look up at me and forget about your
feet." Perdita looked up and met his eyes smiling down at her.
She missed a step and he said softly, "I absolutely forbid you
to stumble! No, don't look down again. Look up!"

His arm was about her waist and, though they were dancing
a strictly correct distance apart, they could not have been closer
in spirit. They moved as one, in a world of their own, their eyes
locked together and their difficulties forgotten in the enchantment of the waltz. They dipped and swayed, turned and re-
versed without conscious effort, lost in each other. When the
music ended they stood quite still for a moment, and the Earl's
hand tightened round Perdita's as he gazed at her in a be-
mused fashion. They came to to find themselves an object of
interest to three pairs of eyes. Eliane was looking on in admiration, but the Countess and her sister were unable to hide their
sympathetic curiosity. The Earl looked slightly self-conscious
as he led Perdita to her chair, but by the time she was seated he
had resumed his remote air. He bowed and withdrew without
further conversation.

"That was wonderful! You both looked so graceful. I should
like to learn to dance like that," cried Eliane at Perdita's side.

"I shouldn't," said Perdita sadly. "It's too dangerous."

"Oh, but it didn't look for a moment as if you would fall,"
said Eliane. "Edward seemed to be holding you so securely."

"That's what I meant," replied Perdita. Then she pulled
herself together, and to Eliane's puzzled query she would only
laugh ruefully and shake her head.

To Perdita's profound relief Monsieur de Marantin did not
approach her again that evening, but neither did the Earl.
Somehow, after the waltz, she found the zest had gone from the
ball and she felt tired. She was glad when it finally came to an
end and the guests had either departed or were in their rooms.
Eliane, too, was pale and heavy-eyed, and worried them all
when she almost fell at the foot of the stairs.

"She is still not strong, Edward," Madame d'Harcourt said.
"I hope the dancing has not been too much for her..."

Edward swung Eliane into his arms and started up the stairs.
"Send for her maid, Tante Marguerite. She will be in bed in a

very short time. And after we have gone to England you can see that she does not exert herself unduly. I cannot believe one evening's enjoyment can have a lasting effect." But when he returned to his mother and Perdita, who were waiting in the salon, he said, "It's this damnable business with young Fourget. I sent the Fourgets an invitation—"

"Edward!"

"Why not, Mama? It's time the old loyalties were forgotten. If the King would only realise it, France needs men of principle such as old Fourget. At present he's surrounded by sycophants and time-servers, men of the old regime, eager to restore their private fortunes." He sighed, then added, "But the Fourgets refused to come, and I cannot blame them. They would have had a cool reception from most of our guests. It would seem that Eliane must once again be unhappy."

"No!" cried Perdita. "I will not accept that. Philippe loves Eliane!"

"Oh, love!" said the Earl contemptuously. "That is a much overrated emotion, believe me. I am increasingly of the opinion that one should have a good dose of it in one's early years, much as one has the measles, and then it should be decently forgotten. Do you go to bed now, Mama? I will escort you upstairs."

The Countess rose wearily, and together with Perdita, preceded her son up the stairs. They bade each other goodnight and went their separate ways to their rooms. The ball was over, and all attention must now be on the voyage to England.

CHAPTER FOURTEEN

IT WAS A SUBDUED PARTY that set out three days later. The Countess was still tired after her exertions for the ball, and was as disgruntled as her sunny nature permitted at her son's adamant refusal to spend any time at Ambourne before going to London. He knew she was not a good traveller and, considerate son that he was, would normally have indulged her instantly in her desire to break the journey. But he had proved completely inflexible on this point. Hers was not a nature to repine, however, and she would have been in better spirits if she had been more sanguine about the affairs of the young people about her.

Eliane was far from happy, and her aunt was afraid that Philippe was proving to be a reluctant suitor. Then there was Perdita. The Countess considered the white face of the girl sitting opposite her in the chaise. Perdita was clearly distressed at leaving Belleroi. She had walked in the woods and round the lake and had visited Madame d'Espery and Père Amboise before she had left. The servants had been sorry to see her go, and Colette and Jeanne had been inconsolable. There was another thing! Edward had rejected her very reasonable suggestion that Perdita should take Jeanne with her as her maid. He seemed to want to cut all ties between Perdita and Belleroi.

She could not study Edward, for he had decided not to travel with them in the chaise and was riding alongside. But for a long time now he had been abstracted and short-tempered. What was he proposing to do about Perdita? The Countess feared that her son might be throwing away his chance of happiness in this pursuit of Piers Carston. But then, Perdita had said that even when it was over they could not marry. The Countess set her mind to think of something more cheerful, for she could do little enough for the moment about the problems the young were facing. At least they would have as comfortable a crossing as the Channel would permit. Edward had his yacht moored at Honfleur. She closed her eyes and tried to sleep.

Perdita too tried to rest. The last two days had been painful, and she had slept little at night. It was most unlikely that she would ever see Belleroi and the people in Normandy again. After the loss of her home in Somerset and the death of her mother there had been a large gap in her life, and during the last five months Belleroi had begun to fill it. Now she must forget it again. The future seemed dreary, and even the fact that she would at last face Piers Carston with his crimes failed to console her. With determination she turned her mind to what she would do in London.

As for the Earl—it was fortunate that he did not meet with any unexpected hazard on the way to Honfleur, for he was so deeply wrapped in his own thoughts that it was doubtful he would have coped with it. He dealt with the changes of horses, escorted the ladies into the inns on their way, but it was all done without real thought. To the casual observer he looked his normal authoritative self. But in fact he was still no nearer to recovering the calm certainty with which he had faced the world until such a short time before. Was there a way to ruin Piers Carston without involving Perdita in a distasteful marriage? But all his plans had been perfected with this in mind, and surely Perdita herself was not so squeamish? For all her dainty ways now, she must have lived roughly with the pirate gang. He thrust away the thought that, whatever Perdita's views on the subject were, her forthcoming marriage to Piers Carston was highly distasteful to him.

They arrived at Honfleur in the evening and wasted no time in embarking. Tom was there to help them on board and show the ladies to their cabins. The Countess retired immediately. Perdita would have helped her, but she said with a wan smile, "No, child. I fear I am very poor company on a sailing vessel, and my maid will do all I need. I shall see you again in Portsmouth."

Perdita was taken to a small cabin on the opposite side of the ship from the one in which she had lain ill six months before. Then she had been determined to reject all contact with others, to remain detached, not even bothering to communicate. Now she had just cut the ties of a whole web of relationships and involvement—Eliane and Philippe, Colette and Jeanne, Madame d'Harcourt and Madame d'Espery, and a host of others. She had a short time longer to enjoy the Countess's friendship, then that too would be gone. It hurt, and would hurt for some time, but she could not regret her friendships with these people. She avoided thinking of the Earl, for that was something different and had still to be resolved. A rocking motion told her that the ship had set sail and she lay down. Her tired mind gradually relaxed and she fell asleep.

THEY SPENT TWO NIGHTS on board and landed at Portsmouth early in the morning. It took some time to manoeuvre the yacht alongside and Perdita stood on deck watching the busy life on the quayside. This was England! In her darker moments on the pirate ship she had doubted that she would ever see it again, but now it looked as if she was home for good and she was grateful for it.

Tom came up to her. "Mind your dress on them ropes, miss. His lordship would have a fit if he saw them, they're that dirty."

"I'm not afraid of a bit of dirt, Tom," said Perdita, smiling slightly.

"Yes, well, things are a bit different now, aren't they? I mean, you're a lady now, and some of the things that happened in the past should be forgotten, Miss Perdita—if you'll forgive my saying so. Particularly baths and the like." Tom spoke severely, and his rugged face grew slightly pink. Perdita was sorry she had teased him, but she had forgotten his efforts when she was in the bath—she only remembered the way the Earl had dumped her into it.

"I'm sorry, Tom. I was wrong to mention it. But I was grateful for your care."

"Well, just you make sure you don't get into any more scrapes. I'm not sure how his lordship will take it, him being so out of sorts, like."

Perdita gathered that the sea voyage had not improved the Earl's frame of mind. She was glad; he ought to suffer a little. However, when he appeared a few moments later he spoke with his usual calm authority.

"I'd like you to stay below till we berth, Perdita. The less you are seen, the better. Perhaps you would like to join my mother? She seems to be recovered and would like your company."

Perdita went to the Countess's cabin. It was the one she had been in on her journey to Tangier, and she looked round it, remembering her fever and pain she had suffered.

"There you are, my dear! How have you fared on the voyage? I feel ashamed of myself for looking after you so badly. But it's always the same—Charles used to say that I felt queasy when I saw the lake at Ambourne!"

They heard footsteps approaching, but it was Tom who had come to collect the first valises. With a great deal of bustle the Countess's belongings were slowly taken ashore and loaded on the chaise. Then Perdita's bag was fetched, looking pathetically small by the Countess's pile of luggage, and in a very short time they were on the road to London. The last stage of Perdita's long journey had begun.

They spent the night at Godalming, where the Countess declared, quite without foundation, that the sheets at the inn were not properly aired.

"You are only annoyed, Mama, that we did not stay at Ambourne. The rooms at the King's Arms were very decently prepared."

"When I am in my bed with a rheumatic disorder you will remember, if you please, that I was not happy with them!" said his mother crossly, and then, as Edward smiled at the idea of his mother with rheumatics, she sighed in relief. It was the first time Edward had smiled in a fortnight.

They reached London at the end of the week, and, though they had travelled in comfort, they were all glad to reach Rotherfield House at last. This was a handsome building quite near Green Park in Arlington Street, Piccadilly. It had been built in the 1730s for the Earl's great-great-grandfather, when the barony had been elevated to an earldom. Though its style looked somewhat heavy to the modern eye, its large rooms and splendid central staircase were impressively grand.

The Countess shuddered as she came in, and hurried quickly into the small parlour.

"How anyone could live here in comfort I do not know. I was always asking Charles to modernise it or even to move to the other side of Oxford Street. There are some very pretty new houses near Portman Square and I quite set my heart on one of them, but Charles would not hear of it. He said they weren't big enough or some such nonsense, and would keep talking of family tradition and boring things like that. In most things I was able to persuade Charles into a more reasonable frame of mind, but not in this.''

While the Countess was talking she handed her cloak to a footman and settled herself on the day couch, which stood by the fire. Several other personages had appeared on their arrival, and these were now engaged in carrying luggage and clothing to the bedrooms.

"Now, Perdita, we shall have a little refreshment here; Purkiss shall see to it, won't you, Purkiss? And then we shall restore ourselves to good order in our rooms till dinner. You know London keeps late dinner hours, do you? We dine at seven.'' Perdita nodded, and watched Purkiss's stately approach to the door as the butler went to do the Countess's bidding.

"Can you imagine what it was like when I first came here, Perdita? You know how small Belleroi is. The salon there is its largest room, but it would fit eight times over into the ballroom at the back of this house. And Ambourne is even bigger! I was petrified, especially by Purkiss there. Charles's parents were the friendliest people imaginable and I was soon on good terms with them, but it took me three years to overcome my awe for Purkiss!'' Perdita laughed and said she could not imagine anyone taking three hours let alone three years to fall under the Countess's spell. "You are a darling, Perdita. What shall I do without you?''

They both fell silent. The Earl had announced that Perdita could not stay at Rotherfield House for long, as it would rouse Carston's suspicion if she and the Earl were seen to be connected. When Perdita's chaperon arrived they would remove to the house he had engaged for them in Dover Street on the other side of Piccadilly.

The Countess's voice grew sad as she said, "Perdita, Edward says I must not visit you in Dover Street, so it is possible I may not see you again for some time. I have a small gift for you here. I hope you will remember your Belleroi friends when you wear it—it comes with our love and friendship. We shall think of you.'' A lump came into Perdita's throat as she looked down at the prettily painted box with the letter 'P' in gold on the lid.

"I need no souvenirs of Belleroi, ma'am. They are in my heart. But this gift means more to me . . . more to me than I can . . .''

"Come now, Perdita! It is a mere trifle. Open it and see what is inside," said the Countess in bracing tones.

Perdita took out a small gold brooch set with seed-pearls and sapphires. She went over and sat at the Countess's feet. "I shall never forget your kindness, ma'am. It's not just the brooch, the dress and the many other things you have given me. You have made me feel part of a family again..." She could not continue.

The Countess said warmly, "Well, of course you are! What sister could have cared more for Eliane? What daughter could have been better company? Don't thank me for that, Perdita—and please do not give us up! Wear the brooch when you come to see us again."

Perdita only smiled and nodded. How could she tell the Countess that her intention was to disappear once she had seen Piers Carston? Better by far that they part now while the Countess remained in ignorance of the ugly facts connected with her stepbrother.

Purkiss entered the room, so there was no time for more. When they had drunk some tea they went upstairs to wash and change out of their travelling garb.

Dinner was a quiet meal, for the Earl had excused himself and was dining at his club. The two ladies were still tired and somehow low in spirits. They were glad when the tea-tray was brought in at ten o'clock and they could retire gracefully to bed.

The maid had gone, and Perdita was in bed, examining the brooch in the light of her candle, when she suddenly realised that she had left its box in the parlour. She leapt out of bed, threw on her wrapper and crept downstairs. The Countess had told the servants not to wait up for the Earl and they had all gone to their own quarters. The house was silent. A lamp burned in the hall, but the small parlour was in darkness except for the dying fire. She made her way over to the table, retrieved her box and started for the door.

"Perdita!" Perdita turned round with a jump. The box fell unnoticed to the ground as she became aware of the long figure sprawling somewhat inelegantly in the wing chair by the fire. "Perdita," he said again. She waited for more, but he seemed to have finished. She took a stealthy step towards the door but kicked the little box, and had to bend to pick it up. The Earl sat up and carefully focused his eyes on her. His cravat was loose and his hair slightly dishevelled. "Stealing the silver, perhaps?" he suggested, without any real conviction.

"No, Lord Ambourne. Rescuing a box given to me by your mother. I left it here earlier this evening. I did not expect to find you here."

"A box?"

"I have the brooch that was in it upstairs, but I would be sorry to lose this box. It is very pretty."

"Why did my mother give you a present?"

His tone annoyed her, and she replied sharply, "For reasons you could not possibly understand, my lord. It was a token of her affection, her trust, her friendship. And because I love her I shall treasure it."

A spasm of feeling passed over his face. He thought and then said, "In the best circles, Perdita, it is considered unsporting to kick a man when he is down. I had thought better of your sense of fair play. Show me this box. Please." A sudden suspicion occurred to her and it was confirmed as she came closer. There was an unmistakable aura of alcohol about the Earl's person. "Yes, I must reek of brandy. If it offends you you'd better keep your distance. But, Perdita..." There was a pause.

"Yes, Lord Ambourne?"

"Perdita, let no ignorant fool tell you that sorrows can be drowned in alcohol. It's an illusion, a myth, a chim...a chimera." He seemed to like the word, for he repeated it. "Yes, that's it—a chimera. I must have consumed more brandy this evening than I normally drink in a month, and here I am—stone-cold sober!" He emphasised these last three words by thumping the arm of his chair, and the small wine table next to his arm rocked dangerously. Perdita removed the brandy bottle to a safer place.

"Yes, my lord, I can see," she said, with only the faintest of smiles on her lips. "What sorrows have you failed to drown?" she sat down on the stool near by. At first his reply seemed irrelevant.

"Belleroi. Belleroi was always a happy place for me. The house, the woods, the apple orchards, the people. A place of peace...yes, truly a place of peace." He was so absorbed in his thoughts that he seemed to have forgotten she was there. "But, whenever I think of Belleroi now, I see Perdita running down the lawn to the house, Perdita limping along the lane, Perdita licking her fingers in the dining-room, Perdita in the music-room, in the library, at the ball . . .'' His voice died away.

Perdita could hardly breathe. Was he at last going to renounce his plan?

The disappointment when it came was bitter. ''But, try as I might,'' he went on in a sombre tone, ''I cannot forget those other pictures—Eliane at Ambourne on the threshold of womanhood, full of innocent gaiety. Eliane in London, half starved and cowering in a corner of the cellar. Eliane in Paris, indifferent as to whether she lived or died. I cannot let Piers Carston go unpunished.'' He covered his eyes.

Perdita got up. ''Of course,'' she said woodenly. ''Of course. I will wish you goodnight, Lord Ambourne.'' She walked wearily towards the door.

''Perdita, don't go!'' He leapt up from his chair, knocking the wine table over in his haste. ''Don't go yet.''

''I must. It is late and I should not be here dressed like this. If your mother or the servants—''

''Damn my mother, damn the servants, damn the world, Perdita! There's so much I want to say to you, so much we have shared . . .''

''I was of the opinion we had shared a great deal, too,'' she said sadly. ''But it is not enough to cause you to change your plan to marry me to Piers Carston, is it?''

''Perdita, I have explained to you why I cannot—''

''Then there is no more to be said. Goodnight, Lord Ambourne.''

''Can you not treat it as a game, Perdita? Can you not gull London society with the same impudent enjoyment as you gulled Champollion and the rest?''

''And marriage to Carston? Am I to treat that as a game too?''

''The stakes are high—and the rewards—''

''I beg you not to talk to me of jewels and dresses, establishments and rewards! You do me an injustice, Lord Ambourne! When this farce is played out I shall seek only peace.''

He took her hand and said slowly, ''Perhaps we could find peace together, Perdita?''

''And what part would I play in that idyll?'' she asked, her lip curling in scorn. ''Your mistress? Would the large discreet establishment be replaced with a small one, just for two? Or were you planning a modest retreat in the country? No, Lord

Ambourne, I shall seek my own life in my own place. You will play no part in it!"

He let her hand fall. "You are right. I shall have no claim on you when the Carston affair is over. I shall see that you have your independence, Perdita, in your 'own place'."

"Thank you, my lord; I believe I can find one for myself."

He smiled ruefully. "Gallant to the last. But you will need some help. We shall see." As she got to the door he said, "Perdita, have you no gift for me? A final kiss—for consolation? I am persuaded that would help more than any brandy."

"I will not kiss you again Lord Ambourne. Not while I am destined to become Piers Carston's wife. Goodnight."

That night Perdita dreamt she was in a corridor from which there was no escape. As she went further along it she found herself moving faster and faster, unable to stop, and she knew that something grotesquely terrifying lay in wait for her at the end. She woke up in fright with tears on her cheeks, and lay shivering for a long while before falling asleep again.

The next day Mrs. Frith arrived. Perdita regarded her with interest, for this lady was to introduce her to London society and eventually lead her to Piers Carston. She was a tall, queenly woman with slender hands and feet. Her hair was almost hidden under a lace cap inside her grey velvet bonnet, but the little that could be seen was an unusual shade of dark red. Her face was dominated by her green, almond-shaped eyes fringed with dark lashes. She was soberly but fashionably dressed in French grey corded silk trimmed with bands of grey velvet ribbon. Her gloves and slippers were of fine kid, and a dark green cashmere shawl was elegantly draped over her arms. She regarded Perdita with a detached but kindly air, and greeted the Countess with cool amiability.

For the next hour Mrs. Frith sat in the salon at Rotherfield House, displaying considerable tact. The Countess had taken it into her head that Perdita should not leave her protection until she was satisfied she would be safe. It said much for Mrs. Frith's powers of persuasion that within a short time the Countess permitted it. No one, least of all the Countess, was unaware that Mrs. Frith had been engaged by the Earl, but as Perdita's friend she was determined to see that Perdita was going to be well looked after, even if her son was not there to see to it himself.

At the end of half an hour the Countess confessed herself satisfied, and Mrs. Frith smiled politely and rose to take her new charge to Dover Street. The moment of parting had arrived. Calling on all her lessons in deportment, and what was left of her self-control, Perdita took a fond but restrained farewell of the Countess. She must not betray by any undue emotion that this was probably the last time she could see her, for the Countess would be returning to Ambourne before Perdita's entry on to the London scene. Somehow she managed it, and she and Mrs. Frith entered the closed carriage the Earl had provided to make the short journey to Dover Street.

The house the Earl had hired was small, but beautifully furnished and decorated. It was in a highly fashionable quarter and was a perfect setting for Perdita's role as a rich heiress. Her mother might well have hired just such a one for Perdita's season if fate and Piers Carston had not intervened. The two ladies admired its airy hall and pretty parlour, its small library and well-proportioned drawing-room. It was already staffed with a butler, who was nearly as imposing as Purkiss, a housekeeper, two footmen and several maids, one of whom was for Perdita.

In the bedroom she found several dresses laid out for her inspection, and more in boxes on the bed. All the rest of a young lady's wardrobe was disposed in the drawers and cupboards round the room. She was gazing in wonder at this lavish display when she was disturbed by Mrs. Frith, who was standing at the open door of the bedroom.

"Miss Taver, if you wish my help in selecting some dresses I shall be happy to advise you. They will then be altered to fit you, since the modiste has worked only from one of your previous dresses."

Perdita could not be other than impressed by Mrs. Frith's low voice and quiet manner. But she was sure that there was more to this woman than that, for, apart from the red hair and green eyes, had she not seen her handle the Countess at her most wilful? With a promise to deal with the dresses the next day, Perdita persuaded Mrs. Frith to come down to the salon. She was determined to discover what lay behind this understated façade. She was embarking on a difficult, even dangerous, game, and wanted no hidden complications.

They met the housekeeper in the hall and Perdita exchanged a few words with her. Mrs. Frith watched for a short while, and then with a smile went into the drawing-room.

Perdita followed a few minutes later and said, "I have ordered some tea—I hope you will take some with me? I could send for chocolate, if you prefer?"

"I usually drink coffee Miss Taver, but tea will do very well. It is more refreshing, perhaps." Perdita was surprised, for coffee was not a customary drink during the day in an ordinary house.

"I lived for some time in Eastern Europe, where they drink vast quantities of coffee. I'm afraid I developed the habit—I am Hungarian by birth, Miss Taver."

"Your English is excellent. I would never have suspected it." The housekeeper appeared at that moment with the tea, and the two ladies talked generalities until she had once again left the room, shutting the door behind her. Perdita spent some time serving the tea, for she was trying to gather her thoughts. She finally decided to be frank.

"You will forgive me if I speak plainly, Mrs. Frith. I am not sure what Lord Ambourne has told you of me, but you have certainly observed that I am not a nervous seventeen-year-old just out of the schoolroom. I defer to Lord Ambourne's insistence that I have a chaperon because I myself see the need for one here in London."

Mrs. Frith smiled at this forthright speech and replied, "Am I to understand, Miss Taver, that you are happy if I confine my chaperon's duties to providing a socially acceptable background? While I am very willing for this to be the case, I ought perhaps to tell you that Lord Ambourne has given me some details of your past and was of the opinion that I could be of help to you—and himself."

"Lord Ambourne gave you details of my past . . . ?" asked Perdita in astonishment.

Mrs. Frith put her cup down and said with a smile, "He knows he can have complete trust in my discretion. We have been friends for several years." When she saw Perdita stiffen, she said carefully, "Lord Ambourne and my husband were close friends and colleagues, Miss Taver. They acted as observers in a diplomatic mission to Vienna in 1814. It was not all simple diplomacy, I assure you, nor even simple observation! The Napoleonic Empire was being disbanded, and it was es-

sential that England was in a position to protect her own trad-
ing interests. The three of us—Lord Ambourne, my husband
and I—worked very well together to keep Lord Castlereagh informed. In times of stress and even danger, Miss Taver, one
grows very close to one's companions—and, above all, one
learns to trust them. That is why Lord Ambourne knows he can
trust me.''

This matter-of-fact statement intrigued Perdita beyond
measure. What sort of woman was this who looked and spoke
like a conventionally fashionable society lady, but who was
Hungarian and mentioned so casually that she had taken part
in dangerous activities? But she must find out how much the
Earl had told her.

As if in answer to the question, Mrs. Frith went on, ''I think
he has told me everything he knows, including his plans for
Piers Carston. I met that gentleman last season. I cannot say I
admire him, for, apart from what I have heard of him from
Lord Ambourne, I have had one or two indications from other
sources of his character. I believe him to be an unprincipled
villain.'' With that startling statement she picked up her cup, sat
back and calmly sipped her tea.

''H-how...how do you propose to help me?'' asked Perdita, somewhat daunted by this quiet Amazon.

''First and most obviously I shall introduce you to society. I
have the entré to most circles—there should be no difficulty
there. Then I shall see that Mr. Carston learns that there is a
rich and charming heiress at large in London. I think it would
be better, Miss Taver, if you could manage to appear rather
naïve—as much like a nervous seventeen-year-old as you can
manage.'' She smiled, and Perdita was forced to respond to her
charm.

She said ruefully, ''Lord Ambourne did not doubt my power
of dissimulation for an instant.''

''Nor your intelligence, from what he has said,'' was Mrs.
Frith's surprising response.

Though Perdita's curiosity about this Hungarian lady was
still unsatisfied, she found it impossible to question her further. There was a certain air of detachment, which was difficult to overcome. Mrs. Frith had drawn up a list of the sights
which might interest a young lady on her first visit to London,
together with directions and where to apply. She had also made
appointments for the modiste, the milliner and coiffeur to come

to the house. She had arranged invitations for Perdita to visit
some of the great ladies of London society...

Perdita grew increasingly impressed with Mrs. Frith's abilities, but did not know whether they pleased or frightened her
more. A scheme in which this woman was engaged would be
almost certain of success. But would Mrs. Frith see through
Perdita's own plans? There was much to be done, including at
least one visit of which the Earl was to remain in ignorance. She
would have to exercise extreme caution with Mrs. Frith.

CHAPTER FIFTEEN

WITH ALL THE ACTIVITIES planned by Mrs. Frith, Perdita had little opportunity during the next day or two to find out more about her chaperon or to pursue her own interests. She was forced to exercise a great deal of self-discipline to hide her impatience to be free, for Mrs. Frith was sure to be curious, even suspicious, of such a desire. She tried, therefore, to enjoy the sights and sounds of a London that was still celebrating the end of the Napoleonic wars and the resulting growth in trade with new buildings, new entertainments and a lavish display of goods of all kinds.

They visited the Pantheon and the shops in Oxford Street, and they went one day to the City, to the older, more traditional shops on Ludgate Hill. After examining the splendid mercer's shops there, Perdita insisted on visiting some of the bookshops. Mrs. Frith could not reasonably deny her, though she did point out that, since Perdita's goal was to entrap Piers Carston, pretty dresses and shoes might be of use, but books certainly would not!

At no point did Perdita have any money. The Earl must have been explicit about this, for it would otherwise have been quite normal for Mrs. Frith to provide her with a little pocket-money. Perdita bided her time. Somehow or other she would find the means of seeing the lawyers at Lincoln's Inn.

They had just returned from one of their shopping expeditions, and were having tea and coffee in the salon, when one of the footmen announced that Perdita had a visitor, who was waiting for her in the parlour downstairs.

"Who is it?" asked Mrs. Frith swiftly. "The Countess of Ambourne, ma'am," replied the footman.

Perdita leapt up before Mrs. Frith could say any more and said, "Don't stand there, Forrest! Show Lady Ambourne up here immediately."

He turned to go, but was swept aside by the tiny figure of the
Countess. She strode in imperiously, hesitated, then turned to
look at the footman with a stony face. Perdita had never seen
her look so like the great lady she was. Perdita dismissed the
footman, and then turned to the Countess and said urgently,
"Ma'am, Lord Ambourne said you were not to visit m—" But
she was not allowed to finish.

"I have something I wish to ask you, Perdita. I would prefer us to be alone, if Mrs. Frith will permit?"

She stood while Mrs. Frith rose, looked quizzically at Perdita, then said, "If you have no objection, Miss Taver, I will
return the sample silks to the modiste. It will only take me half
an hour, and Lady Ambourne will be here to keep you company. You will be here when I return, Lady Ambourne? If not,
I will take my leave of you now." She went out, not without a
questioning look at the Countess, who stiffly bade her good
afternoon.

Perdita invited the Countess to sit, but she refused impatiently and said, "Perdita, I cannot believe what my son has
just told me, and I am here to hear you deny it. He is surely not
going to marry you off to Carston? Tell me it isn't so!"

Perdita's face grew scarlet then white. She stammered that
she could not deny it. The Countess had been told the truth.

"But surely you haven't agreed?" When Perdita stood in silence she cried, "I told Edward he was mad, Perdita! That,
even if he had forgotten every decency, you would never agree
to such a shameful thing..." She walked away from Perdita as
if she could not bear to be near her, then turned on her. "What
sort of monsters are you? I thought I knew you both, but I
realise now that you are strangers to me. Up till this minute,
Perdita, I would have sworn there was not a man in the world
who had more integrity than Edward. And not a woman for
whom I had more regard. I am sadly disappointed in both of
you. My son to do this! My son..." Her voice trembled as she
said these last words.

"Ma'am, you do not understand—"

"I understand very well, Perdita. I understand that Edward, who I would swear loves you, will see you married to
Piers Carston, whom he hates. And that you, who love my son,
will marry this...this...*salaud*, will live with him...I cannot speak of it." She turned away again, then cried, "But why
are you doing this? It is insulting to suggest you are being of-

fered money for this betrayal. But what else could have persuaded you to agree to such an infamous scheme?'' When Perdita hesitated she said, ''Oh, do not bother to tell me. Nothing could have forced you against your will, not even my son. You make a fine pair!''

There was a slight pause. Perdita was in an agony of indecision, but, before she could say anything, the Countess continued, ''I loved you as a daughter, Perdita. I was foolishly taken in by your charming ways and your lovely face.'' She took a deep breath and said, ''Now I never want to see you again. As for my son...it will be a long time before I will forgive him for his shameful plans. It is the worst thing yet that Piers Carston has done to our family.'' A sob escaped her.

Perdita cried, ''He had his reasons, ma'am. It isn't as you think, I swear it!'' Then when the Countess started to the door she made up her mind and said, quickly, ''Ma'am, I beg of you, please wait here while I ensure we are not overheard. I know I can ease your mind on one point at least, perhaps more. Will you wait?''

The Countess stopped and turned round. What she saw in Perdita's face seemed to convince her that she was being sincere, and she nodded. Perdita hurriedly checked that the servants were all out of earshot and returned to the salon, where she found the Countess standing at the window.

''Ma'am, what I am going to tell you is in part known to your son, but only in part. I would like your assurance that you will not reveal to him anything he does not already know. Indeed, I think it would be better if you did not tell him that you had seen me at all ... Will you promise?''

''I will not promise anything until I know what it is, Perdita,'' said the Countess coldly. ''And Mrs. Frith is almost certain to tell him I have called. However, at the moment my son and I are not in communication. I have already informed him I am returning to Ambourne tomorrow, and I do not expect I shall see him again before I go. What is it that you have to say?''

''Will you sit, ma'am? It is a long story.'' The Countess reluctantly sat down and Perdita began hesitantly, ''First, your son has good reason to believe that I would not regard marrying Piers Carston as abhorrent. I told you once that I had associated with thieves and murderers, and I do not think you really believed me. Lord Ambourne knows it to be true. For

over two years I lived on a pirate ship in the Mediterranean.''
She went on to describe in detail the circumstances in which the
Earl had discovered her. ''You know of his determination to
ruin Piers Carston, ma'am. Believing me to be worthless, he
bought me to be a tool, no more, to achieve that end. To his
mind, my marriage and subsequent separation from his enemy
was of benefit to me, for I would then have the means to escape from a life of cruelty and crime and...and...be able to
live in comparative affluence. I beg you, do not blame your son
for this. He may have developed some feeling for me, but he is
determined to conquer it, for how could the Earl of Ambourne be associated with a pirate's...a pirate's whore? Forgive me if I have offended you, but I must speak plainly. It is
important that you do not think so badly of your son.''

She waited, but at first the Countess was deep in thought.
Finally she said, ''I still do not approve of his intentions, but I
can understand them, at least. But what of you? I do not understand why you should have agreed, for, whatever the circumstances in which Edward found you, Perdita, I refuse to
believe you would not in fact find marriage to Carston repug-
nant.''

''Now we come to the point at which I must trust you,
ma'am, not to tell Lord Ambourne. Mrs. Frith, who is his associate in this matter, is out of the house, so she will not know
anything. Can I trust you?''

The Countess considered Perdita's anxious face and said, ''If
I can see my way of keeping Edward in ignorance I will, Perdita. Continue.''

Taking her courage in both hands, Perdita told the Countess the unhappy story of her family's involvement with the
Carstons. She held nothing back, even giving her real name and
the place of her birth.

The Countess was deeply shocked. ''The man is a monster!
Indeed, I think Eliane was lucky to escape as she did.''

''Do you understand now, ma'am, why I have agreed to help
your son? I think if I had insisted he would have dropped this
dreadful idea. Do not blame him too much, I pray.''

''Well, I do still blame him, Perdita, for his willingness to
expose the woman he loves to that kind of danger. It does not
reflect well on him. But how will you go on? You will surely not
pretend to marry Carston?''

"Oh, no, ma'am. All I have to do is reappear. If I could only get to our lawyers I could soon ruin Mr. Piers Carston, I assure you. The difficulty is that I do not wish to take Mrs. Frith into my confidence, for I believe her loyalty will lie with Lord Ambourne. And I have no money to go there myself—apart from the difficulty of escaping her vigilance."

"I am sure I can remedy that, at least. But, Perdita, why do you not wish my son to know what you have told me? Surely it would be much simpler if he knew?"

Perdita hung her head, then looked up defiantly. "I do not wish to make it simpler for him, ma'am. Though he is not the 'monster' you thought him, it is true that he is prepared to see me married to someone he hates in order to further his own plans. I know he could never marry me himself, but it has caused me some pain that he can contemplate such a thing. He does not deserve to have his path made smooth sooner than necessary."

The Countess regarded Perdita ruefully. "Oh, what a match that would be—you and Edward! Can it really not be so?"

"It is kind of you even to think of it, ma'am, but do not forget yours is an old and proud family. And I too have my pride. No, it cannot be."

The Countess thought for a minute.

"In one thing at least I can help you, Perdita. I can provide you with some money—enough and to spare for a hackney to Lincoln's Inn. Has my son really not given you any?"

"He does not trust me, ma'am," said Perdita sadly. "Not in London."

The Countess pursed her lips, but said nothing, while she considered. Finally she said, "We must make haste, Perdita. It cannot be long before Mrs. Frith returns, and we have to decide what you can do. Does Mrs. Frith always accompany you when you go out?"

Perdita nodded. "Always. But she usually rests in her room in the afternoon."

"Then you must slip out of the house unobserved tomorrow afternoon and take a hackney carriage from Berkeley Square. I can arrange to have one waiting for you if you tell me when you wish to go. And I'll make sure the driver is trustworthy."

The Countess was becoming quite her usual self in the interest of helping Perdita to outwit Mrs. Frith. By the time that lady returned they had arranged it all and were sitting amicably chatting in the salon. The Countess did not stay much longer, but thanked Mrs Frith for giving her this time alone with her son's ward. She had wanted, she said, to have one last cosy chat with Perdita before returning to Ambourne. Mrs. Frith was too well bred to express surprise or disbelief. She smiled slightly and said she hoped to see the Countess again—when she returned to London and had another cosy chat with Perdita.

ALL WENT AS THEY HAD planned. The following day Perdita slipped out of the house, her money wrapped in a handkerchief in the deep pockets of her cloak, and ran round to Berkeley Square. The Countess had not failed her, for as soon as he saw her a middle-aged, red-cheeked hackney driver came up and handed her into his cab. He already knew where he was taking her, and gave her a running commentary on London life as they bowled up Oxford Street with its numerous shops, through the dirt and misery of St. Giles, and into High Holborn. From here they turned into Chancery Lane and thence into Lincoln's Inn. Asking her driver to wait, Perdita hurried into the building.

When she entered the poky little ante-room the elderly clerk standing at a tall desk came over to ask rather testily what she wanted. But when he saw her face he clutched the side of the desk and said, "It can't be! Not after all this time. I don't believe my eyes! Who are you?"

"I'm Felicia Taverton, Burgess. Have you forgotten me?"

"Miss Felicia? Oh, Miss Felicia! Forgive me, what am I thinking of? Well, my goodness, I can't believe it . . . Miss Felicia, after all this time . . ."

He would have continued in this vein, but Perdita knew her time was limited. She asked, "Would you take my name in to Mr. Rambridge, Burgess? I should like to consult him on a matter of some urgency." Still muttering, the old man went into the inner room. Perdita heard more exclamations, and a white-haired gentleman came out in a most undignified rush.

"Miss Felicia! Miss Felicia Taverton! This is happy news indeed. Come in, come in. Burgess, fetch some wine. We must drink to this. But my dear young lady, where did you disappear to? What happened? We searched the country for you."

Perdita was made to sit down with a glass of wine, and after more exclamations and questions, which she was not given time to answer, she finally managed to give him a short account of her adventures.

The lawyer already knew that Piers Carston was a villain, but was very shocked at his unbelievably callous treatment of Perdita. He kept interrupting to ask her to repeat what she had said, and shook his head each time in amazement and distress. When she came to the end, he said gravely, "And what do you wish me to do now? Of course, we can lay this information with the authorities. There can be little doubt that your evidence would incriminate him, though if he denied it it might be difficult for you... I suppose we might show what he had done with the estate..."

"I think I have a better scheme, Mr. Rambridge. But first tell me about my mother."

His face grew sad. "She died shortly after you disappeared..." Then he burst out, "I knew that young villain was lying, but your mother would have none of it. He couldn't say he had seen you die, though, so, in spite of what he implied, she was convinced you would return. Poor lady, she died believing in that ruffian. You know she left him to look after the estate until you came back? We could do nothing. Oh, we stopped him selling any of the land, but he has milked it dry, Miss Felicia. The tenants and workers are in a poor way; I don't know what you can do. There will be a great deal to repair and not many resources to do it..."

"After I have dealt with Piers Carston here in London," said Perdita, "I shall return to Somerset and do what I can. Meanwhile I want you to help me here." She went on to instruct Mr. Rambridge. He was very doubtful of the wisdom of her actions, but was forced to agree that taking Piers Carston to a court of law would be an uncertain business.

"As we all know," he said at last, "Carston is a plausible and attractive-looking rogue. He just might convince a jury you were lying, Miss Felicia. Perhaps you are right, after all. He might, if surprised, convict himself. Well, I will do as you say. Just send me word when you are ready." He renewed his expression of joy at seeing her alive and well and looking, "as pretty as a picture, Miss Felicia, if you will permit an old man to say so. Whatever you have suffered, it has not done your looks any damage."

He led her out to the hackney carriage and handed her in,
telling the driver to take great care of her. She saw him standing at the gate until the carriage turned into Holborn.

Perdita asked the driver to put her down at Green Park, and
when she tried to pay him he told her that her ladyship had already done so. She established that he would be prepared to
take a message to Mr. Rambridge when called on. Then she
went into the park. Thanks to the Countess's forethought, she
now had a slender store of money to help her in any emer-
gency. For a short while she watched the nursemaids and their
charges, then went back to Dover Street. This enabled her to tell
Mrs. Frith without a blush that she had taken the air in the
park. That lady gave her a sharp look, but merely said mildly
that she was surprised Perdita had not felt cold, and went on to
tell her that her dresses had been delivered.

Perdita was glad of the excuse to escape upstairs to her room,
and spent the time until dinner trying on her new wardrobe.
Very soon now she would be launched. The first ball of the
season was in two days' time at Glasham House. According to
Mrs. Frith, Piers Carston was unlikely to be there. But at least
it would start London talking about the new heiress.

IN ALL THIS TIME she had not seen the Earl, but he came on the
night of the ball. When she entered the salon after dressing he
was waiting for her, looking pale but very handsome in the dark
blue tailcoat and white breeches. A diamond gleamed in his
starched cravat... Her eyes closed as she suddenly remembered the evening at Belleroi after he had saved her when the
branch fell. Madame d'Espery had been there too, and he had
worn a diamond then. She remembered how it had sparkled
throughout dinner. Then afterwards he had kissed her...

She came to with a start as his cool, well-bred voice said,
"Are you quite well, Perdita? You look a little pale, though, as
always, ravishingly lovely." The indifferent tone in which he
uttered the extravagant compliment was like a slap in the face.

She rallied and said with deliberate malice, "You are equally
pale, Lord Ambourne. I hope nothing has made you unhappy.
Your mother is well, I hope?"

His indifferent air was lost as he said, "You know very well
what has happened, Perdita, so don't sharpen your claws on
me! My mother probably told you all—if she kept her temper

with you long enough, that is. I gathered from her somewhat intemperate comments that you had an equal share of the blame in her eyes. Was the interview with her very bad?''

"Not at all, Lord Ambourne," said Perdita airily. "Your mother now knows me for what I am, and it is better so." He looked surprised, but did not comment. Instead he produced a thin box and passed it to her.

"This may be a bizarre come-out, but it is one, nevertheless. I wish you to wear these tonight, Perdita." She could not reply, for her throat was choked and her eyes full of tears. He had given her a long rope of perfectly matched pearls with a sapphire clasp. Its velvet-lined box, with the name of one of London's foremost jewellers on it, was exactly like the one her father had given her on her fifteenth birthday just before he'd died. The pearls then had been equally well matched, but that necklace had been a small one, suitable for a young girl. She wondered fleetingly what had happened to it . . .

"Perdita?" When she looked up he said roughly, "You're crying. Why on earth should you cry over this? You need not wear them if you do not wish to. Do not, for heaven's sake, give yourself a red nose and blotched eyes for a trumpery necklace. Was my mother very hard on you, Perdita?''

"No," she replied truthfully. "The Countess was very kind, but she went away quite soon."

"She has gone to Ambourne. I do not remember seeing her quite so angry before. Certainly not with me . . .''

For a moment he looked so unhappy that she longed to go and comfort him. But then she hardened her heart. His mother's anger might have distressed him, but it had not caused him to change his mind. He recovered his indifferent air in an instant, and asked if she was intending to wear the necklace. She sensed that her answer was important to him and did not have the heart to disappoint him.

"Thank you, Lord Ambourne. I will wear it with pleasure."

As he fastened it round her neck she felt his fingers tremble slightly, and then his hands rested on her shoulders. Their grip tightened as he said, "Perdita . . ." But when she turned round to him again his face was impassive. Only his eyes gave him away. "It is nothing."

Mrs. Frith came in at that point, looking elegant in brown silk, lace and emeralds.

"Ah, Edward, how nice to see you. Are you not pleased with your ward?"

She took Perdita by the hand and twirled her round like a doll. The dress to Perdita's mind was a trifle overdone, with its white lace robe over a pink satin slip, its pearl embroideries and knots of satin ribbons. A half-garland of lace and small pink roses was tucked into her back hair, and she was wearing white corded silk shoes and white kid gloves.

The Earl looked at her through his glass and finally said, "Perfect, my dear. Just the effect we want—lavish, rich and naïve. Now, if Perdita can play her part, we shall have Carston sniffing at her heels in no time."

With a sort of gallows humour Perdita decided to enjoy this last act in her relationship with the Earl. She ignored his last remark and said gaily, "Have you seen my pearls, Mrs. Frith? Are they not splendid? I vow I have never seen prettier beads in my whole life!"

Mrs. Frith examined the pearls with indulgence at first, and then with real surprise. She raised one eyebrow at the Earl—who, to Perdita's great pleasure, was looking outraged—and murmured, "Worth a king's ransom—or at least a prince's! I am surprised you consider it necessary to make the props so genuine, my friend. They are extremely pretty 'beads', Miss Taver. You must look after them, for they will give you a rich old age!" Then she looked at the Earl and Perdita with amused speculation in her green eyes.

IT WAS OBVIOUS from the first moment that the Duchess of Stockhampton's ball would achieve everything they had hoped for. Mrs. Frith's information was sound—Piers Carston did not appear. But the rest of the polite world was there, and Perdita's beauty, Perdita's naïve charm, and above all, Perdita's apparent wealth were clearly about to form the topic of conversation in most of the clubs and houses that Piers Carston would frequent. No one doubted her credentials, though no one could remember actually hearing of the Taver fortune before. A few hints that the family had connections with the East India Company...that the French wars had kept them abroad...soon put an end to any speculation. After all, who was going to question the origins of a lady sponsored by Mrs.

Frith who, as everyone knew, was related to the Esterhazys and was a princess in her own right?

Perdita was soon pronounced to be a pretty, well-behaved girl who did not put herself forward in spite of her vast fortune. It was noticed by the observant that, though the Earl of Ambourne meticulously avoided any hint of gossip, never dancing with Miss Taver more than twice in one evening and never paying her undue attention, he seemed to be aware of her all the time. And any unfortunate young man who was unduly pressing in his attentions often found himself edged out of her presence by a grim-faced Earl. Miss Taver, for her part, seemed to treat her suitors with charming deference. They were all enchanted with her childlike innocence.

CHAPTER SIXTEEN

WORD FINALLY CAME that Piers Carston had reappeared on the London scene. Mrs. Frith's informant was certain that he would attend the ball to be given the following Tuesday at Lady Francombe's Palladian mansion in Berkeley Square. Now that the climax of her London season was so near, Perdita suddenly felt nervous. The feeling behind her conversation with Mrs. Frith when they heard this news was therefore unfeigned, though she would have pretended if necessary.

"I have been considering my initial meeting with Piers Carston, Mrs. Frith, and have some thoughts on the subject that might interest you," she began as they were sitting one afternoon in the drawing-room. Mrs. Frith looked up from her work and smiled encouragingly. "My suitors have grown to such numbers—drawn, no doubt, by the growing size of my reported fortune—that it might prove difficult for Mr. Carston to approach me as easily as he would like. I am seldom free of a crowd of admirers when I am in public."

"You think he will be frightened away by the size of your entourage? But surely the size of your fortune will outweigh that?" said Mrs. Frith cynically.

"I am sure it will. But it will take him time, and I would be happier if the business was settled as soon as possible. I do not find it easy to sustain this deception . . ." Her chaperon raised one eyebrow in elegant disbelief. Perdita said earnestly, "I assure you, I do not, ma'am. I am constantly in dread of being found out."

"I am sorry you find it such a strain, Miss Taver. I had thought you were enjoying it. So you would like to end the affair quickly? That would need some special thought, I agree. Let me think . . ."

Perdita sat there, crossing her fingers and praying for the right opportunity. She could hardly believe her good fortune when it came.

"How could Mr. Carston meet you away from your followers?" said Mrs. Frith slowly. "He would certainly be suspicious if you arranged a meeting alone with him too soon after making his acquaintance."

"Oh, I could not do that, ma'am. Nor would I wish to see him without your presence. If only there was someone who could offer to arrange such a meeting—perhaps even for a suitable sum? Is there anyone in your acquaintance who would act as a go-between?

"There might perhaps be just the person..." said Mrs. Frith. "I must speak to Lord Ambourne."

The result of Mrs. Frith's consultation with the Earl was everything Perdita had hoped for. Mrs. Frith herself would act the part of mediator, for it was not thought politic to introduce any other party to the scheme. Now that Piers Carston was actually in town they must practise extreme caution. Perdita joined in the planning of the deception with enthusiasm. If the Earl had been present he would surely have suspected her motives, but he was taking care to stay away from the house. Mrs. Frith, having no reason to doubt the truth of Perdita's anxiety, took her helpful suggestions at face value, and it was finally settled that Mrs. Frith would allow herself to be suborned by Carston into introducing him to Perdita in a private room at Lady Francombe's ball.

"Can you do that, ma'am?" asked Perdita.

"Oh, there will be no difficulty in persuading Mr. Carston that I can be bribed," said Mrs. Frith, "for he judges everyone by his own corrupt standards. Nor need you fear that he will suspect I put the idea into his head. Allow me some subtlety, Miss Taver." Once again Perdita reminded herself that Mrs. Frith was a dangerous woman. But she must continue.

"Do you know of a suitable room, ma'am? How will I know where it is?"

"After you enter Lady Francombe's house there is a great staircase in front of you, which rises up the centre of the hall. To the left of the staircase on the ground floor is an ante-room, followed by the library. This would seem to be an admirable place for you to meet. A small waiting-room opens out of the library on the far side, where Lord Ambourne can, if he wishes, conceal himself.''

Perdita felt the Earl would like to witness this first meeting to see that his 'tool' was prepared to carry out his wishes. Well, he would see more than he bargained for!

"I should like that," she said nervously, "for I do not know how this Piers Carston will treat me. You have said he is a villain, have you not?" She thought she might have overdone it, but Mrs. Frith said gravely that he was indeed.

The next days passed swiftly. Perdita managed to send her message to Mr. Rambridge, and spent the rest of the time alternately worrying about her plans and her appearance. Woman-like, she wanted the Earl to see her at her best on this last evening, and she had saved her prettiest dress for the occasion. It was of white silk gauze woven with a thread of silver, and was worn over a white satin slip. Little ornament was needed for the material itself glinted and shone as she moved, but thin bands of pale blue silk caught the folds of the gauze round the bottom of the skirt, and were tucked round the white satin bodice at the waist. It was a triumph of lovely simplicity, and had cost more than any two of her other dresses together. With it she would wear her rope of pearls, wound twice round her neck, with the sapphire clasp at the front.

In her room on the night of the ball, while the maid arranged her hair and reverently put the dress on her, Perdita was as nervous as any débutante. It would not be too much to say that tonight would determine the rest of her life. Her heart was thumping as she came down to the salon, where Mrs. Frith waited. She hoped everything was done. If only Mr. Rambridge had done his part—and Piers Carston would do his—she would answer for the rest!

Mrs. Frith was standing in front of the large mirror to the side of the fireplace. She looked superb in dark green silk and diamonds, but Perdita sensed a most unusual excitement in her. Her green eyes were glowing like a cat's and her whole air was slightly feverish. She complimented Perdita on her appearance, and they were about to depart when the Earl was announced.

"Are you mad?" was Mrs. Frith's greeting. "What if Carston should observe you coming into this house?"

"He will not," said the Earl briefly. "I would like to speak to Perdita alone, Ludmila." Mrs. Frith looked from one to the other and then shrugged her shoulders.

"I'll wait downstairs, Miss Taver," was all she said before she went out.

As soon as the door had closed the Earl said abruptly, "Perdita, I have to speak to you before you meet Carston tonight. My mother was right. It is a vile thing I have asked you to do—you must not marry Carston. After tonight you are free to do as you please. If you wish to leave London and live elsewhere in England, or France, or even Africa, I will arrange for you to do so."

"But what of your wish to punish Carston? Have you forgotten what he did to Eliane?" asked Perdita in astonishment.

"No, I have not forgotten," was the terse reply.

"Then why do you wish to abandon your scheme? Is it because of your mother's anger?" Her eyes searched his face.

"No," he said. "She has merely crystallised my own feelings in the matter."

"Then why—?"

"Is it not enough that you no longer need to do something you have found so repellent?" he said harshly.

"No, it is not enough, Lord Ambourne. It is not nearly enough. After weeks of preparation you arrive here to tell me to abandon all our plans—"

"They are my plans, Perdita. Mine alone."

"Oh, I am fully aware that you have always regarded me as little more than your tool," cried Perdita angrily. "You have made that very clear from the first—"

"It isn't so, Perdita. I have come to have regard and respect for you—"

"Regard and respect! You do me too much honour, Lord Ambourne! What would a pirate's drab do with your 'regard and respect'?" Perdita was growing angrier by the minute. The unhappiness of the last weeks at Belleroi and the tension that had built up inside her in London culminated in a burst of rage towards this man. His plans had caused her so much heartache and anxiety, and now he wished to throw them all out of the window—for a caprice, as far as she could determine. "Are you afraid that your aristocratic friends will condemn you for associating with people like Piers Carston and me? A thief and

seducer of young girls, and a strumpet from the Mediterranean? Is that it?''

"Be silent, Perdita. I—''

"I will not be silent! I am not an inanimate object to be used
or rejected at your whim. And unless you can give me a better
reason than your 'regard and respect' I will tell the whole of
London what sort of girl you have foisted on all the ambitious
mamas and their fortune-seeking sons!''

"Be quiet, you little termagant!'' He snatched her to him and
kissed her savagely. As she struggled and kicked he gave a short
laugh and kissed her again, holding her so closely that she was
lifted off her feet. "There's your reason! Mad though it is, I
cannot tolerate seeing you married to Carston—or any other
man!''

Shock held her still for a moment. Then she released herself
from his hold, but still held on to his sleeve—she could not have
stood otherwise.

Seeing how dazed she was, he led her gently to a chair and sat
her down. Then he walked to the fire and gazed moodily into
the flames. Still not facing her, he said, "I admit that when I set
out on this enterprise I thought it would be simple. I would trap
Carston with his own ambition and greed. You were merely the
means by which I could achieve this. You seemed perfect for the
purpose—lovely, abandoned and, as I thought then, de-
praved. But Sheikh Ibrahim warned me not to attempt to use
you, and he was right. Believe me, Perdita, I have been well
punished for ignoring his words. Can you forgive me?''

Perdita's thoughts were racing. There was so little time. She
could not now abandon all her own carefully laid plans. And
yet she must respond to the Earl's words. Should she tell him?
She must! But at that moment Mrs. Frith came into the room,
and the opportunity was lost.

"Edward, I must interrupt you. Miss Taver will arrive un-
pardonably late at Lady Francombe's. It is too bad of you, after all our work. Come, Perdita, you must tidy yourself up a
little before you are seen in public.''

Perdita looked at the Earl and said softly, "I will meet Carston tonight. We shall talk about my future after that. You will
be there?'' He nodded. She smiled at him. "Then I will not be
in any danger.''

He started towards her but Mrs. Frith said sharply, "Perdita!" and with an apologetic glance at the Earl she followed Mrs. Frith upstairs to her room.

While Lucy fussed around her she stood lost in a dream. Her chaperon contemplated her for a moment, then said, not unsympathetically, "Pull yourself together, Perdita. You have much to do tonight. I cannot imagine why Lord Ambourne could not have postponed the affecting talk he has obviously had with you till another time. But men are often incomprehensible creatures. They do not keep their minds on the task in hand. Women are much more practical. Come, my dear."

She took Perdita down to the waiting carriage, and they were soon in Berkeley Square. When they entered the house Mrs. Frith pointed out the library, and as they gave their cloaks to the footman Perdita managed to remain unobserved as she handed him a note and some money. At the top of the stairs she was introduced to their hostess, who was most gracious and chatted to her for some minutes while the line of guests built up behind her. Then they went into the ballroom. It was half-past nine.

Perdita was surrounded almost immediately by her crowd of admirers, and Lady Francombe's affability was explained when later a callow youth came up to her and said, "Your servant, Miss Taver. I am Gervaise Francombe. My mother has told me so much about you..."

THOUGH PERDITA DANCED every dance, the minutes till eleven o'clock dragged and it was a relief when Mrs. Frith came to her and it was time to go downstairs. With a pretty smile of apology to her waiting court, Perdita left the ballroom with her chaperon. She had not seen the Earl since arriving at Lady Francombe's, but trusted he was in his place in the writing-room. As she passed the footman he gave her a small nod. Good! Mr. Rambridge had arrived. She asked Mrs. Frith to wait for one minute outside the door, and then, forcing herself to look calm, walked into the library...

The man at the far end of the room had been examining himself in the mirror over the fireplace, and when he turned Perdita saw that time had started to take its toll of Piers's handsome face. His features had coarsened, the guinea-gold hair was fading, and his blue eyes were beginning to look bloodshot. A glass of brandy was in his hand and his face was flushed.

When he saw her the carefully practised smile vanished and his jaw dropped.

"Felicia!" he exclaimed in horror. "No, it can't be! How did you get here? You're dead. Felicia's dead!"

"Legrand brought me here, Piers," said Perdita softly.

"You're lying! Legrand is dead! He was drowned last year— and so were you!"

"Oh, no, Piers, I wasn't. As you see, I am here. And Legrand asked me to give you a present. Look!" He stared at the pearl held out to him in a slender hand. The soft voice continued, "I was worth more than the half-pearl he paid for me, Piers. And I've come back to give you this."

He backed away from her and said loudly, "I don't want it! Take it away! What sort of game is this? Legrand said he'd make sure you never came back..."

"What did you tell my mother, Piers? That you'd sold me to a pirate for half the price of a pearl? That you'd left me to be beaten and starved? That you'd given me into the hands of a twisted maniac? You surely didn't tell my mother that as she lay dying, did you?"

The tremendous shock that Carston had undergone had caused him to lose all sense of self-preservation. If he had kept a cool head he might have bluffed his way out of the trap Perdita had laid. But the shock, and the brandy he had drunk, made him reckless.

"Don't be so stupid!" he said with a laugh. "Of course I didn't! I was her golden boy! I had a damned sight better story than that, and she swallowed the lot—the bloodstained scarf, how bravely I fought... after all, I had been injured, hadn't I? You threw me out of the chaise, remember? No, I could wind her round my little finger—except that the stupid bitch wouldn't believe you were dead!"

"So I heard. So you couldn't sell the estate after all—Taverton, with all its rich lands and farms?"

"No!" he said resentfully. "And after my father died I found it damned hard to keep myself going with it, I can tell you. Those meddlesome fools of lawyers wouldn't let me sell off any of the land. I've had a rough time of it this last year."

"Poor Piers," said Perdita sarcastically.

He took another drink of the brandy, gave her a calculating look, and carefully put down his glass. Then with conscious charm and an air of frankness he walked towards her, saying, "Felicia, I know I behaved badly, and I'm sorry... Legrand frightened me and I acted in panic..."

"What about the pearl, Piers? Was I really worth so little?"

For a moment he stopped and thought. "You made me angry," he said finally. "You should have married me when I asked you."

"My mother trusted you to take me to safety, not to try to force me to marry you!" Perdita cried.

"Yes, I know that," Piers said impatiently. Then he remembered his role and spoke charmingly again. "Felicia, can't we forget all this? Remember the good times we had at Taverton? Can't we go back to what we were? Even now, after all that you've been, I'm prepared to marry you. Come on, can't we kiss and be friends?" He was close to her now, and she could smell the brandy on his breath. He grabbed her roughly and she screamed.

In a flash three people came into the room. The Earl went straight for Carston, knocked him to the ground and stood over him menacingly, his face white with rage. Mr. Rambridge hurried from the ante-room, closely followed by Mrs. Frith, who took Perdita's hand and led her to the side. Carston groaned and tried to get up. The Earl pushed him back.

"You'll stay there, Carston, if you're wise. I'd be delighted to knock you down again!" he said. Carston lay back.

"I think you should let him go," said Perdita. "You can't keep him there all night, and he can't do any more damage."

"Let him go?" exclaimed Mr. Rambridge. "Let him go? My dear young lady, he should be handed over instantly!"

"Have you given the envelope to the magistrates? To be opened tomorrow?" Perdita asked.

"Yes, I have. I took it myself today. However—" But Perdita did not let him finish.

"Then tomorrow they will have a full list of his crimes, including the betrayal of shipping information—"

"But Miss Taverton, I still think he should be handed over tonight," protested Mr. Rambridge.

"I am giving him twelve hours' grace to enable him to leave the country. After that he will be a wanted man, but twelve hours he will have," said Perdita obstinately. "Lord Am-

bourne, let him get up, if you please.'' Reluctantly the Earl,
who looked slightly dazed, allowed Carston to get to his feet.
They watched in silence as Carston, without another look at
any of them, went out.

"Perdita," said the Earl, "my love…" And he took her into
his arms and kissed her passionately.

Mr. Rambridge gave a small cough, and when Perdita finally looked at him he said, "I cannot agree with your actions, Miss Felicia, but your clemency does you credit. There
is much to discuss, and I'm afraid there will be many papers
dealing with the estate to sign. Shall I see you tomorrow in
Lincoln's Inn?"

Perdita hesitated, but refused to look at the Earl. Then she
said she would be there at eleven. Mr. Rambridge, too polite to
do more than glance curiously at the tall figure standing silently by his client, turned to go. He was immediately knocked
aside by a frantic figure in a greatcoat. It was Piers Carston.

"You lied!" he shouted wildly. "You said you'd give me till
tomorrow, but you lied! There are men out there—Runners!
You lying devils! You did this, Ambourne!" He suddenly
pulled a pistol out of the pocket of his greatcoat and pointed it
at the Earl.

"No, Piers, no!" screamed Perdita and threw herself at him.
There was a loud report, and Perdita staggered.

As she twisted round and fell she heard the Earl cry out,
"Oh, God! Perdita!" But then his voice died and blackness
overcame her…

WHEN SHE CAME TO she was lying on the couch and the Earl
was bending over her. Mrs. Frith was in the background, and
Mr. Rambridge was standing at the foot of her couch, looking
very anxious.

"Thank God!" said the Earl as she opened her eyes. "No,
don't try to get up. We've sent for a doctor."

"Did the men come for Piers?" she whispered.

He nodded gravely and said, "They arrested him immediately after he shot you."

"But who…?" Perdita struggled to sit up, but fell back with
a cry as she felt a knife-like pain just below her shoulder.

The Earl swore under his breath and put her gently back on
the couch. Then he said firmly, "You must lie back and rest,

Perdita! Your wound is not serious unless you make it worse by your own unconsidered behaviour!''

He smiled at her to soften his words and got up to move away. But Perdita caught his hand and said, ''No, don't go! It's better when you're here. But do tell me who sent for the Runners.''

''They were not Runners, Miss Taver,'' said a calm voice behind them. Mrs. Frith came forward to the couch. ''They were constables, hired by my friends at Lloyds. And I apologise. I should, of course, have called you Miss Taverton.''

''From Lloyds? Well, bless my soul! I quite thought the magistrates had refused to wait till tomorrow to open Miss Felicia's letter,'' said Mr. Rambridge, his elderly face creased with worry as he regarded Perdita. ''I must see that they are informed straight away. Will you excuse me, Miss Felicia? I think you are in good hands.'' He bowed to all of them and left.

''On whose authority did you send for these men?'' demanded the Earl. Then, as Mrs. Frith remained silent, he said grimly, ''We have a lot to discuss, Ludmila.''

''And I will willingly tell you all you wish to know, Edward, but not, I think, here and now. Miss Taverton needs some rest.''

''Do not, I beg you, shut me out!'' pleaded Perdita, faint but game. ''I must know why those constables came to arrest my stepbrother.''

''I will see that you know everything,'' promised the Earl, smiling at her. ''But for the moment I must give way to the doctor, who is even now coming through the door.''

There followed some extremely painful moments when the doctor removed the pads the Earl had placed over the wound and examined it. He advised Miss Taverton that the bullet was lodged in the flesh near her shoulder, and recommended that she should be carried carefully to her own home, where it could be removed.

''I'll take her,'' said the Earl quickly. ''Ludmila, please make our excuses to Lady Francombe and follow us to Dover Street. I will arrange for a carriage to fetch you.''

''Of course,'' said Mrs. Frith.

Throughout the excitement that was taking place in Lady Francombe's library the ball had continued uninterrupted. The music and chatter of the guests had drowned any untoward noises—even the sound of the shot—and the Earl, with Mrs. Frith's aid, was able to carry Perdita out with no other excuse than that she was feeling faint. This was no less than the truth. The pain of the last hour, together with the strain of the preceding interview, had drained all Perdita's resources. The doctor had not given her anything to deaden the pain because, as he kindly put it, she would need that solace later in the evening. In due course she found herself in her room, and the Earl was giving precise instructions to her maid. Then he went to escort the doctor upstairs.

"Oh, your dress, miss! Your lovely dress! What a shame!" was Lucy's contribution to Perdita's comfort. Fortunately the doctor arrived straight away, and after an even more painful time the bullet had been removed and Perdita's shoulder bound up. No serious damage had been done, but Perdita was past caring. The doctor had given her some laudanum, and she was smiling sleepily when the Earl pushed a scandalised Lucy aside and came in to see how she had fared.

"Are you comfortable? You look it." Perdita tried to nod but her head felt too heavy. The Earl smiled and said softly, "Goodnight, Perdita. We shall see how you are tomorrow." As he left the room he bowed to the maid, who was staring saucer-eyed at the gentleman in her mistress's bedroom. And him an Earl!

CHAPTER SEVENTEEN

IT WAS NOT TO BE expected that Perdita would feel comfortable for the next day or two. The bullet had gone deep into her arm, and she dreaded the doctor's daily visit to examine and dress the wound. But on the second day she insisted on getting up in the afternoon, and the day after that she was downstairs as soon as the doctor had gone. Mrs. Frith protested once, and then helped to make her comfortable on the day bed in the salon. The Earl had not visited Perdita again in her bedroom, but had left a bottle of claret and some flowers. As soon as Perdita's admirers heard she was ill the house was besieged with callers, none of whom were admitted, and who left whole gardens of flowers, some with very fanciful notes.

"How nauseating!" was the Earl's response to a particularly effusive communication. He had been surprised to hear that Perdita was up and ready to receive him when he came round on his daily visit to the house that afternoon. On being invited into the salon he had examined one or two of the billets with an expression of distaste.

"You are not very kind," said Perdita, laughing.

"You will allow that this poem could not possibly help anyone to feel better. If one were not sickened by the sentiment, the quality of the verse would be enough to cause an instant relapse!" he replied. "And it has caused me to forget my manners—how do you go on, Perdita?"

Perdita assured him that she was almost better, at which he raised an eyebrow and asked her to raise her right arm.

"Well, that's a little difficult," she protested, laughing again. "It will be a while yet before I can use my arm freely."

"I don't think the services of the Sheikh are called for, are they?" he asked, smiling down at her.

"No, no. Time is all it needs, Lord Ambourne."

"As to that, I am charged with all sorts of messages from my mother, the gist of which is that you should come down to Ambourne as soon as Dr. Barnes pronounces you fit to travel."

"Amb...Ambourne?" faltered Perdita, looking doubtful. After all, the Earl had been very firm in his refusal to go there when they were travelling from France. She had thought that he didn't want to see Ambourne contaminated by her presence. "And what about you, Lord Ambourne?"

"I, too, would like you to come, Perdita. We have much to discuss, have we not?" said the Earl. "But now I think we should hear what Mrs. Frith has to say. Some of it I have already heard, but I insisted she wait until you were downstairs before she told us everything. Ludmila?"

Mrs. Frith came forward and sat down in front of them. For two days she had visited Perdita's bedroom constantly, but had always refused to discuss the events at Lady Francombe's ball. Now Perdita knew why. The Earl, as usual, had given his orders!

In her usual calm manner Mrs. Frith began, "First I should tell you both that I have known of Piers Carston's various activities for some time."

Perdita broke in to ask, "His various activities? You mean, not only about Eliane, but about his behaviour to me, too?"

"More even than that, Miss Taverton," Mrs. Frith said patiently.

"What—even the business of the shipping? But how?" asked Perdita.

"I think it is better if you let Mrs. Frith tell her story without interruption, Perdita," said the Earl, and Perdita subsided.

"I think I told you, Miss Taverton, that my husband spent some time working for the government at the Congress of Vienna. His special interest lay in routes for shipping and trade, and after the war he continued this work. Piracy was always a problem, though the situation improved after the Royal Navy bombarded Algiers, which was a centre for these criminals, three years ago. However, it came to my husband's notice that, though there were fewer pirate ships, the value of the cargoes lost—especially from ships registered with Lloyds—hardly diminished. He set out to discover why this was so. Unfortunately he died before his work was complete, and it has since been continued by others."

Mrs. Frith paused and pressed a small handkerchief to her lips. "I knew he suspected Piers Carston of selling information about shipping to a certain Michel Legrand. When Edward asked me to find someone to act as chaperon to you, Miss Taverton, I volunteered myself. His desire for you to meet and marry Mr. Carston seemed to provide me with an opportunity to get closer to the man."

Mrs. Frith's normally pale cheeks became slightly pink.

"I have to confess that I acted somewhat deviously. Though I did not inform Lord Ambourne, I knew more of your story than you suspected, Miss Taverton, and in particular I found what you had to say about the meeting that took place in Bristol between Piers Carston and Michel Legrand extremely interesting."

"How did you learn of that?" Perdita had to interrupt, even if it meant incurring the Earl's displeasure. When Mrs. Frith's colour deepened she exclaimed, "You listened! You listened at the door to my conversation with the Countess? But you were out!"

"I'm afraid returning the samples to the modiste was only an excuse to leave you alone. I knew you would not talk freely if I were present. In fact I stayed in," said Mrs. Frith calmly.

"But that was not honourable!" said Perdita in a shocked voice.

Mrs. Frith's tone was contemptuous as she replied, "I do not have this stupid English approach to honour. Piers Carston was a villain, and I wished to expose him."

The Earl gently pushed Perdita back against the cushions when she would have argued. "Let Ludmila finish," was all he said.

Mrs. Frith went on, "The evidence I gathered was almost enough to convict him—and Mr. Rambridge will now supply the finishing touches. You need not be involved at all, Miss Taverton."

The Earl leaned forward and asked, "Is that why you acted so precipitately, Ludmila—because you knew from Perdita's conversation with my mother that there would be only one meeting with Carston? You surely had very little time to arrange for the men to be there to arrest him."

Mrs. Frith's aristocratic lip curled in scorn. "I arranged that earlier than you think, Edward. For some time I had been doubting your resolve to carry the matter through to the end. I

suspected that your feelings for Miss Taverton were becoming
more important to you than your scheme to punish Mr. Carston. And I was right! Where would all my plans have been had
I not anticipated this? But then, you always did allow sentiment to interfere with policy."

The Earl frowned, and Perdita wondered about their activities in Vienna. Had Mrs. Frith been as ruthless there?

"You and I have always differed on the rival claims of honour and expediency, Ludmila," he said in a cool voice.

Mrs. Frith drew in her breath and said sharply, "And I dare
say we shall do so in the future, too, Edward. But I do not
propose to argue old issues." With an effort she returned to her
former calm. "Well, there you have it. Piers Carston will almost certainly be convicted of conspiracy with pirates, and I
expect he will be at worst hanged, or more probably transported. My husband's work is vindicated," the quiet voice finished.

Perdita had always suspected that Mrs. Frith was not all she
seemed, but she was appalled at the woman's ruthlessness.
There was an awkward silence, which was broken by the Earl.

"It is time for Perdita to rest again—she is looking very
pale." He paused and said deliberately, "I will wait down here
while you see her to her room, Ludmila. Then we shall talk
further."

Mrs. Frith rose and escorted Perdita upstairs. Neither of
them spoke, and when Mrs. Frith merely gave her into Lucy's
hands and returned downstairs almost immediately Perdita was
glad. It was some time before she fell into a troubled sleep.

PERDITA NEVER KNEW what passed between the Earl and Mrs.
Frith after she was safely upstairs. No one referred to it again.
But when she came down the next day she discovered that the
Earl had arranged to take her to Ambourne the following
morning and that Mrs. Frith would not be accompanying them.
She was slightly annoyed at this high-handed behaviour, but
could not in all honesty find another solution. She was still too
weak to be alone, and it would be some weeks before she could
use her arm at all easily. So it was not difficult for her to acquiesce, and she merely asked Lucy to have her things packed
and ready when the Earl should call. It was more difficult to
know what to say to her chaperon. She had been kind in her

way, and, though Perdita could not approve of her methods, her swift action against Piers Carston had solved a number of problems.

Mrs. Frith showed no consciousness of any awkwardness between them, and after luncheon settled herself in the salon by Perdita's couch.

"I have enjoyed our acquaintance, Miss Taverton," she began. "I seldom have the opportunity for close association with another woman, and it has proved interesting." Perdita stammered something, and Mrs. Frith, looking at her in tolerant amusement continued, "It is, of course, obvious that Edward is devoted to you. I have never seen him in love before—it has been a most enlightening sight. However, I hope you will not make the mistake I allowed my husband to make."

When Perdita asked her what that might be, she said, "I allowed him to marry me, knowing I was his social superior in every way. You know already that I am Hungarian. Do you also know I am a princess, closely related to the Esterhazys?" She looked at Perdita, who nodded. Then she said sadly, "I rarely allow my feelings to rule my head, Miss Taverton, but I would have walked barefoot to marry David Frith. I was passionately in love with him, and even now I am unable to consider any other man. But, though I never told him what I felt, I was never totally happy in our marriage."

Perdita said, "I don't understand. Did he not love you in return?"

"Oh, yes," was the reply. "As much as I loved him. Can you imagine what it was like, loving someone so much and yet always regretting what one could no longer have—the social position, the respect of one's equals, the status that one feels one is owed? I assure you, it was very difficult, especially as one could not share these feelings of resentment with the partner whose own inferior birth had led to the situation. I never became resigned to it."

Perdita caught a glimpse of the burning ambition which drove this woman. She had used the word 'vindicated' of her husband's work. It was more likely she was using the words of her own actions. Perdita felt pity for her, but Mrs. Frith's next words made her angry.

She continued, "I wonder if Edward is the same? Or will he tolerate what I could not?"

Perdita said coldly, "Mrs. Frith, what are you trying to im-
ply? Any warnings you may be giving me against marrying
Lord Ambourne are unnecessary, I assure you. But my birth is
not inferior to his. He is the son of an Earl. My mother was the
daughter of one, and my father's family have owned estates in
the south-west since records began."

"And your reputation? Your life with the pirates? If that
should become general knowledge, Miss Taverton, your noble
birth would be of little consequence! Do not misunderstand me.
I shall remain discreet—the polite world will never know from
me where you have lived these last three years. But there is always the possibility that someone else will learn of your
past..." Mrs. Frith spread her hands in a totally foreign gesture and shrugged.

Perdita restrained herself and said merely, "These warnings
are totally unnecessary, believe me. We will say no more on the
subject. If you do not mind, Mrs. Frith, I should like to stay in
my room this evening. The journey tomorrow will need what
strength I have. Will I see you tomorrow morning?"

"Oh, I think so, Miss Taverton. I shall depart after you, so
we shall be able to say our goodbyes tomorrow. May I help you
upstairs?"

THE JOURNEY TO AMBOURNE could have been one of unmixed
delight for Perdita. It was a lovely day, sunny, but not yet hot,
and the Earl's carriage was not only well sprung but had been
loaded with cushions and rugs, so that it looked, as he re-
marked, like a scene out of the *Arabian Nights*. He swore he
was afraid he would lose her among them all.

He was a charming travelling companion, and pointed out
sights and scenes to amuse her on the way. They passed through
several pretty villages—Brixton, Streatham and others—and
the wayside was lined with may blossom, late bluebells, cam-
pions and the fretted network of cow parsley.

If only Mrs. Frith had not reminded her of her true situation she could have given herself up to enjoyment of the day.
As it was, she did her best to let no trace of unhappiness show,
but the Earl glanced sharply at her once or twice, and asked if
she would like to stop, or if he could provide her with a more
comfortable cushion. They took the journey at an easy pace
and arrived at Ambourne in the middle of the afternoon. Be-

fore Perdita was out of the carriage the Countess was waiting for her on the wide steps in front of the house.

Larger than Belleroi, Ambourne Place had been rebuilt in the middle of the previous century by the second Earl. It was an imposing building with its many windows and spreading wings, but it was made beautiful by the colour of its rose-red brick and its lovely proportions. Perdita was to discover that the house was eminently comfortable to live in in spite of its apparent grandeur.

"Perdita, my poor child!" said the Countess, running down the steps to her visitor. She stopped short just in front of Perdita and said anxiously, "Will it damage you if I kiss you?" Perdita was tired and low in spirits, but she could not help smiling at this. She bent down slightly and the Countess gave her a warm greeting. "Now carry her in, but carefully, Edward."

"Ma'am, I don't need to be carried!" protested Perdita.

"Perhaps not, but Edward needs to carry you, Perdita!" said the Countess, with a wicked look at her son. The Earl glanced at the impassive footmen standing waiting on the steps, told them briefly to carry in the valises, and lifted Perdita gently into his arms.

"Hold on to me with your good arm, Perdita. My mother would disown me if I dropped you," he said.

The little procession wound its way through the marble entrance hall and into the guest wing. Here, a room facing south over the park had been prepared for Perdita. It was quite large, but very prettily decorated in soft blue and white, following the taste for chinoiserie in vogue in the previous century.

Perdita was put down on a day bed by the long windows, and, with a slightly concerned look at her wan face and dark-ringed eyes, the Earl withdrew. While her luggage was being unpacked and put away the Countess sat by her and told her something of Ambourne and its estate, but as soon as the other servants had gone she called the maid who had been assigned to Perdita and told her to get her mistress undressed and into bed.

"I am not an invalid, ma'am."

"Your face tells me differently, Perdita. Dr. Barker will come from Reigate tomorrow to have a look at your shoulder, but tonight you will rest here for an hour or two, and then we shall see whether you are to join us for dinner."

She went out, and the maid—a capable but rather solemn country girl—saw to Perdita, drew the curtains and left. It was fortunate that the journey, short though it was, had exhausted Perdita, and she slept soundly for two hours.

When she awoke she found she was able to come to a decision about her stay at Ambourne. She would enjoy it for what it was—a short interlude of happiness and recreation before she began with the hard work of renewing the Taverton estate. Mr. Rambridge had arranged to come down to Ambourne to see her soon, but she did not doubt for an instant that her heritage had been seriously damaged by Piers's depredations. For the moment, however, she would forget the problems waiting for her in Somerset. Mrs. Frith had suggested that the Earl would ask her to marry him, but she did not really believe that. He might be in love with her, but he would hardly commit the folly of marrying her. So for these two or three weeks she would live for the moment.

When the Countess came in to see whether she was awake Perdita was eager to get up and dine with them. She did not want to waste a single moment of the time left to her.

APART FROM A MORNING spent with Mr. Rambridge, which proved to be every bit as disheartening as she had expected, the days that followed were magical. Ambourne was an enchanted castle, where time did not count and all unpleasant thoughts were forbidden. They spent a great deal of their time out of doors, for the weather was perfect, too. At first Perdita could not walk far, and the Earl drove her round the estate in a light chaise, often in the company of the Countess. Under her benevolent eye the Earl showed Perdita the rudiments of fishing, argued with her over the merits of Byron's verse, taught her to play piquet and laughed as she recklessly gambled away several paper fortunes. He constantly watched over her for any sign of fatigue or pain. If he suspected she had done more than she should activities were instantly suspended and she would be ordered to rest. When she lost her temper at his high-handed behaviour he teased her into good humour again. On one occasion, when she had fished too hard and long in her efforts to catch a particularly large perch, he took note of her pale face and removed the fishing rod from her hand. Then he lifted her up and, in spite of her protests, deposited her on the garden seat near by. It took some time and all his skill to charm her into a good mood again.

"All the same, Edward, I think you are the outside of enough," she said eventually. "If I were a man you would not calmly remove me as if I were a parcel! And deprive me of my best chance to date of catching that fish. He was almost on the line!"

The Earl, stretched out on the grass before her, looked up, laughing, "If you were a man, Perdita, I would not now be prostrate at your feet, admiring the ridiculous straw hat on your lovely head and desperately longing for you to stop frowning at me. And why are you so sure it was the perch? It was probably an old boot." At Perdita's gasp of outrage he hastened to retrieve his position. "No, of course it wasn't. It was a giant of a fish, a champion swimmer. But aren't you secretly glad I saved his life?" Then his face lost its teasing expression and he grew serious. "As you saved mine—I believe I have not yet thanked you for that. What made you do such a foolhardy thing? You could have been killed."

All the things she wanted to say were forbidden, so she contented herself with saying lightly, "Your mother would never have forgiven me if I had allowed Piers to shoot you. Besides, you have saved my life more than once, I think. I still owe you two lives."

"It's not enough, Perdita," he murmured. "Two lifetimes is not enough." But at the sight of her puzzled face he only laughed. "Come, the sun is getting too strong. We must go into the shade."

"Edward, you more than anyone know that I am well able to support strong sunlight! Have you forgotten my past history?" She looked at him steadily, for she had not brought up the subject of her past by chance.

"How could I?" he said. "I am ashamed of the part I played in it. And it is my fervent hope I can help you to forget it all in time. I can only admire the indomitable spirit which enabled you to survive and thank God for it . . . But this is not a matter for a sunny afternoon. And we are moving into the shade all the same, Perdita. Think of my complexion, if you are indifferent to your own!"

Later, when she could move her arm more freely, she played to them in the evenings, while the Countess sewed and the Earl sat and watched them both. An idyllic time, one which she never forgot for the rest of her life.

It came to an end one evening after dinner. The rector had dined with them, and he and the Earl had disappeared into the library to discuss the matter of the church organ. The Countess had gone to her room for some more sewing silks, and Perdita was left alone. The long windows of the salon opened out on to a broad terrace, and she wandered into the soft June night.

She was beginning to feel it was time to leave Ambourne, and the thought was almost unbearable. It was not quite dark, but the moon had risen, bathing the lawns and trees with a soft radiance and laying a streak of silver over the lake. Ambourne looked incredibly beautiful, and Perdita felt she never wanted to leave it again. From the woods beyond the lake came the exquisitely unmistakable song of the nightingale.

The Earl saw the rector on his way, having convinced him of his interest, largely financial, in the church organ, and returned with relief to the salon. He caught his breath at the sight of the girl standing in the moonlight on the terrace, her head lifted as she listened to the nightingale's song. He was transported to Algiers, and the sight of the same girl in the courtyard of the Dey's palace. But this girl was now so infinitely dear to him that he could not envisage life without her. Ever since the night at Lady Francombe's ball he had been certain of his own feelings. But he had remained silent in order to give Perdita a breathing space, time to get to know him in different circumstances, time to learn what sort of life she would lead in the future with him here at Ambourne.

Suddenly he could wait no longer. He was as certain as a man could be that she loved him, but he had to be sure. He stepped forward on to the terrace.

They looked at one another, and somehow they had met and were frantically kissing each other, murmuring little terms of endearment and then kissing again. The Countess came to the window and hastily retreated, unobserved by either.

"My love, my darling, my lovely one," said the Earl, somewhat incoherently. Perdita's answer was to pull his head down to kiss him again.

"I love you!" she whispered. "I shall always love you, wherever we are."

The Earl held her even more tightly, and then hastily released her as he said, "Oh, God, I'm not hurting you, am I? I'd forgotten your shoulder."

Perdita shook her head impatiently. "No," she said. "Kiss me again!"

Lost in a world of delight, they stayed out on the terrace for some time, until the moon went behind the hill and it was dark. The nightingale's song still filled the air.

"We must go in, Perdita," said the Earl, stroking her hair back from her forehead.

"No, please! Let's stay a little longer," pleaded Perdita. "The night is quite warm and...and it's so beautiful out here."

He smiled and they stayed for a few minutes more. Then the Earl said firmly, "Perdita, has it not occurred to you that my mother must have been looking for us long before now?"

"The Countess!" gasped Perdita. "I had quite forgotten her! I said I would meet her in the salon, and she will surely be wondering what I am doing!"

"I doubt that very much, my sweet innocent! My mother probably knows very well what you have been doing for the last hour!" laughed the Earl, and at Perdita's self-conscious look he kissed her again. They were at the window by now, and a burst of clapping startled them. The Countess stood in a ring of lamplight, looking as excited and pleased as a child at Christmas.

"Famous!" she cried. "Edward has lost all sense of propriety and is busy trying to seduce my guest under my very nose."

"Then I must make amends and marry her out of hand, Mama," he said, gazing down at Perdita, a smile in his eyes. "How soon can you be ready, my darling?"

Perdita looked up, startled. "Marry you?" she said. "You want me to marry you?"

Edward looked injured. "It's time you knew, Perdita, that, in spite of my treatment of you in the past, I am essentially a conventional man. If I kiss a young lady in public I expect her to marry me!"

He could hardly have used a more unfortunate phrase. Perdita stared at him. Conventional! What was conventional about her history?

The Countess saw her stunned distress and said hastily, "The poor child is worn out, Edward. All this emotion is very wearing!"

The Earl held Perdita's face in his hands and looked at her
searchingly. "Sleep well. We have the rest of our lives before us,
Perdita. Don't allow doubts to spoil it. Goodnight, my darling." He kissed her tenderly, infinitely sweetly, and then said,
"But don't imagine for a minute I'm going to let you gamble
my fortune away playing piquet with anyone else, my love!
We'll keep your losses in the family!" Then he lowered his voice
and added, "And I'll keep my wife's company to myself."

Still in a daze, Perdita allowed herself to be led upstairs by
the Countess. At the door of her room, the Countess stopped
and said to her, "I suspect you are more than tired, Perdita.
Perhaps you are apprehensive about the future? You have no
need to be. Edward will love you and cherish you, just as his
father loved and cherished me." When Perdita would have
spoken, she said, "No, I won't hear of any objection. I truly
believe that you and my son are made for one another. I beg
you not to make any hasty decisions. Sleep now, and in the
morning it will all seem very easy. Remember, you have the
power to make Edward the happiest of men—and the unhap-
piest. Take care how you use that power. Goodnight, Perdita,
my dear."

What was the echo those words had aroused? The Sheikh!
"You have the courage and spirit to help Lord Ambourne. Use
them wisely...wisely..." The words echoed through her head
all night.

In the morning she had decided what she must do...and two
days later she was huddled in a corner of Lord Ambourne's
carriage, being carried to an uncertain future far away from the
two people she loved most and had hurt most.

CHAPTER EIGHTEEN

EVERY CARE had been taken for Perdita's comfort. The carriage was large and well sprung, and the Countess had sent Mary, the girl who had acted as Perdita's maid, to remain with her for the journey. Two of the Earl's best men, who would deal with accommodation and changes of horses on the journey to Somerset, were riding alongside. Perdita had nothing to occupy her mind other than the misery she had inflicted on herself and others. She tried to console herself with the thought that the Earl would eventually be grateful to her for his escape, but she could not persuade herself that this was the case. Throughout the long journey, with its tedious stops at posting houses and inns and its jolting progress along indifferent roads, her mind returned again and again to the scene the previous morning.

It had begun romantically enough with a note and a rose from the Earl, brought in by Mary. News had travelled round the great house that the master was at last intending to marry, and there was an unusual air of excitement about Mary's sensible person. Perdita's resolution was severely shaken when she read the note. The young men who had left their effusions in Dover Street could have learned much from the Earl, for it was everything a lover's note should be—romantic without being sentimental, and, though it was written with a light touch, it was full of the writer's happy anticipation of their future together. She went downstairs, reluctant but determined to put an end to these dreams.

She found the Earl with his mother at breakfast. He rose immediately and came over to her, bringing her hand to his lips and kissing it.

"Good morning, Perdita," said the Countess. Her tone was bright but her eyes were worried. "Edward, put Perdita down and continue with your breakfast, if you please." They smiled at her words and joined her at the table. After breakfast Perdita asked to see the Earl alone.

"Perdita," said the Countess urgently, but Perdita looked at her with stony determination and said,

"No, ma'am, I must speak to your son first." The Countess shook her head sadly and went out.

The Earl had observed this little exchange, and his mouth tightened slightly. He said nothing, but led Perdita into the library, where they would be undisturbed. Here he took her into his arms and kissed her. Then he held her away from him and said, "Now tell me what it is that is making you so thoughtful, Perdita."

There was no easy way to do this. "Lord Ambourne, I cannot marry you," Perdita said bleakly.

He looked searchingly at her for a moment, then said, "I thought as much. I find it hard to believe, but it's what I feared you would say. But how can you? How can you, Perdita?" Without waiting for a reply, he turned suddenly and went over to the window, where he stood gazing out at the woods. "I lay awake all night thinking of you, of what happened on the terrace, and of our future together, Perdita. It seemed to me that our understanding was so complete that nothing, nothing at all, could stand in its way. Why do you say that you can't marry me? Are you trying to tell me you don't love me? I won't believe you, you know."

She made a mute gesture of appeal, but he went on, "It's not just last night, Perdita, perfect though that was. It's all the other times—the excitement of being together, the laughter, the interest, the way the world becomes alive when we're with each other. No, I will never believe you don't love me." He swung back to face the room again. "So tell me why you can't marry me." His voice was calm enough, but his hands were trembling. If he had ranted or raved, if he had tried to persuade her differently by forcing her to kiss him, she could have borne it more easily. Her own spirit of resistance would then have been aroused and she would have fought him back. But this reasoned approach to the very heart of the matter disarmed her completely.

"We are not suited, Lord Ambourne," was all she finally said. But she should have managed something more convincing. He was at first astonished and then angry.

"Not suited, Perdita? Not suited? After the way you re-sponded to me last night? Held me as closely as I held you, as reluctant as I was to part? Pray, do not insult my intelligence! Do you call this not suited?"

He strode over as he spoke and pulled her to him. He kissed her with no tenderness or restraint—and yet she found herself responding once again, not fighting him, but only wanting to assuage his anger and pain. Their kiss deepened and changed, and when after a long time they finally drew apart they were both breathing quickly. The Earl still held Perdita's arms as if he could not relinquish her completely. He rested his cheek on her hair.

"Perdita," he murmured, "you can't deny this. There is something which binds us together. This feeling has always been between us, from the moment I first saw you. I didn't recog-nise it immediately, but it was always there, right from the start. I think it will be with me for the rest of my life. I shall never forget it."

"Nor shall I," she said quietly and sadly. "But the circum-stances of our first meeting are such that I can never agree to marry you." She gazed at him steadily. "I must go away, Lord Ambourne."

"You were on that pirate ship through no fault of your own, Perdita. No blame can attach to you for your imprisonment in the Dey's palace."

Perdita pulled herself away from him and cried, "It is not, however, a place in which to find the future Countess of Am-bourne." She spoke with such desperate determination that he was stopped from further protest. He looked at her penetrat-ingly, saw how she was trembling, and led her, protesting, to a chair.

"Sit there while I think for a moment. No, don't get up to go. I am not going to attack you again. It doesn't seem to help ei-ther of us," he said ruefully. They sat in silence for a full min-ute, then he said, "You are really determined to give up all the happiness we could have? To bid farewell to me, and my mother, and Ambourne? In spite of anything I can say, you are resolved on this course of action?"

"I must," she cried, "I must! I could not bear to see you turn away from me when you came to your senses again. I'm sure you love me now, but I must not let you make a dreadful mis-

take. You will be glad of it when you have had time to reflect!''

"And you, Perdita? Will you be glad?"

A sob escaped her, but she said valiantly, "I must be—for
your sake if not my own."

For once neither her tears nor her gallantry moved him. He
said slowly, "I would have wished you to have more confidence in my love, Perdita. I have no doubts, and nor should
you. But, since you will not be swayed at the moment, here is
what I have decided."

She looked at him in surprise. "Decided?"

"Yes, why not? I reserve the right to have some say, too, in
something that affects our happiness so greatly, Perdita. You
may be prepared to cast it to the winds for a totally unnecessary scruple, but I do not have to acquiesce tamely—nor will I,
by God!"

For a moment he looked so fierce that Perdita gave a gasp.
He heard it and softened his tone immediately, picking up her
hand and holding it in his. "But I do in some measure understand your hesitation. It must be that you do not yet know me,
or yourself, well enough. I thought three weeks here at Ambourne would be enough, but it is clear you need longer. It is
not surprising. The events of the last three years have hardly
encouraged confidence in your fellow human beings." He
carefully put her hand back in her lap, and said, "So you must
go to Taverton, not, as I had hoped, with me, but alone. I will
give you time to reconsider, to come to understand how real our
bonds are, time to develop faith in me. I believe you will learn
to trust me in the end. I hope to God you do, for I see a very
unhappy future for all of us if you do not."

"I will not change my mind, Lord Ambourne. I love you too
well."

"Perfect love has perfect trust, Miss Taverton. And you do
not trust me well enough. But you will come to do so. I shall not
let you escape. Come, we must find my mother—she will be
sadly disappointed, but not, I think, surprised."

At the door he turned her to him and kissed her again. The
kiss was not passionate but deeply tender, each of them reluctant to end it. Perdita was saying a final farewell to her love, the
Earl sealing his promise to seek her out again.

The Countess was sad, but she would not let it show. Her
brave face tore at Perdita's heart, and her concern for Perdi-

ta's safety and comfort on the journey was only rivalled by the Earl's. Neither could supply the only comfort Perdita needed—the conviction that what she was doing was for the best. Indeed, the Countess's last words were, "You are so wrong, my child. And you are creating so much unhappiness. But you must promise not to be afraid to admit you have been wrong. I know Edward's affections will not change. Come back to him if you can."

OCCUPIED WITH THESE and other equally gloomy thoughts, Perdita found the journey unbearably long. Mary was not really amusing company, for not only was she normally rather a stolid girl, but she was also shocked and disapproving of Perdita's treatment of her master and mistress. Added to this was a tendency to coach-sickness. Perdita was glad of her company in the inns at night, but found her presence in the carriage during the day no comfort.

They spent the last night of their journey not far from Taverton at Warminster in Wiltshire. When she entered the inn she had a pleasant surprise.

"Why, I declare, it's Miss Felicia, isn't it?" The landlord's wife came up to her, half uncertain at first, then with a warm welcome. It was Abby, the Taverton coachman's daughter. She glanced curiously at the Earl's carriage in the yard, but made no comment. Instead, she led Miss Taverton up to a pretty bedchamber on the first floor, well away from the noises of the bar. A trestle-bed was found for Mary, and the two travellers were soon refreshed and ready for a meal. After supper Abby could restrain herself no longer and came to have a chat with Miss Felicia.

"It's a good day for Taverton when you come back, Miss Taverton. The estate has gone down dreadful since you've been gone."

"How is your father, Abby?"

"Oh, he's fair, Miss Felicia. He's living with my brother over at Sherborne now, you know. When he had to leave Taverton along with the rest he had a hard job to find anything else."

"Are there no servants at Taverton now?"

"Well, none that need money to live on. Old Joan and Samuel Lupton still keep an eye on the place. They keep theirselves going with the pigs and hens at the home farm. There's no others. They wouldn't stay, would they? Not for your step-brother, they wouldn't—begging your pardon, Miss Felicia. But after your poor sainted mother died they didn't treat servants right at Taverton. Shouting and cursing, the old man was, and the son was not much better—except when he sweet-talked the girls. But where have you been all this while? We all thought you was dead.''

Perdita gave her some sort of answer, which, though not very satisfying, at least stopped further questions. She and Mary went to bed not very long after supper, and as Perdita lay in bed, listening to Mary's adenoidal breathing, she wondered what she would find at Taverton the next day.

In fact she found desolation. Outside, the house looked much as it had for centuries. But what a scene of chaos greeted her inside—broken windows, invisible from the drive, shattered pictures, rooms empty of furniture, and bird droppings everywhere.

Upstairs, where the lead had been removed from the roof and fallen slates had never been replaced, the rain had run down behind the panelling and caused great patches of rot and decay. In her mother's bedroom, the huge bed was leaning drunkenly to one side, its curtains ripped and torn.

Numb with shock, Perdita wandered from room to room, each one worse than the one before. Old Joan followed her, her back bent with rheumatism, excusing, complaining, railing against the Carstons until Perdita could bear it no longer.

"Are there any refreshments for Lord Ambourne's people?" she asked. With much debate Joan decided she could produce some healthy farm fare, and Perdita asked her to feed Mary and the two men in the kitchen.

"The kitchen, Miss Felicia? You wouldn't feed the tinkers from Bartholomew's Fair in that kitchen! I'll take them to the farm. That'll do for them. But where are you going to live, Miss Felicia? You can't stay here. It's not fit!"

Perdita had to acknowledge this was true. Grasping Joan's arm, she said urgently, "Joan, you must not let those people see this house! Keep them away! And don't talk to them about the state of the house or the Carstons or anything, do you understand? I don't want the Earl and his mother to know what it is like here. I'll find somewhere to live, but can you put me up at the farm for tonight? We'll send Lord Ambourne's carriage back to Warminster. It's still early in the day and they'll be glad

to be on their way." Joan tried to demur, but had to agree that
there was nowhere for Miss Felicia to sleep tonight other than
the farm.

After bidding farewell to Mary, who displayed a surprising
disinclination to leave her, Perdita set the Earl's coach on its
way. She gave the men some money from funds provided by
Mr. Rambridge.

As the carriage disappeared she felt that her last link with the
Earl and his mother had gone with it, and such a feeling of
desolation overcame her that she was hard put to it not to cry
in front of Joan. But she pulled herself together and asked Joan
to take her to her room.

Still bemoaning the state of Taverton and the poor accommodation to be offered to its mistress, Joan tried to take her to
the Luptons' own bedroom. This Perdita would not have, and
in the end insisted on a tiny attic bedroom at the top of the
farmhouse. It had the advantage of a small window, which
overlooked the rolling Somerset countryside. At least the
Carstons had not put their dreadful mark on that.

For the rest of the day she inspected the house and the
buildings round it more closely. Apart from the walls and panelling on the upper floor, the damage was mostly superficial.
Repairing it would take a great deal of work, but should not be
beyond the resources of the estate. It was impossible, however, to replace the missing furniture—some of the chests and
presses had been in her family for generations. She wondered
what had happened to them, for they were only of value because they were part of the Taverton family history. She later
found some of them in pieces at the back of the stables.

The next day she sent for the workers still living on the estate, and found that most of the young able-bodied men had
left to work for better pay near by. Rescuing the estate seemed
a daunting business, with few resources and hardly any men.
She would have to sell some land, but which? Her experience
in estate management was small, based on her early years with
her father, but somehow she would have to learn!

The first evidence of the Earl's continued care for her wel-
fare came two weeks after she had left Ambourne. With help
readily given by the women on the estate, who were all unaf-
fectedly glad to see her back, she had sorted out the kitchen, the
breakfast parlour and a small sitting-room in the main house
for her own use. Here she lived and slept. The conditions were

by no means luxurious, but at least she was in Taverton Hall again. She laughed ironically—Miss Taverton of Taverton Hall, indeed!

She was sitting in her parlour one afternoon, worrying over the question of land, when Joan announced a visitor. She jumped up apprehensively, for she was expecting no one. In came a youngish, respectable-looking man with brown hair, the red cheeks of a man who was used to working out of doors, and a quietly confident air.

"Miss Taverton? His lordship sent me . . . Lord Ambourne, I mean. My name is Seth—Seth Ashwood. He thought I might be of some use. Here's his letter."

He handed her a sealed letter, but, without opening it, she asked, "Why should Lord Ambourne think I need help?" Before he could stop himself Seth Ashwood looked round the room with its meagre furniture and patched-up furnishings. His open face was expressive, and Perdita's cheeks grew red. "I need no help," she began stiffly, but he said pleadingly,

"Please, Miss Taverton, read Lord Ambourne's letter. I'm sure he will explain. I'll sit outside, if I may. I like the fresh air."

The Earl's letter began abruptly, with no greeting.

> Perdita—do not turn Seth away. He's a good man—one of the best I have. I trained him myself in helping to manage the estate and he has aptitude for it. You will say you do not need him, but, from what John the coachman told me, you most surely do. If you send Seth back I shall come to find out for myself how you go on. And even I feel it is too soon yet for any substantial change in that obstinate will of yours. My mother sends her love.
>
> Ambourne

The businesslike tone of the letter did much to reconcile Perdita to accepting Seth's assistance, and it was true that his arrival was like a miracle. The women might have welcomed Perdita back, but their menfolk, fond as they were of "Miss Felicia", were more doubtful of her ability to cope. Seth proved to be like an answer to a prayer—tactful with the remaining workers, knowledgeable about the farms, a good manager of land.

She found herself leaving more and more in his capable hands. At first she followed him, trying to learn from him, but in the end she gave up. The men responded better to Seth when she was not present, and anyway there was enough work elsewhere to keep her fully occupied.

In a curious way it could have been enjoyable, this gradual restoration of Taverton Hall to some of its former glory, except that, wherever she was and whatever she was doing, Perdita's thoughts returned constantly to the Earl. Her unhappiness was like the toothache—she could numb it for a while with hard work and the sleep of exhaustion that resulted, but it never went away. No lovely view of the Somerset hills, no exquisite birdsong, not even some amusing incident on the estate could pass without a passionate wish to share it with him. Sometimes her longing for him was so powerful that she was on the point of setting out for Ambourne. Then Mrs. Frith's words would return to haunt her.

"Can you imagine what it was like, loving someone so much and yet always regretting . . . ?"

That was not for her! And she would return to work even more frantically.

She was not without company. The neighbouring families, who had stayed away from Taverton for more than three years, gradually started paying calls. But Perdita was usually so tired that she seldom returned the visits, and when she did she found the somewhat restricted conversation left her cold.

So THE SUMMER CAME and went, and autumn had just started to change the countryside to gold. Perdita started to worry about the roof of the Hall. Where was she to find the money to pay for that? If she sold more land the Taverton estate would be diminished even further. The anxiety over this question and sundry other estate matters gnawed at her mind until she could no longer sleep, however tired she was. She walked the house at night like a restless ghost, and, like any other ghost, she mourned her love. The last time she had heard from the Earl had been several weeks before, when he had sent her an account of Piers Carston's trial. Her stepbrother had been sentenced to transportation for life, so they would not see him again.

But since then there had been silence. She was afraid now that she had, after all, achieved what she had set out to do in the library at Ambourne in June. The Earl had come to his senses and was forgetting her. She was forced to call on all the strength of character she possessed to withstand the pain of this thought.

MEANWHILE, AT AMBOURNE, the Earl was finding the enforced wait a strain. He had done what he could to make sure that Perdita had arrived safely at Taverton, and had provided her with some much needed help on the estate. To a man who wanted to cherish her for life and to give her the world, this was a woefully inadequate substitute.

The strain showed in his manner, and his mother was often reminded of the difficult time at Belleroi when Edward's temper had been equally uncertain. Her heart ached for her son, and she was quite relieved when he decided they should go to Normandy for a while. On his return, however, he was even more restless. He threw himself into the work on the Ambourne estate with such vigour that his agents wished he had remained in France with his mother! Finally, unable to bear Ambourne with its echoes of Perdita everywhere, he went to London. The capital was almost empty of people he knew. The season was over, and most of them were enjoying the late summer and autumn in the country, or at Brighton, Bath or some other watering place. But he did find Mrs. Frith, who was preparing to leave England and return to Vienna.

"Edward, I am glad to see you before I go," she said coolly. "I did not enjoy our last parting. You were unnecessarily harsh."

"I cannot believe that anything I said has had a lasting effect, Ludmila, but I too am pleased to be able to wish you well in your future life. I think you are right to rejoin your family in Vienna, but is there a special reason for doing so?"

"I have finished what I had to do in England," she said. "Mr. Carston's trial and sentence have put an end to my ambitions here. But tell me, how is my protégée, the little Taverton girl? She must have been gratified at Piers Carston's end."

"I am not in her confidence, but I do not believe that Perdita would think of it like that, Ludmila. If you remember, she would have given him time to escape elsewhere, which you denied him.''

"If I had been as sentimental as she he would no doubt be cheating and lying his way to another fortune at this very moment. God help Australia if he ever gets free, is all I can say. But have you, then, parted with Miss Taverton? I congratulate you. You have more strength of mind than I would have credited. Or did she take my advice?''

The Earl suddenly grew alert. "Advice? What advice?''

"Oh, come, Edward, surely you can see for yourself that, however besotted you were at the time, her somewhat lurid past would certainly have caused you embarrassment in the future? Even if it did not become public. I merely pointed this out to her.''

There was a silence while the Earl regarded Mrs. Frith with growing anger. Finally he asked in clipped accents, "May I ask what I have ever done to arouse such malice, Ludmila?''

"You are wrong. I did not dissuade Miss Taverton from marrying you solely out of malice. You have been very discourteous to me and I was angry with you, it is true. But I also sincerely believed it would be wrong for you to marry her. You forget how I felt in my marriage to David.''

"You ruined David, Ludmila. You ruined him, though I know you loved him. He could have been a brilliant diplomat—was on the way to becoming one—but you destroyed him with your empty ambition and consciousness of position, your scorn for honour and your lack of principle. Did you really think you kept your true feelings hidden from him? In the end he took himself, at your valuation, as inferior and unworthy.''

She was white with rage. "Take care, Edward! The story of your dealings with Miss Taverton would entertain London society for months if I chose to reveal it!''

"Do you think I care? I will not discuss my feelings for Miss Taverton with you, Ludmila, for I do not think you could possibly understand them. But if she marries me, then I will count myself more fortunate than I deserve. I think we have said enough to each other. For David's sake I will wish you a happier future in Vienna. Goodbye, Ludmila.''

The Earl turned and left her standing there. For a moment her face was a tragic mask, then she resumed her normal expression of calm indifference. She went back to her packing and set off for Vienna that afternoon.

The Earl also left London that afternoon. At last he could
understand why Perdita had been so determined to refuse him,
so reluctant to trust his constancy. That cold-hearted woman
had done her best to destroy something infinitely precious.
Well, she wouldn't succeed. Perdita was his; there would be no
more denials, no more hesitation. When he got to Ambourne
news was waiting for him from Normandy, which, if he needed
one, gave him the perfect reason to go to Taverton. A few arrangements had to be made, and then he set off early the next
morning.

CHAPTER NINETEEN

EDWARD ARRIVED at Taverton late in the afternoon. The Hall lay in its valley, the warm gold of its stones glowing in the autumn sun. He met Seth Ashwood at the gates, talking to an elderly lady who was introduced to him as Mrs. Lupton.

"Sam's wife, isn't it?" She curtsyed and smiled and looked flustered. He went on, "Is Miss Taverton in the house?"

"Yes, sir...my lord. She'm be having a rest, sir. She works too hard, does that poor maid."

"Thank you. I'll see myself to the house, Mrs. Lupton. You stay here and keep Seth happy." He strode up the drive, half expecting Perdita to appear at any moment, but the house lay silent and still in the sunshine. When he came into the parlour he could see why she had not heard him. She lay in a chair, fast asleep, her cheeks brown but thin, and her whole body expressing unutterable weariness. He walked softly over to her and kissed her. The dark blue sapphire eyes flew open and once again he was lost in their magic.

"Edward," she murmured, smiling sleepily. "Oh, Edward, my love." He kissed her again, but she pushed him away and sat up. "Lord Ambourne, why are you here? I have not changed my mind!"

He sat back on his heels. He was going to enjoy this.

"I haven't come to ask you to, Perdita my darling," he said. She looked at him suspiciously. "Then why are you here?"

"To ask you to come to France with me," he said, his eyes dancing.

"Come to France with you?" She stared at him in amazement. Then an expression of understanding came over her face. "I see. You don't want to marry me, yet you're asking me to come to France with you—as your mistress, I suppose? I am not yours to command now, Lord Ambourne!"

He replied ruefully, "Believe me, Perdita, if that was the only way I could persuade you to live with me I would. But my intentions in this instance are perfectly, boringly honourable. My mother wishes you to come. Eliane needs you."

She flew out of her chair and grasped his arm. "She's not ill again, is she? Oh, poor Eliane!"

He put his hand over hers reassuringly. "No, but she needs you. You will see. Are you coming with me? I will engage to behave admirably."

"Of course. But what about Taverton?"

"I think Seth can manage Taverton in your absence. He seems to be on good terms with Mrs. Lupton. Are you satisfied with him?"

"I cannot thank you enough, Lord Ambourne, for sending him. He has been the saving of Taverton."

"I could wish he had saved you more," he murmured. "What have you been doing to make such a wreck of yourself?"

"Working," she said briefly. "Are you sure you wish to take a 'wreck' like me to France?" She was hurt, but she would not show him, nor would she tell him that sleepless nights were more to blame for her appearance than any amount of hard work. Besides, though she wasn't going to say so, he looked a bit worn himself!

He looked at her with a smile in his eyes. "I can't console you in the only way I should like," he murmured. "But I do want you to come to France with me. Please come, Perdita."

In a surprisingly short time Perdita was ready to leave, and in two days they were on their way to Portsmouth. The Earl had stayed at the local inn and spent the intervening time viewing the work Seth had done on the estate and inspecting the house. After an argument with Perdita he had persuaded her to accept help with the re-roofing of the Hall. He found it strange to meet people who had known Perdita in her early years. They all called her Miss Felicia, of course, and he asked her one evening whether she would prefer him to call her by her original name.

"After we have been to France you will have no need to call me anything, Lord Ambourne. 'Perdita' will do till then."

He saw her looking at him to see how he was taking this provocation, but kept his face impassive. Her attitude provided him with no little amusement. He was now in no doubt that Perdita would marry him, whatever she was saying at the moment, but he refused to rise to her challenges. Perdita was no longer as determined as she had been, he was sure. Those dark-ringed eyes, her thinness, and above all her reaction at his arrival—all told their own tale. But at the moment she would welcome a chance to put him down. She was not going to have it, not if he could help it.

Again they travelled together in the Earl's coach, but he confined his attentions to ensuring she was comfortable and to making light conversation. Once he caught her looking at him, when she thought she was unobserved, in a puzzled and wistful fashion. He longed to take her in his arms there and then, but instead, exercising severe self-control, he said, "You are looking tired, Perdita. Perhaps you would like a short sleep. There is little of interest on the journey."

Convinced that the Earl thought she looked a hag, Perdita turned away with a suppressed sigh and tried to do as he suggested. Memories of the loving care he had taken of her on their journey to Ambourne and the laughter and interest they had shared kept her awake, however, and when she did fall into an uneasy slumber the lurching of the coach woke her again. Finally she let herself fall over to lean on the Earl. She felt an immediate sense of well-being, which was cut cruelly short when he gently but firmly put her back against the squabs on her own side. The journey to Portsmouth seemed very long to Perdita.

They had a good crossing with a following wind, but this time Perdita was thankful to stay in her cabin. The carriage that waited for them at Honfleur was comfortable but small, and the Earl elected to ride alongside in order, he said, to give Perdita more room to rest. It was with relief that she saw the chimneys of Belleroi on the horizon.

Colette was waiting at the gates, and ran up the drive by the carriage until Perdita ordered the coachman to stop and let her in. Madame Lebrun had been warned of their arrival and was waiting in the entrance hall. It was an indication of the change in Perdita's status that Madame Lebrun curtsyed and greeted her formally as an honoured guest. She also apologised for Colette.

"That child has spent hours waiting at the gate for the last three days, *mademoiselle*, but she shouldn't have been so importunate. I'm afraid her behaviour doesn't improve with time. May I show you to your room?''

Perdita followed Madame Lebrun to the foot of the stairs, but here she was detained by the Earl, who had just come in from the stables.

''Georges wishes me to convey his pleasure at your return, Perdita.'' She turned and smiled at this sally, but he went on, taking her hand and kissing it, ''Welcome to Belleroi, Felicia Taverton of Taverton Hall. All your Norman friends are very happy to see you here at last. My mother is at Beau Lac at the moment, but by the time you are downstairs again she will be back. I'll escort you to your room.''

At the door of her room he handed her over to a smiling Madame Lebrun and an excited Jeanne, and left her.

As soon as he had gone Jeanne cried, ''Oh, *mademoiselle*, I'm so happy to see you again! Look at your room!'' Madame Lebrun made a small sign of disapproval at this undisciplined outburst, but Perdita smiled and greeted Jeanne warmly. The girl dragged her into a room that was full of flowers and messages—less pretentious perhaps than the notes in Dover Street, but much more welcome. Her eyes filled with tears at this evidence of the affection that waited for her here, but she was soon laughing at Jeanne's insistence that she remove her bonnet and allow her to arrange her hair. Madame Lebrun gave Jeanne a warning glance and excused herself, then Jeanne set to work, talking all the time. It was clear that the girl was bursting with news that she was not allowed to pass on. Several times she began a sentence that she cut short, until Perdita's curiosity got the better of her.

''What is it, Jeanne? What are you hiding?''

''Oh, it's wonderful news, *mademoiselle*! But I can't tell you. Madame la Marquise could be angry with me if I did. But you'll be pleased, I know.'' Perdita refrained from testing the girl's discretion any further. She would have to wait till the Countess told her. If it was what she hoped, then it would be joyful news indeed.

The Countess came into the house with a flurry of silk skirts, demanding to see Perdita and the Earl immediately. She swept into Perdita's room and embraced her enthusiastically.

''My child, my dear child, it's wonderful to see you here again. Heavens, you're so thin, Perdita! You've been working far too long and hard, child. No matter, Rosanne's cooking will soon remedy that, and then we shall see you as you were. How is your arm?'' She accepted Perdita's assurance that her arm was as good as ever and went on, her face alive with happiness, ''We have such good news for you, Perdita—and but for you it might never have happened. Eliane is about to marry Philippe! Is that not wonderful?''

Perdita's reception of this news was as rapturous as the Countess had hoped. To have such a happy end to a story which had begun so miserably was all she could have wished for her friend. ''But, ma'am, what about Monsieur Fourget? Does he agree?''

''Oh, yes, though I should think he would be relieved to have the entrée once again to decent society, the traitor! Oh, but I forget—Edward says I mustn't call him that any more. Monsieur Fourget is about to become an important man in politics here in Normandy. I don't really think that is a great improvement on his former position, but Edward seems to think it is, and he has spent a great deal of time with Monsieur Fourget. So all is forgotten and forgiven, and Eliane and Philippe are going to be very happy together.''

Perdita exclaimed without thinking, ''So that is why I heard so little from your son! He was in France.''

''Did you think he had forgotten you?'' asked the Countess. ''Oh, Perdita, when will you learn? Edward's feelings will not change. You should know that by now. Why are you so cruel to him, so cruel to us all?''

''But, ma'am,'' cried Perdita, ''you do not understand. He might come to regret marrying me if my story becomes known and he is ostracised for it! What love could stand that?''

''Edward's!'' said the Countess promptly. ''Do you mean to say, Perdita, that you are making Edward so unhappy for this reason? I could be angry with you, I think. You claim to love him, and yet you know him so little?''

''I do love him, ma'am. I want to spare him pain.''

''No, you want to spare yourself pain, Perdita. You're prepared to sacrifice any hope of happiness for yourself or Edward because you won't risk the pain of losing him. I don't call that love—love is not so selfish! Of course you might lose Edward—you might lose him in a riding accident, you might lose him, as I did my husband, through a sudden illness, you might die yourself at an early age. These are all risks we take when we love someone enough to marry. But you will not lose Edward's affection because of some trivial question of social position. How dare you even think it?" The Countess got up to go. "I thought you had more spirit, Perdita. Think of the courage Eliane and Philippe have shown. You are not the only one to have an unhappy past. But are you ready for an unhappy and lonely future? It is certainly not what I wish for my son."

She went out, leaving Perdita deep in thought.

Outside, the Countess paused and looked back at the closed door. She smiled and crossed her fingers. Then she went downstairs to greet her son.

"Edward, dearest boy. Have you seen Masson's new grandson? He's a delightful baby. They are so taken with him that they have persuaded their daughter and her husband to live with them. Of course, Masson will need more room and I have told him you will see to it. How was your journey? I congratulate you on getting Perdita to come, at least."

"Mama, poor Etienne will have to deal with Masson, but I'm sure he'll manage. I must tell you something I learned in London before I came over..."

By the time Perdita came down, still thoughtful, the Countess knew of Mrs. Frith's intervention in the Earl's affairs. She was both furious and relieved.

"So that is why Perdita is such a coward!" she exclaimed.

"Perdita is no coward, Mama," said Edward swiftly. "You forget how badly life has treated her."

The Countess laughed. "I should have known better than to say anything about Perdita to you, Edward. Perdita is perfect in your eyes."

"No, not so. She is often perverse, sometimes obstinate, and can be completely maddening," he said with feeling. At this interesting point Perdita walked into the room.

"And at the moment I look a wreck, too," she said composedly.

"You devil, Perdita! You were listening!"

"I cannot emulate Mrs Frith's talents in this respect," she said demurely, "but when something is said so loudly that the household now knows I am maddening I cannot avoid hearing it, too."

The Earl came over to her and took her hand. "My apologies. I should have said 'maddeningly lovely.'"

"A maddeningly lovely wreck, perhaps?"

"That is enough, Perdita. You refine too much on what I said in Taverton. You are already looking a great deal better than you did. It was your health, not your beauty, I was concerned with."

The Countess regarded this exchange with deepest satisfaction. Perhaps, after all, there would be two happy couples at Belleroi this autumn.

A few minutes later Eliane came running in. Perdita gasped when she saw her, for she was transformed. The hesitant, melancholy air had vanished, and Eliane was brimming with happiness. She looked more beautiful than ever, in her pale green muslin dress.

"Perdita! I'm so happy to see you. Have you heard? Philippe and I are to be married quite soon. Oh, I must thank you for acting as our good angel."

Perdita looked sharply at the Earl, who was murmuring, "An angelic, maddeningly lovely wreck..."

"Rubbish, Eliane," she said, leading her friend away from the sound. "I am sure you would have made it up in time. You're made for each other..." The two girls sat down at the far end of the room and chatted together.

The Countess said, "Are you going to manage it this time, do you think?"

"Manage what, Mama?"

"Don't be so annoying, Edward. Manage to persuade Perdita to marry you, of course."

"Perdita will be given no alternative, Mama. But I need your help..."

THE PREPARATIONS for Eliane's wedding took three weeks. Perdita enjoyed every minute of being back at Belleroi, seeing her friends again, being jealously looked after by Jeanne, living in the comfort of a large, well-run house. She found it all the more pleasant because it was such a contrast to the gruelling time she had been having at Taverton. Jeanne exclaimed over the state of her hair and hands, and set to work to recreate the beautiful *mademoiselle* who had left Belleroi. Strangely, she was sleeping better too, and she was soon pleasing her friends by looking as lovely as they remembered her. With one exception they all said so, but the fact that the Earl made no reference to her improved appearance piqued her. He remained a charming host, engaging her in conversation at dinner, showing her improvements in the château, but never again referring to their relationship. It was true that Eliane's marriage seemed to be taking a great deal of his attention—almost an excessive amount for what was to be a very quiet wedding. But Perdita reminded herself that in France a marriage was a civil contract first and a love-match second. No doubt there were details of dowries and jointures to be settled. She accidentally broke in on one such discussion shortly after she arrived. The Earl was in earnest conversation with Eliane and Philippe in the library when she went in to look for a book.

As she entered she heard the Earl say, "I have spoken to your mother, Eliane, and she has no objection if you agree. Do you?"

Then she saw Eliane throw her arms round the Earl and say, "Edward, it's a wonderful idea! Don't you think so Philippe? Do say you'll agree to it, Philippe, please."

Philippe kissed his bride-to-be on the nose and assured her he would be very happy to agree. Eliane danced round the room in excitement, but stopped dead when she saw Perdita hesitating at the door.

"Ah, Perdita," said the Earl. "Er—you don't yet know perhaps—Eliane and Philippe have agreed to live here at Belleroi after they are married. They will be doing me a great service—Belleroi needs more attention than I can give it at the moment, and Philippe will learn all about managing the estate from Etienne in order to take over from him in due course. And our two love-birds will still be near their families. Will you not congratulate us?"

Perdita hastened to say how happy she was for all of them. It gave her a pang, all the same, to see how close these three were—Eliane was gazing at her cousin in open admiration, and Philippe was smiling broadly. They talked for a short while, but Eliane seemed rather distracted and soon went off to see her mother, taking Philippe with her.

The Earl also seemed slightly abstracted, and Perdita went to collect her book and go.

"Perdita," he said suddenly, "come for a walk. I'm sure you need some air, and I must see Georges. Then I'll take you to visit Madame d'Espery."

She agreed immediately and ran for her bonnet. It was a particularly fetching one of Leghorn straw trimmed with for-

get-me-nots and dark blue ribbons. Jeanne had commented
that they were just the colour of her eyes, but no such compar-
ison appeared to occur to the Earl. As she followed him out to
the stables, Perdita was full of gloomy thoughts. He thought
she needed some air...hadn't noticed her bonnet...was more
interested in Georges than he was in her! He was probably taking her to see Madame d'Espery out of kindness to the old lady.
The Countess was wrong—the Earl had lost interest in her. He
had fetched her from Taverton only because his mother wished
her to be here for Eliane's wedding. And it was no more than
she deserved—she had had her chance and had thrown it away.

Georges was walking a handsome black Arab horse round
the stable-yard. When the Earl saw the horse he drew Perdita
back to the gateway and told her to stay there.

"This one is wicked," he said. "He runs like the wind, but
is full of nasty tricks. Look at him there—butter wouldn't melt
in his mouth, but he's had me off more than once, and even
Georges can't do a thing with him. You have to watch him all
the time. He's a killer."

"Can nothing be done?" asked Perdita. The Earl shook his
head,

"We've had him gelded—that usually works, but it hadn't
changed this one's nature. There are horses like that—you can't
do much with them. Pity, he's a handsome brute."

"I don't like him," said Perdita with a shudder. "I feel he's
evil. He reminds me of Legrand."

Even as she spoke the horse suddenly reared up, and if
Georges hadn't been on his guard it would have kicked him
with its flailing hoofs. The Earl waited to see that Georges was
in control of the brute, and then took Perdita away.

They spent a pleasant afternoon with Madame d'Espery,
who was delighted to see her *"mademoiselle"* again. Naturally they talked of Eliane's wedding, while the Earl sat looking relaxed and slightly bored.

"Of course, you will be Mademoiselle Eliane's attendant.
What are you wearing?" When Perdita told her madame nodded her head in approval. "Very pretty! I do not approve of the
new idea of wearing white for bridals. Such a dead colour. It's
fitting for royalty, of course, but the old way of dressing in
pastels is much more flattering. And *'Rêve d'Automne'* has
such a pretty sound, *mademoiselle*. Is Mademoiselle Eliane
wearing the same? I heard her dress was ivory."

Perdita corrected her, "It's called *'Rêve d'Or'*, madame. She is wearing ivory roses in her hair..."

Finally the Earl rose and announced it was time to return to Belleroi.

"You have failed me, Madame d'Espery. I had hoped for some reasonable conversation from you. Belleroi is swamped in silks and laces and the set of a sleeve or the placing of a bow has become more important than the state of the nation! However, in two weeks it will be over, and Belleroi will become a fit place for a sensible man again. We shall see you before then, no doubt. Come, Perdita, you will miss your fitting with the modiste, and I shall be in Coventry for the rest of the month with all four of my ladies."

There was a measure of truth in what the Earl said. Belleroi was a hive of activity, and the two weeks flew by. Though the wedding was to be quiet, Père Amboise and the notary came and went, the neighbouring families were invited to dinners and evening parties, and the people on the two estates were invited to a huge gala in the park. Rosanne was in her element, and the girls of the village had never worked so hard before.

Finally the last preparations were done, the last ribbon sewn on the dresses, and Belleroi was *en fête* again, every room polished to perfection and all the ground floor decked in flowers. It seemed rather excessive to Perdita. No guests were staying the night, and the Earl was taking the Countess and herself back to England the following morning.

The wedding-day was an Indian summer day—mellow sunlight shining on trees turning gold to copper, clear blue skies, and just a hint of autumn crispness in the air. The ceremony was to take place late in the morning to enable the few guests to make their way home in daylight, but there was plenty of time for Eliane to get up late and dress at her leisure. Perdita, on the other hand, rose early and walked to the lake. She might come again to Belleroi—to see Philippe and Eliane—but the likelihood was not great. How different it would have been if she had now been married to Belleroi's owner!

As she stood watching the water rippling over the lake and thinking of Eliane and Philippe, of the happy ending of their story and the dismal future that awaited her, she was startled by a voice behind her.

"Are you remembering your past, Perdita? It was here you met Philippe, was it not?" It was the Earl. He came and joined her at the lakeside. She smiled, but made no answer. He waited a moment; then he said, "Do you love me, Perdita?" Then before she could say anything he added hastily, "I'm not asking if you will marry me. You have said you cannot, I know. But, if things had been different, do you love me enough to have married me?"

She nodded, looking sadly away from him. Was he about to ask her to be his mistress? What would she answer? The last months had taught her that living with the Earl, on whatever terms, could not be as bad as living without him.

He turned her round gently, lifted her chin, and gazing into her eyes, he said, "You fool. You idiotic, quixotic fool, Perdita," and kissed her. Then he said briskly, "Come, we have a great deal to do before Philippe is finally made the happiest of men. I like him, Perdita. I believe Eliane will at last be happy as she was born to be. And old Fourget is a very decent fellow when you get to know him ..."

They returned to the house, where the Countess met them with a curious look and scolded Perdita for being up so early.

The dresses were laid out in each girl's bedroom, ready to be put on. The modiste and her assistant, who had been brought from Paris for the occasion, first dressed Eliane and then Perdita, but only after a slight contretemps with Jeanne. Both dresses were to be worn over ivory slips, both were made of a delicate butterfly silk, based on ivory and shot with another colour. It had been specially woven in Lyons, and a piece of the same material was later put in the museum there as a supreme example of the weaver's art. Eliane's dress was shot with pale gold, Perdita's with a kind of copper-rose, and in the depth of each fold was a delicate shadow of colour. Brussels lace edged Eliane's dress and covered her hair. Jeanne had arranged Perdita's hair in a simple topknot, with a few tiny curls escaping at the side. Over this she had placed a fall of Honiton lace anchored with a cluster of copper-pink roses.

The Countess and her sister had tears in their eyes when they saw the two girls. And indeed it would have been hard to find a more exquisite sight. When the four came down the stairs the assembled household gave an audible gasp of admiration.

Perdita didn't hear it, didn't see the crowd in the hall, for she had eyes only for the Earl. He looked pale, she thought, even rather grim. He led Eliane into the flower-decked salon, where Philippe waited, together with Père Amboise and the notary.

Everyone present at the ceremony that followed was moved by
the simple sincerity with which the young couple exchanged
their vows. Then, after the civil formalities had been completed, they were surrounded by a crowd of well-wishers, and
for a while the salon was filled with laughter and noise. This did
not please the notary, who was a self-important man, determined not to be overwhelmed by his aristocratic clients.

He stepped forward fussily, clapped his hands, and cried,
"*Messieurs*! *Mesdames*! Please!" When the noise grew less he
said, "I understand there is a second couple to be married here
today. Where is the lady, Monsieur de Belleroi?"

A puzzled murmur grew among the guests, and the servants, who had crowded outside the salon to see Mademoiselle
Eliane married, looked at one another questioningly. The
family, on the other hand, waited in happy anticipation as
Perdita's startled gaze met the Earl's. As if in a dream she allowed him to lead her forward.

"This is the lady who will be my wife. Is that not so, Perdita?"

All her doubts, all her fears, melted away in the love shining
from those steadfast grey eyes. Secure at last, she looked at the
Countess, smiling encouragement, at Eliane's delighted face,
felt surrounded by the warmth and friendship of the others—
Madame d'Harcourt, Madame d'Espery, Père Amboise and
the rest. How could she reject all this? Her eyes returned to the
Earl, who was still holding her hands firmly in his.

"Edward, I will marry you, and love you all the days of my
life," she said.

Under the shocked gaze of the notary, she was seized in the
Earl's arms and passionately kissed. The guests recovered from
their astonishment and applauded loudly. The notary had some
difficulty in restoring order to these unconventional proceed-
ings. This was not the way business was conducted in the town
hall at Bayeux!

In spite of the notary's disapproval, Edward and Perdita were
duly married, and at the enormously successful feast that followed Eliane laughed at the dazed look on Perdita's face.

"I was sure you would guess," she said. "Did you really
think Edward was telling us about Belleroi when you interrupted us in the library? He was asking us if we objected to
sharing the wedding, you goose! We've known about Belleroi
for ages! Oh, Perdita, I could burst with happiness—married

to Philippe and having you for my new cousin... Isn't it wonderful?"

AT LAST THE GUESTS had departed, the Countess had taken a slightly tearful Madame d'Harcourt to Beau Lac, Eliane and Philippe had gone to their room, and the Earl and Perdita were walking in the grounds.

"Tomorrow I take you to Ambourne, my love, where we shall be undisturbed for as long as we wish."

"And the Countess? I thought she was coming tomorrow."

"My mother is far too tactful, Perdita, my darling. She will stay here for a while to console my aunt. And now, my wife, shall we go in?"

"Edward, there's something I ought to tell you, but I don't know how..."

He smiled down at her anxious face and raised an eyebrow. "More secrets? Can't it wait?"

Perdita said desperately, "No, it can't. That's just it." She took a deep breath and said in a rush, "That gelding you have in the stables—Legrand was like that. He...he...he made me sleep in his cabin to fool the other men on the ship. He didn't want them to know what he was like. But...but...he couldn't...couldn't...I mean, he beat me and burned me instead of...instead of anything else." Her face was scarlet when she had finished.

The Earl said, "Are you trying to tell me that Legrand was impotent, Perdita? That you are, strictly speaking, untouched?" She nodded and then jumped as the Earl let out a great whoop of joyous laughter. Then he picked her up in his arms and whirled her round. "Oh, Perdita, Perdita!" he shouted. "You wonderful, wonderful girl!"

"Put me down, Edward! Put me down, I say. You'll have the whole château out here asking what is wrong!"

"Everything is perfect! And I don't mind if the whole world knows it," said the Earl, keeping firm hold of his bride.

"Well, I do," said Perdita. "It's not the sort of information I want to share with anyone but you. Now there's one more thing I want you to do. Will you promise to do it?"

"Anything, anything, my angel—you've just made me feel ten feet tall."

She whispered in his ear as she lay there in his arms. He
laughed again and took her indoors and upstairs. The next
morning the scandalised staff of the château heard from Madame Lebrun how the Earl had taken his lovely new Countess
and dropped her, in her shift, into the bath in his dressing-
room. But no one ever said what happened after.

Relive the romance...
Harlequin and Silhouette
are proud to present

by Request

A program of collections of three complete novels by the most
requested authors with the most requested themes. Be sure to
look for one volume each month with three complete novels by
top name authors.

In June: **NINE MONTHS** Penny Jordan
                                Stella Cameron
                                Janice Kaiser

**Three women pregnant and alone. But a lot can
happen in nine months!**

In July: **DADDY'S**   Kristin James
             HOME   Naomi Horton
                             Mary Lynn Baxter

**Daddy's Home... and his presence is long
overdue!**

In August: **FORGOTTEN**   Barbara Kaye
            PAST   Pamela Browning
                            Nancy Martin

**Do you dare to create a future if you've forgotten
the past?**

Available at your favorite retail outlet.

HARLEQUIN   Silhouette

Fifty red-blooded, white-hot, true-blue hunks from every State in the Union!

Beginning in May, look for MEN: MADE IN AMERICA! Written by some of our most popular authors, these stories feature fifty of the strongest, sexiest men, each from a different state in the union! Favorite stories by such bestsellers as Debbie Macomber, Jayne Ann Krentz, Mary Lynn Baxter, Barbara Delinsky and many, many more!

Plus, you can receive a FREE gift, just for enjoying these special stories!

You won't be able to resist MEN: MADE IN AMERICA!

Two titles available every other month at your favorite retail outlet.